P9-EDL-770

The Gravity of

Sunlight

The Gravity of

Sunlight

ROSA SHAND

Copyright © 2000 by Rosa Shand.

All rights reserved.

Permission to use four lines by Dylan Thomas from *Under Milk Wood*,
Copyright © 1954 by New Directions Publishing Corp., reprinted by
permission of New Directions Publishing Corp., is gratefully
acknowledged.

Published by
Soho Press, Inc.
853 Broadway
New York, NY 10003

Library of Congress Cataloging-in-Publication Data

Shand, Rosa.
The gravity of sunlight / Rosa Shand
p. cm.
ISBN 1-56947-192-4 (alk. paper)
1. Uganda—History—1971-1979—Fiction. 2. Spouses of clergy—
Uganda—Fiction. 3. Married women—Uganda—Fiction. 4.
Americans—Uganda—Fiction. 5. Poles—Uganda—Fiction. I. Title.

PS3569.H3288 G73 2000
813'.54—dc21   99-088023

10 9 8 7 6 5 4 3 2 1

In Memoriam:

Mary Boykin Heyward, my mother

Gadsden Edwards Shand, my father

And

For my children and their father,

who've known this African hill,
who'll see:
the traits of the characters here
are insubstantial air—
no sorry act resembles fact,
but the spell of the place is real.

Man himself is mute . . . it is the image that speaks.

—Boris Pasternak

Contents

❧

CONTENTS

Prologue

❧

Uganda is a green land. It lies at the source of the Nile—the shapes of its green so multiform you sense the exuberance of chaos. The yellow-green leaves of banana plants flop indolently, saucily. Papyrus swamps lie flat, white-green, vast. The rain forest towers in deep black-green, while red and gold and orange shriek through openings.

The country was never a colony. It was a British protectorate, once known as the Pearl of Africa. Its land could not be bought by European settlers. So the expatriates who flooded into this country were traders and missionaries and teachers and adventurers and a few odd governors and district commissioners and such. By the 1960s, with independence nearing, these persons were no longer English and Goan and Indian—or not solely. They were Russian and Chinese and French and Yugoslav and German.

One couple was American. They came out on the crest of fascination with new-emerging nations—the foreign arm of the civil rights movement, some might think to call it. They taught at a school in the countryside, learned languages, and moved with their children into the capital city, Kampala. The two of them were still young. They lived on the grounds of a college.

ONE

From an Upstairs Porch

I T'S COMFORTABLE IN THE SHADE. Afternoons, the birds are not so raucous as the mornings. But they surprise you. A great blue ibis bends its S-neck, dignified, slow, back and forth along the grass. In the middle of Visram Avenue.

※

"I can *will* to be faithful, okay. I can *will* to love him—no."

She was alone at the café table, so no one disputed her assertion.

This was at the Nile Café on Visram Avenue, Kampala. It was actually the upstairs porch of the Uganda Bookshop, but the café required its own distinctive name.

"Him" was John, her husband. John was a college teacher and a Lutheran deacon (from an obscure midwestern branch) on top of that. She was Agnes. Words popped up with her. They popped up soundlessly, unless she were more or less alone, or more or less distracted. Whichever way, she might ignore her eruptions or she might consider them. This one surfaced from the fighting in her head. John had said "You *can* keep loving if you choose. You simply make up your mind."

There was some huge gap between herself and John over little matters like this—like can a person *will* to love. It gnawed at her. Still, she more or less ignored her eruption since the afternoon was soft, since her elbows rested on a red-checked tablecloth and her mind on a Finnish man downstairs, who was not her husband and who she expected to be up the steps to the café and here beside her any minute now.

The buzz was British voices, larded with Luganda and maybe Gujarati. Sometimes a hornbill shrieked. Her side was pressed against the railing of the veranda. She could look out on Visram Avenue where a car without a muffler drowned out the Indian tinsmith who was squatting on the pavement clanging buckets.

The waiter filled her cup and moved away. He was gray-haired. She knew him as Erasmus—she could speak Luganda and that made him happy with her. Over his shoulder he eyed her now and gave her a quick fat smile before his face went back to droops.

Her Finn was studying the books downstairs. He and she were under a single roof just now, but he was being slow about acting on the fact. She was certain he had seen her come upstairs, and he ought to be following her.

She'd never yet spoken to her Finn. She had no idea who he was or where it was he'd come from, but she assumed he dreamed of her because she dreamed of him. Or at least, in her dream, she had seen strange writing that she knew was this Finn's language—even if, in her dream, the man was black. Even if, in her dream, the man had naked rock-hard calves that had to be Odinga's calves— Odinga was her ex-houseboy. But that was the way of dreams. It didn't mean she wasn't dreaming of this Finn.

She went still at a male's steps on the staircase. She could numb out the tinsmith's racket and manage to hear such sounds if she concentrated on the staircase creaks. Now she sensed him in the café and felt blood heat her cheeks.

Her back was to the doorway. She studied crumbs and listened—he was sitting at the table behind. So he meant her to be the one who'd twist around. Of course. He played games. She'd suspected that, from the play around his eyes. His eyes gleamed and crinkled when he'd almost nodded. He'd made her remember she missed play. At home she knew each movement John would make—she could say John's words before he spoke. John did not have crinkles around his eyes.

It was rainy when she first caught sight of her Finn. It was afternoon at Lubega College. They were both in the semi-outdoor mailbox aisles (underneath Main Hall), and he was dressed in white. He was talking British English—he said "been" to rhyme with "seen" and "past" to rhyme with "oz"—but with some foreign accent. She'd spun around at the strangeness of the voice and stared at a tall thin man, a little bit stooped, maybe latish thirties. He had a bony face, a short beard, and blondish semi-long hair. She thought even in that shadowy spot the man looked strained, with circles under his eyes; but she very much liked the way his hair curved down the back of his neck. Her spinning round—her plait twirling out—had clearly caught him, too. Their eyes locked. Long enough to start this thing.

She'd strained, when he was leaving, to make out the writing on a newspaper he was holding. The look of the language was absurd. She had to make some sense of it, so she called it Finnish—because Finnish wasn't much of anybody's language and because there were oddities about the man. The white he wore for one thing, as if he'd read some antique books about the tropics. And his walk was curious—and who knew how Finns walked. He held himself close in, looked down as if he meant to keep his face from getting cold. It was not a walk she recognized. But she recognized the way he looked at her. And the crinkle round his eyes each time he almost nodded. And each time she ran into him she was aware he watched her when she left the dim-lit aisles. It spurred her into fetching mail more often than the mail came in.

So he taught at Lubega College, like John did. But the college was big. The faculty could come from any country. It didn't mean she'd get to know this man, or not in any formal way. And it shouldn't mean she'd be so conscious of her neck right now, feeling this man's eyes burn on her back.

He was studying her plait perhaps. Her braid was fat, unstylish, brownish. Finnish women might not wear braids halfway down their back, or not loose sluttish braids raveling apart like hers.

He hadn't spoken yet. She was stiff with listening to hear him speak. Erasmus was a quirky waiter—he was paying her Finn no attention whatsoever.

She heard shouts before she heard one sound from the table back of her. She looked up quickly at the street, saw a stream of people running. They were yelling in a jumble of languages—Swahili, African English, Luganda. The street and pavement and the grass-strip in the middle were crowding up. She saw one man fling a broom and another jump a motorcycle with his ripped shirt flying. She saw the long-mat-hair man grinning at the melee, dressed in his heavy army coat in eighty-five degrees. She heard the tinsmith's buckets rolling off and banging down the street. Traffic stopped. Tea drinkers at the Nile Café sprang up to gawk, to press up to the rail where she was sitting.

It took her seconds to catch on that it was a lynching—a thief had stolen something. It seemed to be from Udham's Used Goods shop because Mrs. Udham was standing shouting in the doorway in her yellow sari. Men and boys were plowing down an alley and in minutes the thief would be a puffed-up blood-wet heap being dragged along the street. She was thinking Come somebody, Stop this thing, There'll be chopped-off hands and chopped-off feet, and she twisted round to tell her Finn who would not know about thief lynching. But it wasn't her Finn. It was a fleshy man she'd never seen. She looked quickly around the whole veranda, but not one soul looked Finnish. No white male had a crinkle round his eyes.

She went still in the middle of the hubbub. People bent across her, but she paid no attention to them. She lowered her head. She pressed her fingers on her eyes and stayed that way a minute before she looked up and back out on the street.

A Muganda in a white *kanzu* had taken over. The man had set himself the job of protecting this thief. He was shouting at the mob to keep away. The crowd quieted—and she saw Prudence. Even in the dark she'd know that Tutsi head. The girl was pulling rags out of her basket. She was bending down to bandage the cowering thief.

They—meaning her family: she and John and Michael and Lulu and Anne—had left Prudence behind when they'd deserted Mityana and moved in town to Kampala. And here was Prudence on Visram Avenue underneath her nose. When in heaven's name would they get rid of Prudence.

She put down a shilling for Erasmus and collected her bags. She had to fetch her children.

TWO

On Darkness

NIGHT DROPS UNEXPECTEDLY. BUTTERFLIES FOLD up. Birds hush. Colors drain from jacaranda groves and then you don't see jacaranda groves. The wall of insect screech begins to rise.

Out of town the black is seamless. If it's a moonless night your headlights are the one pinprick, and the beams dwindle, leave the weight of darkness. You sense the flimsiness of manmade things. Your words space out, stop altogether. You go still, listen, strain to catch what's there. You tense to hear the motor, use the force of all your will to keep it turning over.

If you sang you could press down the fear.

She sang to put the girls to sleep. When she didn't have this fear she didn't sing for Michael, not because he was a boy but because he was ten years old (he'd been born when she was twenty-one). When she didn't have this fear she wished no child would grow up so she could keep on singing when the house was dark. Now she sang to Michael, boy or not. The only sounds were her own voice and the flap of some banana trees and insects thudding screens. The

girls were sleeping. John was in the living room. The one light
came from down the hall and it was dim in here. Windows lined
the wall by Michael's bed. It was brighter out the windows than in
here because the moon threw shadows as sharp as the sun.

She meant to get up but she didn't. She didn't want fake light.
If Michael objected to her singing he could tell her, but he was not
telling her. He was tossing, breathing fast. Winifred didn't know
what it was. Winifred was the doctor friend who gave quinine for
malaria when anybody had a fever but they'd never had malaria
that she knew of. Michael had penicillin now, and aspirin. But it
wasn't working.

Fuweesiky the cat curled under Michael's arm. (Fuweesiky was
black, christened "Frisky," but Hesita their housegirl—Hester
before her name got eased into Luganda—couldn't say "Frisky"
and now his name was "Fuweesiky.")

She didn't want to move away from Michael because she was
scared. She couldn't remember the second verse of the song she
was meant to be singing. She didn't normally sing this one.
Generally she sang lullabies and hymns but she was singing Pete
Seeger because Michael loved Pete Seeger. Pete Seeger's songs had
sent them out to Africa and she was useless to forget the verses. She
started over:

> I saw Adam leave the garden
> With an apple in his hand.
> I said . . . what are you gonna do? . . .
> He said, Talk of love not hate,
> Things to do—it's getting late
> We're all brothers and we're only passing through.

Michael made a violent toss. He said, "No no no—Raise Cain."

She leaned close to him. She didn't at first catch it. Then she said
"Oh yes" and sang:

> Plant some crops and pray for rain
> Maybe raise a little Cain
> Yankee, Russian, white, or tan
> Lord, a man is just a man . . .

Michael let it pass. Never mind it wasn't right. She kept humming. The words didn't matter so much anymore because Michael had stopped tossing. Was he sleeping? She needed to hear him breathing—she was as scared as that. She leaned nearer. He moved, reached out for her. He never reached for her—he was the oldest and he was a boy. He was the potent long-distance runner. He endured on principle, had ironclad principles already. But he reached for her arm and he held it. She dared not move or take his hand or he would pull away. He mumbled. She guessed at what he said—"Don't stop." She sang again. She drew out notes as long as they would stretch, as faintly as she could. She let them die when she could hear he was asleep.

His breathing was fast, but regular. She sat silent where she was, hearing cicadas, waiting for one flank of insects to go soft, another flank of insects to grow loud.

She heard John coming down the hall, but she didn't move. He stuck his head around the door. She held her finger to her lip to warn him to be quiet. He said, "Your coffee's cold."

She squinted. The light in the living room was garish, disorienting.

He said, "Shall I heat your coffee?"

She shook her head, mumbled, "No thank you."

He said, "He'll recover. If you're worried in the morning we can take him to another doctor."

She nodded.

She was sitting with her arms crossed. He kept his eyes on her a minute. Then he picked up his book.

She didn't move.

Five minutes passed. Far off, a hyrax screamed. The hyrax sounded like a baby being tortured—you knew there was a torture when you first heard a hyrax scream.

Every half a minute John looked up at her. She did not want to be studied. She wanted the dark. She was scared for Michael and John wasn't. John could not endure it when she was wrapped up in a child this way. Her refuge now was her passivity, and it was not secure.

He slammed his book down hard against the sofa. He said, "Snap out of it. We've gotten through a bit of fever."

"One hundred four is not a bit of fever."

"I remember higher."

"When they're small. He's not small."

"It will be down by morning. He's sleeping. There's nothing you can do now. I'll heat your coffee."

He banged pans, cupboards, trays.

He brought chocolate cake and coffee to the coffee table and pulled the table closer to her chair. He ruffled through records in the corner and set one on the player. The brightest, loudest Vivaldi immediately filled the room, which made her gasp and hop to turn it down while he stood watching her. She said, "I'm sorry. Thank you," and smiled at him before she sat back down.

He perched on the edge of the sofa. His shoulders slumped. She braced. In his own time he said, "Look. I have already canceled two engagements with Wulf. We have to trust the doctor—the child's on penicillin. He's staying in bed. What else? I am going to take Wulf with the girls to Entebbe tomorrow. I cannot cancel again. It will be easier on Michael and you—having the girls out of the way."

She said, "All right."

He said, "That's all you can say?"

"Who's Wulf?"

"The linguist at Social Research—the Royal Institute. The Pole. The new man. I told you."

She said, "All right. I said all right. Don't disappoint your Pole."

He threw his book on the sofa and slammed outside.

It was Saturday, early afternoon. The sun bounced off the walls. The house was a vacuous glare and the whole college grounds, the whole hillside, was silent. Saturdays it was abandoned. Entebbe was the draw—Lake Victoria dotted with sails, lake slopes yellow-green and dotted with birds and monkeys and butterflies. Wildebeests and warthogs in the zoo. Children cried to go there Saturdays. And John was keeping faith with his new Pole.

Michael was sleeping. It was a fitful sleep, but sleep enough so she could leave his room a minute. She stood in the front doorway, looked at the black hawks gliding over the valley, circling assured and slow. She kept her eyes on them. They at least were moving, if ominously.

Their spot was steep. Kironde Heights. The college planners dotted this hill with tiny stucco houses. You looked down on corrugated roofs and banks of gold and white and red and dark pink bougainvillea flopping through the greens. You couldn't see the valley, but you saw bluing hills on the horizon, and vultures keeping watch. You saw a mangy-looking hillside opposite with scrub and cows and banana leaves flapping against tin roofs. One absurd-shaped hump was vine-covered, and looked from here like monastery ruins.

She hadn't fought John over Michael today. She'd felt hollow at John leaving but she hadn't fought. Because it was true what he said—a child recovered. She swallowed her protest.

The difference now from all the other sicknesses was the atmosphere. The world was too bright, too still. It was glaring, useless, vulture-circling light, and she and Michael stranded. She felt it as if she'd stumbled on a once-big city now abandoned. In perfect deadly order.

Hesita was away on Saturdays—Hesita her housegirl, who'd taken Odinga's place. Odinga—the ruling, silent, disturbingly magnetic Odinga—had never come back from Kenya. Megan she would run to always—Megan Schofleur was her English friend who lived just down the hill. But Megan and Piet Schofleur were in Mombasa. No house she knew of had a telephone and now, on Saturday, no house seemed to have people, and she was left without a car. If Michael got worse there was nothing she could do. She couldn't leave him by himself and run somewhere and shout. And even if she did it wouldn't matter. There wasn't anybody who'd know anything, and she could never be certain whether things were critical with Michael or whether she was being silly and making a fool of herself and everybody else—as John was convinced she was doing. She couldn't now run crazily around a vacant hill.

She turned slowly back inside, Fuweesiky rubbing at her ankle.

She could hear Michael's rapid breathing before she reached his door. It came like a pant. What could she do if she waked him? She said, Damn you, John. Please somebody help. But she said it where Michael would not hear.

Michael flung over. His eyes popped open, rheumy bloodshot eyes. She sat on the bed beside him, held his head to sip some ginger ale. He took one swallow and slid back down. She soaked washrags, laid them on his forehead. She said she'd read to him, asked him if he wanted *Kim*. He said "Green." It stopped her. She looked at the pile of books beside his bed. One had green letters. She held it up. She said, "Is this the one you want?"

He said, "Green." She looked further. There was no green book. She looked back at him with a question in her eyes. He barked at her: "Green green green green" and she knew then, and she said as calmly as she could "All right, my darling, it is green outside and it is sunny and I will read to you" and he shook his head with vehemence and he said "Guns—the guns were green" and she said "What guns, Michael? There aren't any guns, but it's all right, Michael my darling. I will read to you. Just keep this on your forehead."

"Lulu. Tell Lulu." He glared at her and cried. Lulu was his sister. Lulu was in Entebbe.

He fell into a fitful sleep. She held her head and closed her eyes and then jumped up and started to the door to go run find some person any person but she got to the next house down and there was only a girl who spoke Luganda and in the house below that the woman's accent was so thick the woman could not understand and she had been away from Michael too long to look further. She ran back. He was calling her weakly. He needed the bathroom. He was leaning on the wall.

She did not leave him anymore. She soaked washrags for his forehead.

• • •

John—when he returned and faced her tears a half day later—said "The nuns—Sister Deirdre, she's the best doctor in the country. We have to get him to Nsambia."

They reached the mission, outside town, when the sun was going down. Sister Deirdre said typhoid fever. She said they were lucky they had come when they did. She said they were lucky that she had streptomycin. A shipment had just come in.

It was two weeks before Michael gained the strength to come back home again.

Tonight he was on the big bed in their room, hers and John's—along with Anne and Lulu and herself.

Anne found the book, said please would Michael read.

Michael set his pillow straight and read:

> Johnnie Crack and Flossie Snail
> Kept their baby in a milking pail
> Flossie Snail and Johnnie Crack
> One would pull it out and one would put it back . . .

Lulu started chanting it with Michael with a loud exaggerated beat.

Agnes lay and looked outside. It was almost dark but it was calm. The crickets were as loud as they had ever been, and everything was good. It was good to lie in this crowded bed. She didn't want to leave this bed when it was filled up like it was.

She would never be the one who would disrupt this thing. Her feelings were exhausted—her feelings always got exhausted when a child was ill. It touched the fear—the rawest fear—that she lived with in Africa.

She would not go stalking a Finn. She would not search mailbox aisles. She'd been demented, following a Finn, merely because he made her insides soft.

THREE

On Paying Respects

SOMEONE COMES TO CALL IN Buganda—which is where the Baganda live—and you don't need to strain for things to say, not like you have to in the West. The greetings are lengthy, ritualized. They don't take thinking. They take up the best part of the visit, and after the greetings you sit without a word. That portion of a visit ought to be as comfortable as the beginning because, after all, it's fundamentally what a person wants—the animal warmth of another creature nearby. At night you want to curl up with some other body, and in the day you want a touch of company without the strain of keeping up a witty exchange. The idea is merely to take comfort in a presence now and then. But how to get that in the West?

The Baganda figured it out, came up with a formula. The trouble comes when you get Westerners mixed up in the ritual. They clog machinery. Their nerves don't get it. A caller comes. The Westerner assumes he'll learn the purpose for the call. When he doesn't, he floats a question. The answer is a word, smiling but flat. He ventures other questions and the answer is a nod. He hops up for food and drink. Then for anything he sees to occupy his hands.

At last the rudest of the type cannot resist the insult. He attacks. He demands: "What is it you want?"

The caller is confused, smiles, doesn't know the answer. She has come to pay respects.

The car was skipping. And a rock had cracked her windshield—she had to drive with her hand pressed up on the windshield. And her clothes were sticking to her skin with sweat and dust.

The boarding school was sixty miles up rutty muddy tracks. She'd had three Tutsi girls piled up in the car and mattresses and bananas and sacks of yam strapped on the car and the trunk of the car roped down. And then the school demanded hundreds more shillings for books and papers and protractors and aprons and labs and bloomers and blankets and no girl was allowed in school without these objects, never mind that she—Agnes—had never set eyes on the other two girls before this very morning—she had taken Gertrude on and that was it (Gertrude was the more or less abandoned daughter of a woman who'd washed clothes for them five or six years before). She refused to think about it. There was no solution but to pay and leave the girls at school. No person, no institution, would take over these stateless, motherless children. And the in-laws of the in-laws that they ended up sleeping with dumped them out at intervals.

Now she would be late getting home, late to go for mail. She would have missed her Finn by now. Like any drug addict she stalked her Finn once more because her child was well again, long since. It depressed her all day long the days she missed the mail-aisle time.

It was as nutty a distraction as it had been from the beginning, stalking Finns—but when it never would and never could come to anything anyway, why shoot down every pleasure?

No, she had not expected, when she married, to be running after Finns. And no she couldn't make it sound like a semi-acceptable activity. If she attempted explanations the rationalizations would be glaring. Where to start?

She could confess that not too long after her marriage she'd begun, in spite of herself, shielding herself from John. Partly she could blame that on an attitude he held, one she'd picked up on pretty early and blamed on his German blood. But that outlook of his came out most pointedly in a certain notorious conversation that John had had with Hugh, an English friend, when she was there on the sidelines. John bullishly defended his stand that there could be no lasting society (he framed his argument as if it affected worlds) if a woman didn't have sex with her husband when *he* wanted, even if she didn't feel like it. It's well known, he pronounced (in his colossal ignorance), that men have more desire than women so how could a marriage last unless a wife submitted? She herself had screamed, of course, at this pronouncement of his—said if that was how a woman was expected to live, she'd soon be nothing but an inert bit of matter, inhuman, a dead extension of a husband's will—since sexuality was clearly at the center of humanness. Even Hugh agreed on that. John didn't budge, only stopped bringing up the subject (verbally) with her around.

Still, that primitive conviction of his went along with the code that he did keep arguing: that you couldn't depend on feelings; that you had to act in the way a situation called for no matter what the feelings. Feelings were habits, he said—to be trained by following good models. Which, interpreted into daily life, meant stop and kiss if your husband wants, no matter what you're doing and no matter what you're feeling or you'll risk your husband's rage (and yes she normally found it easier to simply squash the turmoil of her resistance rather than to fight—and yes she was literally speaking of the simple daily act of kissing with the lips). She'd even forgotten what it meant to actually desire to kiss—since the act was demanded so much more than she could drum up the want. The whole issue was building in her a massive confusion over how any marriage could bring two persons anywhere near peace.

Another raw spot, though undoubtedly a common one: She at times felt pulled into pieces. John tugged one way for her time and attention, her children tugged the other. But then John hadn't wanted children at the time he got them. The children had simply arrived, and quickly, which was not so strange a predicament in the days when the pill was barely known. As soon as they were married, there she was, his supposed-companion wife, now drowned in diapers and ga-ga sounds and so far away from him he needed a telescope. Neither of them had bargained for this—she was supposed to be supporting him through graduate school and now it was a highly hobbled support—though she managed to continue with her obligatory teaching through it all.

So where did one go to pinpoint the source of their discord? It wasn't much help anyway to wonder where fault started. If you wanted to dig in the quicksand of the psyche, you wouldn't call it John's fault. His own mother, after all, had died when he was twelve and he'd detested his stepmother who only smiled at her own beguiling child. So John reached out for marriage when he hit twenty-one, tried to find a mother—and found a naive Agnes, who was as bookish as he was and just as colossally ignorant of the opposite sex. But she was ready to escape her own impossibly protective home in any way she could. And what did John get with this new mother he married? A houseful of diapers and a wife who was slipping away.

Yesterday was just the latest example of the state of their relationship—and this on another issue: what sometimes seemed to her John's mystifying inability to put himself in anybody else's shoes. Their student Jeremiah was brought, moaning, up to the house—they needed John to drive him to the clinic. It was after lunch and John was lying down undressed. It was a clear emergency—Jeremiah could not stand up—but John just took his time, searched the closet for one particular blue shirt, changed his socks, kept rubbing at his shoes, took a full ten minutes in front of the mirror, twisted round to see he had his shirttail tucked in right, brushed his trousers knee by knee, checked his hair again—all sides—in the mirror. She could not endure it. She said, "Hurry up—the man's about to pass out on the sofa," and he kept right on primping. He said, "The man is not about to die." She said, "You have no way of knowing—Jeremiah is not a person who gets sick. They would not have come for you." Her voice was a furious whisper but he kept smoothing down his out-of-place hairs, while she boiled over and dashed out herself to rush Jeremiah and the students to the clinic.

If that spurt of hate had been isolated it would not have mattered much. But the wild defeated feeling crept up on her too often, and at times when she wasn't on her guard. Her answer was the sphinxlike face and closing herself down.

Their chemistry had failed. And it left the raw ends of their nerves a bit exposed.

But they were married. What was done was done. She accepted. She owned a will. She assumed they'd stick to forms and the cobbled-together edifice would have to hold them up, provide a nest for children, ballast for themselves. They had work, interests, causes, arts, friends—the world was big, and not entirely sorry.

And of course the disturbing side of John was far from the only side—John did manage to bring intriguing people to their home and entertain them well, stir them up, get them engaged in debating this and that. He called up passionate responses; he could be brutishly interesting, if you didn't kill him first.

And one part of all this was not in the least bit sorry: though she sensed John was jealous of his children, otherwise he seemed secure enough in himself not to be a jealous husband. He wasn't particularly worried about her escaping into friendships, with women or with men. There'd been a couple of times—when her attraction to one of his friends had been intense, if innocuous— when he appeared so steadily unjealous she suspected he was merely blind, once more, to what went on in people. In itself that was a scary quality, but it was fine and good just then. And it didn't hurt him at all just then, because she was a trustable person. She had willed to be a faithful wife. His lack of jealousy simply meant a kind of freedom in their marriage that made that institution an often tolerable one.

• • •

Today she jolted the car up the drive. Hesita was standing on the grass, shaking her head and bouncing her own black baby. Anne, their six-year old, her mouth gaping snaggle-toothed, was dashing for the car with pigtails flying out. Anne was screaming "Mother Mother Mother, you forgot to get Deborah. You were supposed to pick up Deborah Kibuka-Musoke. She's coming to play with me and you weren't here to get her." Tears were puddling down Anne's cheeks and Agnes, with Anne red-faced beside her, backed the car down the steep drop once again, and limped it down Kironde Heights and up Kololo Hill for Deborah Kibuka-Musoke.

She splashed grape juice in the cups. The drink spread a blue mustache as far as Lulu's cheeks. A sticky-fingered hand came up at her. She poked a cookie at it, and then at another and another.

"*Hodi.*" The call was from the front. It said somebody'd come. She was quite unhideable, with all the kafuffle with the children. Their sorry Peugeot you heard miles away had announced she was at home.

"*Karibu,*" she yelled back. That said, All right, come in, since you know I'm home and I have no escape.

Her hands were purple and most of her hair had pulled loose from her plait and flew out in all directions, but her smile turned bona fide. Two women—Baganda women, dressed in bright *basutis*—stood on her front porch.

It wasn't quiet enough to talk in normal tones, which was all right with her, not talking. Children and sunshine streamed through the room. The floor, red-waxed cement, was squeaking—Lulu and friend Maggie (Maggie was Megan's and Piet's child) were sliding on the floor, on their stomachs, underneath the dining-room table. Lulu and Maggie had taken over Fuweesiky's tailless lizard. Tabula (her ostensible additional replacement for Odinga—it had taken more than one other person to replace Odinga) banged at things behind the dining-room door. The outside noises were only somewhat softer at the moment—dogs, and mortar-pestle *thump thump thump*, and shouts from the college soccer field. So it was easier, with the women, to sip the tea and smile and not try words at all.

She used to be dumbfounded by the callers. They brought vast, swollen, interminable silences and then some simple oh-by-the-way request to please drive them to Mombasa and back.

But these women were not asking things. These women were Edisa and Eseri (Edith and Sarah once upon a time) and she had taught Edisa and Eseri English when they'd all lived out in the country, at Mityana. The women had taught her Luganda, and now they missed those afternoons and sometimes they would find a way to town so they could sit with her. They did not come beseeching her to mend their souls and lives. They came because they missed her.

Eseri said, "*Nyabo*, we have come to beseech you please about a large thing."

Edisa said, "*Nyabo*, the thing it is not a giving for my sister and myself. My sister and myself, we do not ask you."

Eseri said, "We are able to get along ourselves. We do not ask you to help us for ourselves."

Edisa said, "My sister and I, we need only the objects which we have."

Agnes studied tea leaves.

From the kitchen she could hear Tabula (who was ironing now but who was also the gardenboy and waxer of the floors—whose name meant "to stir" because once he was a *toto* to a cook of Sir Something-Buxton). Somebody'd come to the kitchen—Tabula was talking gruffly. She could not tell who had come, but it might offer some escape. Or—she could tell these women that she had to rescue some child stuck in some tree. Or she'd forgotten she had to fetch John—who rather carelessly had broken his neck. Or she could run for vital letters she remembered had just come in.

When she did look up, the women were mildly waiting. She managed to say, "You helped me many times."

She didn't feel it now, but it was true they'd helped her, and once upon a time she had felt it. They'd been saintly creatures in her eyes. Their father had been the first Muganda clergyman, so Eseri and Edisa had been raised to be too bright and upstanding for the men who came their way. Instead of marrying they worked for the church, like they were expected to, but nobody noticed they worked for the church because nobody paid them anything. They raised food and their brother's children. They were highly put-upon saints and now they were acting like anybody else and she did not want to hear any more.

Eseri said, "We have a niece."

Oh Lord, Prudence! Now things made some sense. Mention Prudence and everything was clear. She knew the good aunts had a hand in raising the girl, but she'd tried to forget that bungling act of theirs.

The voice from the kitchen was a man's. Someone she knew well—who?

Edisa said, "You are acquainted with our Prudence."

She opened her eyes. She said, "I have taught Prudence. She is highly intelligent and talented and she is extremely beautiful. But Prudence did not like me teaching her."

The women spoke at once, said Prudence held her teacher in most high regard. Yes, it was true that one man had said their girl did not speak softly enough, and they themselves were not in accord with their good girl always. No, they had one time to give Prudence back to her father's brother, but the girl did not move forward in her father's brother's home. And she aimed to move forward. And Eseri and Edisa aimed for her to move forward. Did she know, Prudence was pointed out for Lubega College?

The women announced it and sat with pride. They smiled quietly. She saw: These women were blind with faith in this most devious niece of theirs.

Once she would have understood these aunts.

That was when they still lived at Mityana, when she'd first met Prudence.

That day she, Agnes, had been walking along the hillside at

Mityana, on the path beneath the palms. Only one other person was on the path. It was a girl with one arm up, with a basket on her head. The girl walked perfectly erect but swaying her hips in the way women walked out here, the way Agnes envied and wanted to walk but felt sluttishly exposed when she had tried. Closer, she was looking at a tiny compact girl, one with a very long neck and a perfect oval for a head.

They approached each other and halted. She began the greeting in Luganda. The girl spoke up in English. The girl was looking for the headmaster because she meant to study at Mityana. It happened to be the April break and the headmaster wasn't at the college. Agnes brought the girl to her house and fed her. John began to make arrangements for this Prudence, arrangements which she now suspected would never come to an end.

The niece of these two women might be going forward, but the smiles of these two women might still be quite misplaced.

She didn't say that. She said, "I have learned that Prudence is attending classes of my husband." She stopped. She was on the point of saying comfortable things, that she'd seen Prudence behave very well at a lynching on Visram Street, and not too long ago. But that would underline these aunts' outrageous hopes for their sweet niece.

Edisa said, "Prudence requested we undertake this journey."

Eseri said, "Our girl is not happy to request from you."

Agnes was listening to something else. The noise from the kitchen was unpleasant. Tabula was loud, which for Tabula was very odd.

Eseri said, "It will be one miracle, for all the clan—if Prudence will attend Lubega College."

Agnes said, "You said she's going to attend."

Edisa said, "There is a matter what is lacking."

Eseri said, "Our girl lacks the things the college commands."

Agnes said, "There are many other things that Prudence can do. She is very clever."

Edisa said, "She will attend Lubega College. One thing only is lacking."

Eseri said, "They command she complete A level language examination."

Agnes said, "There are schools to prepare Prudence for her A levels."

Edisa said, "The schools do not take Prudence."

Eseri said, "They request Prudence prepare by means of tutoring."

Edisa said, "You will take Prudence up to her A level examination."

Agnes stared.

No. She would not take Prudence up to her A levels. She had no time between teaching and play-writing and play-producing and child-raising and hauling mattresses and finding boarding schools for Gertrude—and checking on the mail four times a day. She did not care to fit in taking Prudence up to her A level examination. She did not get along with the girl. She did not trust her. This request was outrageous and demanded a clearcut, guiltless refusal. Give her a minute and she'd figure how to say it.

She was conscious her expression went odd, and confusion came up in the women's faces. She saw a man—out the window, out back. Fleetingly. He'd ducked away—but she saw he'd noted her recognition. Odinga caught those things.

She said, "Yes yes, I will talk this over with Prudence."

She'd say no to Prudence herself, a little later. It was easier that way. She had to get rid of these women. Odinga had come back.

FOUR

On the Household Bonds

IT'S NOT CLEAR WHY, IF you live in Africa and leave the place, you never drop the subject. It could be nostalgia for adventure, or for sun and canna lilies all year round. But it's probable you felt more human—more connected—when you lived in Africa, even when you never quite came out with that in words. The loneliness of Africa—places have their brands of loneliness—wasn't Western isolation. You had no telephone: A living person walked up to you with news. You had no television: You read and talked instead. But most of all, your house was never empty.

You might, if you were single, claim you lived alone, but you'd be lying. Another person, two or three more likely, showed up on schedule. No, it isn't politic confessing that the person you knew best was one you paid. You explain that fact away, say you were besieged, say you were forced to hire somebody.

But your dreams won't keep the categories. You lived with Africans. Africans involved you willynilly in their lives, and your life wrapped willynilly around their lives. The human atmosphere was full, and decades later it comes back as riches lost.

She was hiding in the bedroom, curtains drawn, her arms flung loose across the basket chair. She had no intention of facing this, sprung on her this way. And what could anybody do if she never moved at all.

Odinga was a Luo. Odinga was tall and bright. His legs and arms were always bare and they were beautiful. He carried himself with a stone solemnity but he also carried a sexual magnet and Odinga was aware of that.

Odinga had run their house. He'd asked for leave—business in Kenya, his wife had run away. That obliged him to instigate a search and find the woman and eliminate the lover and discover what had happened to his children. But their own agreement with Odinga was, he'd be back here in Kampala in no more than one month's time. Agreed.

They waited two. She would still be waiting. Yes, the sexual tension was always there with Odinga but it stayed underground—that had been tested over years. And since it stayed invisible, innocent, and unnameable, she'd grown quite used to it. It gave a kind of life to the house. And she could count on Odinga. But John had not been fond of him—not that John picked up the sexual current; he had no antenna for that kind of thing. She thought she saw what it was with John and Odinga: it was as if Odinga's size and masculine beauty, his stoically silent air of confidence, the way he carried himself and looked at you directly—all of that shrank John to a flimsy set of nerves. So, said John, this was enough of this waiting on Odinga. Okay. They redistributed the work. Hesita would cook and clean and sometimes keep the children. Tabula would garden and iron and wax the floors. No one person could manage what Odinga had managed.

She went along with this. And Hesita and Tabula had new status with Odinga gone. Hesita and Tabula had never been disposed toward a Luo. They didn't like each other either, being respectively Muganda and Munyoro, but nothing was simple as that. In the face of a Luo they saw eye to eye.

Still, she herself gained something as well, having Odinga gone.

With Hesita she was completely comfortable, maybe more comfortable than with anybody. Hesita's baby was sometimes a bit inconvenient (it wasn't Hesita's baby—her family dropped Emma off on Hesita to raise), but she herself could be in the kitchen hours at a time with Hesita and Emma and they all three—she and Hesita and the baby—all of them were easy together. The air didn't turn too thick to breathe. She could show Hesita about mango sauce and that was that. There was none of that crazy unease she felt when she had to give Odinga instructions; none of that terror of a sexual offense. Whereas with Odinga, she, the ripe pink bare-armed woman in the sundress, which was tight across her chest—she had to stand beside Odinga at the stove, Odinga stirring groundnut soup, her fat breast an eighth-inch from his arm. They got locked in those positions. She'd be too aware of his brown gigantic arm, the way his veins branched out and glistened dark on the too-large bulk of his muscles. While she taught him custard making.

Now she turned quickly toward the window, the front window. She must have seen a movement there, or intuited one. You couldn't actually see shadows through the curtain, but Odinga could project himself in any situation. Odinga made an art of the minimum gesture that would catch her attention. They danced in step and he was faultless. He didn't waste a flutter of his finger. At the moment he would know, to the centimeter, where she was. He need only come around to where the bedroom window faced. He would never call or knock. He preferred to let her catch his shadow—it was the fine art of the continent.

She kept her eyes on the curtain. It was mottled white. It was once a watery light green, but the sun changed everything it touched.

She stood up stealthily. The basket chair mustn't creak. She reached for the curtain edge. She could pull it back a quarter-inch without him seeing her. But she stopped. She did not dare. He'd be looking straight at her no matter what and there'd be no explaining. She'd been hiding here too long to try explaining.

The high window. Very slowly, very nearly squeaklessly, she climbed up on the bed. Joint by joint she unfolded herself, stood, reached up to the windowsill, grabbed the corner of the curtain, and went still. This window looked up to the commons and the jacaranda trees, and if she got a slanted angle through the curtain cracks without touching the curtain at all, it could be she'd get by with it.

She pulled the curtain open a crack and looked out. His shadow—she saw it before she saw him—he was headed around this side. Abruptly she dropped the curtain. It shook. He would see the shaking. He would know that she was standing on the bed (he'd always picked up on bed-squeaks).

She stood frozen on the bed. If she moved he would hear. She had to reach out, hold the wall to keep her balance. She leaned her head down on the windowsill, felt the sharp cut of the window ledge.

It dawned on her that she was mad. She moved her head up fiercely. What could Odinga do? Odinga wasn't dangerous. Odinga was bound to know—how could he expect to have his job still waiting? Their agreement had been perfectly straightforward. Clarified. Everything.

Still, she could not leave the bed. Still, she could not dare a squeak. And the sense of her absurdity ballooned—that this man knew he controlled her. That this man knew that all he had to do was wait and she would do precisely what he intended her to do— at least about his job.

Children—she could hear them galloping shouting up the hill. They would see Odinga and they would drag her out and she would have to face Odinga.

The closet!

Lunatic. How would she explain when they discovered her?

She heard them battering Hesita for a drink. For *michungwa*, for *michungwa*. They weren't bothering with her. That meant they hadn't seen Odinga. Meaning Odinga must have vanished. He preferred to wait till she came out alone.

For a moment she was safe. She jumped down off the bed. She slid down in her desk chair and ripped back the curtain for what fresh air she needed.

She was not mad.

Of course you got involved with people—in some way, good or bad—if you stayed in a room with them hours at a time. That was obvious. And it was good. It was right you grew attached to the people closest to your body. It would be unlivable to hate the people close to you. This way meant cohesiveness, civilization finally. You lived around Africans—you got attached to Africans.

No one could blame themselves for dreams. Like last night—in some hut in the banana trees—where Odinga'd picked a stem of bananas for her once. Last year, by the football field with John as coach, and once in an unknown place in Kenya. Odinga got in where he wanted and where she did not want but that was inevitable and meaningless.

✂

Next morning, the dream woke her, but she didn't let on. She never let on when she woke up or John would know and the floating feeling would be gone. She needed to hold it. If she kept to a deathly quiet there was a chance, a hope he wouldn't pester her. Though again he might. He would know dead stillness was not sleep—nothing worked well enough. If she had to breathe as if she were sleeping, then she had to concentrate on pretending to breathe as if she were sleeping, and she couldn't feel out what she needed to feel out. The threads of dreams were as wispy as somebody else's mind.

But the dream began to come: A porch with vines, three sides of the house. Low, flush with the ground, without a step almost. A mortar-and-pestle *thump thump thump* somewhere, but in the dream she thought it was drumming. She thought someone in the house was drumming. There was an easy coming and going between the garden and veranda, which was wide with chairs and tables and books and pillows and all that you wanted to live with.

But she had to wax the veranda floor—that was it! Oh Lord, the position! She stopped pretend-deep-breathing.

John said, "I *thought* you were awake. Look, this afternoon . . ."

She said, "Wait." She rolled out of bed and ran away. Some child was in the toilet room. She ran to the bathtub room and crouched on the edge in the corner.

A ludicrous preposterous position! They were stuck together, herself and Odinga. Of course Odinga had to get himself into that dream, since it was all about waxing floors. Only he was white in this dream, and he had hair just like her Finn. For some reason she had to wax the veranda—it was Megan's veranda—with the sheepskins and so she had to tie the sheepskins on her feet. She'd never done that job before. Always, in life, it was Odinga who slid around their house on sheepskins, room to room, while she observed, obliquely, the lump of his calf muscles and the swelling of his thighs. In the dream she wouldn't ask for any help because of course she could tie sheepskins on her feet and skate the floor and it would be fun to skate around the floor. But her legs kept slipping on the oily floor. Her legs kept straddling apart and she kept catching herself with her hands on the floor but Odinga came up behind her and he picked her up and put his own feet in the sheepskins and he told her to put her feet on top of his and she did that, with her back to him, but after only about one yard she felt the movement of his body at her bottom and then his hands were on her breasts and with all of his activity she was having some little trouble standing up and somehow they landed on a tiny cot someplace she did not know, but she knew Michael was swinging on a limb and gawking in at the window and her mortification was so sharp that she woke up throttling a scream.

She raised her head with a jerk—of course. Damn it, forget the sex. If it erupted that way then it couldn't be thought about. It was telling her something important, not sex with Odinga, something she'd forgotten—yes—it was about Megan—Megan, her English friend and Maggie's mother. Megan was losing her housegirl. Megan would need somebody in her house right now. Megan had envied her for having Odinga—she had said so. So Megan would hire Odinga!

She was pulling on her clothes and telling John she had to run—she had to get to Megan quick before Odinga's head popped up behind their curtain. John said, Stop rushing. He said Odinga didn't deserve this rush. He said Odinga didn't keep his part of the bargain and the man could not expect her to find him a job and she was acting like a fool to rush out of here like this.

But it worked. Megan said, Yes, of course she wanted Odinga.

Now she could tell Odinga—she now had him a job. She was free of her guilt about Odinga!

When she got back up Kironde Heights, the car was gone. The doors of the garage were pushed out wide. She passed the garage. She was crossing the porch to go inside, pulling off her sweater and tossing it aside when it registered. She spun around to check the hump in the garage—the red had caught her eye.

A long thin drum. With bundles—and a pattern she knew. It had once been John's cravat. It was the bright red silk cravat that she had given to Odinga. It had a stain and John wouldn't wear a thing that had a stain. She'd pictured the scene—Odinga in a stiff white shirt and the elegant flare of a red cravat. He'd be in a doorway. The room would be crowded. Everybody in the room would hush, turn around slowly, stare at the haughty sullen black man in his bright red silk cravat.

Odinga never wore a tie. But this cravat was right here with his bundles, which meant he'd carried this cravat back and forth to Kenya. Along with a drum—if the drum was his. And deposited them confidently inside her garage.

She walked in over drips of oil to the end of the garage where the bundles were stacked. They were lumpy bits of cloth, knotted around objects. She stooped. She smelled Odinga. She was pondering this small gray-patterned bundle when she sensed, rather than heard, somebody back of her and spun her head around.

Odinga stood in the opening in shorts. His legs were huge. The sun flared off around his legs.

It cost her awkwardness, but she stood up. She said "*Jambo, Odinga.*"

He said, "*Jambo, Memsahib.*"

She said, "Did you find your wife?" She said it in Swahili. Her voice was tentative.

His voice did not have the tentative edge. He said, "I have arranged some few of my affairs."

She said, "Good. *M'zuri.* Oh yes, you have a job."

Odinga smiled. She had rarely seen Odinga smile, but this smile was not a welcome smile. It was ominous—Odinga was making a mistake. He had not understood what she had meant. Now it was going to be harder. She spoke quickly. She told him to come with her—the memsahib Schofleur wanted to see him now.

They walked down Kironde Heights in silence. He would not walk beside her. He walked two steps behind her.

Her hands were misplaced. They merely dangled, and in front of his eyes. She didn't have pockets anymore—she wished she still had her sweater with pockets that she had had this morning. She tried her arms across her chest. She bent to pick a leaf she passed—she could tear that up with her hands. But it didn't seem to help her with her walk. Her hips must not hint movement, any movement whatsoever. Odinga must not see her hips swing side to side a mere two steps from his eyes.

It would actually be a great release—she accepted now—when Odinga was safely away at Megan's house. She'd be free of her absurd self-consciousness.

FIVE

In a Lighted Window

AT DUSK, FOR A MINUTE, the sky hoards light. And then abruptly you can't make out the skyline, when seconds before there were black hills against red sky. Huts are plunged in a viscous dark.

But in stucco houses the light is as blazing as sunshine. In those houses, which are new, people move in brightnesses. The houses have screened windows and lights on the verandas, and the lights draw insects, and the insects dive-bomb lightbulbs and thud screens.

A woman is walking in the dark. She smokes a pipe. She is a barefoot country woman in a mud-dark dress. She stumbles on a house where the windows flame out light. She halts. Her mouth drops open. Who would dare to mock the sun?

She is frightened. Obscurely she senses: If someone turns the night to day, someone will turn the day to night. And then the sky will fall.

The children were in bed and it was time. She rushed down the hall. She passed the bathroom. John stood at the bathroom mirror, his head turned at a slant from the mirror while he strained to eye himself—clean features, trim beard, dark hair and eyes. He fingered the back part of his hair, the one part that never would lie straight.

The kitchen billowed heat and curried-frying-onion smell. Emma's thin bent legs stuck out from under the ironing board. The baby was leaning over, patting the broom, making grunting noises.

She stopped, blank, in the hot thick steam of the kitchen.

Hesita was peeling a papaw. A curl of sticky yellow-green dropped toward a heap of peelings—banana, pineapple, mango, papaw. She could not remember why she'd rushed in here. Hesita eyed her, said *piki*. She hadn't asked Hesita but of course it was *piki* that she wanted—Hesita called the scissors *piki*. She said thank you (*Webale*), pulled open drawers, foraged noisily, and headed out through the front.

John was setting up the drinks but stopped to watch her. When she reached the front door, he said, "Turn around." He observed her closely, said, "I can't remember you looking more beautiful." She made a face at him, but it had a smile behind it. She reached to touch her back self-consciously to check her skirt was right. She'd pinned a long gold-green *kitenge*, dragon-patterned, tight around her waist and stomach and let it bunch and flare and hang free down her back.

The air outside was as saturated as the kitchen. It was cool, but it was soaked with frangipani and gardenia and jasmine, and something she'd never yet tracked down. The porch was thumps and whirs. Beetles, moths, sausage bugs, and unknown bugs, hit at the bulbs and screens, and yellow light cut out through black and over grass and shrubs. The close gardenia bush was high and fat and heavily clumped with blossoms—buds, and adolescent blooms, and soft-ripe, bosomy, grown-up flowers. Some had liver spots. Others had wilted on the grass. She stood on tiptoe. She cut the stiff young blooms, and heard a car and English voices just below the drive.

Hugh Cavanaugh was John's friend. In style he was a monk-thin Oscar Wilde. He stopped some feet below her, made a flourish of a bow. He stood braced with his legs apart, threw his arms out, leaned back, drew his breath in several Ahhhhs and said, "The lady with camellias."

She said, "I will need to practice."

Hugh said, "My dear Agnes, you have never needed practice."

He meant to mock her southernness. Like he sometimes mocked the rhythm of her voice—he drawled it out. They stood smiling while Claudia was saying to Hugh, who happened to be her husband, "Gardenias. It is not camellias, Hugh. You live in Africa."

Claudia was short and pink and had no use for opera. She was a wealthy quick-smiling Texan but with an English father who'd taught Hugh ancient history. That was the subject Hugh now taught out here, in the same humanities department as John and Piet.

Hugh caught Agnes's hand, bent over it, and kissed it. She didn't notice when he dropped her hand because she'd been caught by a figure in a gleaming pure-white jacket, a man in the dark at the bottom of her drive. She was staring at her Finn, and her Finn was staring up at her.

Hugh twisted around to see who she liked more than she liked him. He barked out "Wulf" and scuttled down the drive.

The drive was thickening with people. Her Finn was kissing cheeks, as if her Finn knew everyone.

John's Pole! Her Finn was John's Pole! Her Finn knew her children! He'd been to Entebbe picnicking. This was the man that Lulu mocked—this was the man who rubbed his lip!

She was shifting boulders in her head.

You talked politics when people came to supper. The men and Megan talked politics. Yes the country was collapsing. But could it be? They had made it eight years with Obote, which was not so bad. So what if Obote made his fresh new constitution one more time?

Wulf quietly glanced his amazement at her, again and again and again. He did not talk politics.

Now it was the language confusion they meant to straighten out. The vote was coming up—for the official language of the country. Megan had ideas on language—Megan wrote poetry once upon a time and meant to do it again before she died. She said, "Suppose it's English. That will guarantee we Europeans keep on controlling what's thought and what's discussed. Everything comes through the language. Even what's felt. Subtly. The language dictates who we are. It makes us at home or not at home."

Like Hugh, Megan was English, or Scottish but raised in England. She was large-boned and sturdy, and her way of speaking was assured. You could see it in her face. Her cheekbones were high and her chin was square and Agnes found her miraculously beautiful. Partly it was the straightforward manner. Partly it was the startling blue of her black-rimmed irises, set off against hair that was almost black—long and straight, clipped chastely at the back of her neck. It wasn't classic feminine beauty. There was something decidedly masculine in Megan's face. Agnes, from the very first, had found it hard to stop gazing at Megan.

Hugh said, "Then Swahili? What can you read in Swahili? Such is the style of apartheid." Hugh pursed his lips and cocked his head as if he'd closed the argument. (It occurred to her that all the men but Hugh had beards—Hugh would not stoop to "crazes." John's beard nicely hid some childhood scars on his chin.)

Piet Schofleur (who was Megan's husband) bit his stick. The stick was not a cigarette—it aided him in quitting smoking. He couldn't think without his stick, and Piet would always think. He taught ethics and meant to put it into practice. His eyes were nearly closed right now.

He nodded enigmatically and turned to Wulf. He said, "And you?" It was a habit of Piet's, that question, that way of pulling someone into a conversation. Piet spoke a lovely English with scarcely a trace of an accent—all Dutchmen seemed to be born with five good languages at least. Megan and Piet had met at Stanford though, and had come out to Africa, like them all, with the pull of the new independence. But Piet was the authentic humanitarian, committed to risking whatever he needed to risk. He had that spirit in his blood, if there were such a thing. His parents had been honored figures in the Dutch Resistance in the forties.

Presumably Wulf heard Piet, though his eyes had drifted onto hers and he appeared to be confused. It could be English was a strain. But he pulled himself together, made stray sounds, began to speak his foreign British English. Africa was a hodgepodge of every accent you had ever encountered.

Wulf's style was a watchful one. He'd nodded more than talked so far and she knew his manner by now—they'd been sitting in the living room an hour and a half. That was a good bit of time with gin and cheese, but still some guests were missing. The Sempebwas—the Ugandans she'd invited. She would not begin the meal if the Sempebwas might still come.

Wulf said, "The issues here, they are new to me. But I have begun to consider them."

He seemed to her to have a smile each time he spoke, though the smile seeped out of his eyes and not his lips. And then, instead of continuing, Wulf plunged himself deep into contemplation, like she'd seen him do already. It meant bending his left arm across his stomach, resting his other elbow on that arm, looking up some-where near the ceiling and rubbing his lower lip with his finger, gently, back and forth and back and forth—like she'd recognized since Lulu'd imitated him. He seemed not to know right now that anyone was observing him, not even her, while here she was fixed helpless on his long thin fingers rubbing at his lip. He had no inkling what effect he had, while he seduced the room—herself, and Megan, and Claudia, and who knew—even Hugh and John and Piet as well.

John had started this subject. That was John's job, starting subjects (and John looked elegant in his newly made red cravat, which heightened his dark eyes). But now that Wulf was contemplating, it was hard on John. John had trouble with quiet rooms. He jumped up. He filled glasses. He cut brie. Megan wasn't cutting brie like she usually did. Megan was taken up with Wulf. It was too easy to be taken up with Wulf—while he did not let on he knew they watched.

Now Wulf's eyes began to crinkle. He looked at Hugh. He said, "I agree with you." He looked at John and said, "There is no question—Swahili as official, as the language of the schools— Swahili would be a barrier for foreign study, foreign trade. However," he paused for a surprisingly long time. "New here, I am—however, I will speculate. I do believe a slowing of the Western influence is required. At the moment it is the most required objective."

Oddly she felt relieved. She hadn't had any idea how Wulf thought, about anything. But she saw he thought like Megan and Piet and not like John and Hugh. And that was good.

She heard "*Nyabo*" (madam) from the kitchen. She uncrossed her legs, pushed up, and had to squeeze her hips between the close-set chairs. Knowing he had his eyes on her maneuver.

Hesita was unhappy. The dinner was dry. They would have to eat whether the Sempebwas came or not.

A pure white dinner party once again. That had not been their idea.

Remnants of cheese and butter and bits of crust were littering the table with the half-filled glasses of wine. In a gap of their quiet the insect screams grew louder from out the open windows. Their eyes were fixed on candles, which gave the illusion of a circle that no one meant to break because the house was dark around them, the dark that seemed to press on them and hold them close to the few slight hints of light.

The now-desultory talk was on change in the country. How to bring change to the country. Always change. Wulf was smiling rather pensively. It was Piet who begged to know what she herself was thinking.

She spoke haltingly. She said, "We might think things are changing. But the deep-telling thing is the woman—is the raising of a child. And a change like that's so slow it hardly counts. Because the raising of a child is a bone-deep body memory . . ." She stopped. They weren't with her in the way she meant. She hadn't said it right and the silence was a puzzled one.

Piet started in with a question but John interrupted him. John said, "Education, you are trying to say, is useless."

She ignored him. She didn't care for John to act as her interpreter. She said, "We talk about changing things. But it all comes down to what a mother is. And a mother draws on her bone memory—somebody might tell a mother to do this and do that with her new baby, but when you have ten babies all day long you don't think 'Do this, do that.' You do the first thing you can, and that's what your mother did and what her mother did and what you've seen done a million times—it's there, you do it. The child is raised the way her mother was raised. And we keep hoping for an overnight change. While we ought to be glad nobody listens. It keeps things semi-balanced, that the mother doesn't change. It's the only thing that stops us turning everything upside down—even when we try to turn things upside down. It's the reason change—genuine change— is a slug's-pace thing—it's the reason that a little bit of a culture might be saved . . ."

She was aware of what was happening. Not a soul was listening to her. They weren't being rude to her. They were caught with her, but a little like they'd been caught with Wulf. Not at all in what she was saying. Had they connected her with Wulf? Or was it this silky mood of hers—the way she leaned and the way she smiled and the way she tipped her wineglass back and forth. And her talking let them watch this mood, the way they had watched Wulf.

Her voice trailed off. They kept on staring. She dropped her eyes down to her plate.

Wulf was next to her. The fact was not irrelevant. She never meant to say her state of mind was a disembodied state. She wasn't drunk. But everything around her was near to floating off because Wulf's knee was pressed on hers.

As soon as they'd sat down at the table Wulf's knee had hit hers. It was accidental. She had pulled hers back. Then it happened with her knee, and he pulled his knee back. But after a while the knees settled happily against each other. She sat out the evening in the heat of his knee, and she was glad for candlelight and nothing brighter than the candlelight and she was glad they'd come to an agreement. The settlement was stable. It meant if she jumped up to fetch some rolls and to pass some chutney—then when she sat back down the knees were not confused. They went straight where they were meant to be.

They were on the front drive in the dark. The voices were behind her. She heard John say to Wulf, "Next time your wife will be with us."

She heard Wulf say, "There are many hurdles, but we hope that it is so."

In her, the boulders settled back in place. Her silky movement drained away. She was emptied of fluids. Abruptly she had no way to reach a person and she did not care to reach a person. Ex-Finn Pole with crinkly eyes or any other person.

She saw at once that she had conjured a mirage.

Yes, it once occurred to her that grown-up men were married. For someone well past thirty the condition would be an obvious one. But it had not concerned her—she had not one thing objective in her mind concerning Finns. What was in the air was what was in the air and that was that. The way they'd played around the mail aisle—that had given rise to the illusion she was living. It hardly called for analyzing families—she had her own attachments as it was. Which made this game innocuous.

But this evening, in her own house, she had learned he lived alone. And from his manner—and his knee—that fact was justified. From his manner she could lose the sense that he was playing with her.

When of course he was playing with her all along. At the mail and in her house.

She nodded good-bye, barely perceptibly.

She locked herself in the bathroom, left the light off, sat on the tub edge, and held her head.

She'd built cardhouses, over and over, and each one had collapsed.

Maybe she never believed in her cardhouses. Maybe she never believed herself at all. Maybe that was the trouble.

So grow up. So live her own sweet given life.

On Disseminating John Milton

Y OU'RE AWED BY THE COUNTRY when you land. First you think you're coming in across huge football fields between the hills. It takes months to learn that they're papyrus swamps. Then you can't get straight if you are in the country or a town. It looks pure country, but there are people walking on the road. The women wear reds and blues and yellows and they sway their hips and carry jugs of water on their heads. The men brake on their bicycles and call out to the women. The air is humming with the greetings, drawn-out, musical. The trees are blooming red and blue and yellow. The view is rich with every shade of green, and filled with flat-topped hills.

Still, vaguely you're disturbed.

It takes a while to put your finger on it. And then you see—the land looks chaotic. It's not split into squares. Banana leaves flop anywhere. You can't find one straight line and you can't see where the *shambas* end. It's topsy-turvy. You decide these people don't know how to take control. They don't bulldoze the hillsides or rearrange the rivers. It must be the religion, you decide. Theirs doesn't tell them they're in charge—that they must subdue what they can see. They assume, rather, that they must fit in. You're disturbed by such a passive attitude.

Immense immeasurable emptiness of things.

She was repeating it. Silently, wedging it in gaps around *Paradise Lost,* which Prudence was stammering over.

She was on their sorry sofa, one knee up on a cushion. Prudence perched on a sorrier chair. Both the chair and the sofa were unforgiving boards—Public Works Department fare—with ropes across the bottom. A thin foam cushion hid the ropes, and the two of them sat board-stiff as the chairs, with a thin foam cushion of politeness between them.

Her living room was not a tutoring place. Milton would have interruptions, but that was the way it was since she was forced to say yes to aunts or to abandon Africa. If she had to tutor Prudence then children had to hurtle through their place and demand their juice and tourniquets. There wasn't an office in this house, and the dining room edged into the living room—both exposed to wanderers—and she was not inviting Prudence into their bedroom. This was it. Afternoons she kept children and afternoons was what they had.

Afternoons with *Paradise Lost.* Picked from a sadist's reading list. She'd avoided this piece of misogyny since she left college but here she was in Africa sloshing line by line through Milton. With Prudence. The halting stumbling desperate incomprehensible made-up explanations, every line, was wearing on both of them.

So she would cushion herself with daydreams to do her Prudence-penance, for the sake of aunts, in memory of her own Aunt Haidie and Aunt Addie. But her head would swim with ex-Finn Poles. (He was walking off into the dark, leaving their house, looking up at her over his shoulder, bewildered since she had scarcely said good-bye.)

He could have attempted to see her since that night. But he had not. And it took adjustment, his taking an assumed *no* as if *no* were what she meant. As if he'd never had a will of his own at all. As if she'd invented his interest.

There were further layers behind her depressed mood. Not merely Prudence and Milton and her ex-Finn Pole. The worst was apprehending she was strapped to nothingness. Maybe philosophically. But she meant more immediately—that it was sheerest lunacy to be out here in Africa.

They'd run howling to escape suburbia—to bog down in John Milton. Day after day after day. And it seemed you sat next to each other all day long, Africans and whites, and no connection happened. You tugged and strained at anything—after all, you'd got to call *some* interchange a friendship. Though nothing clicked. What was the point. You didn't have the boots to keep slogging through the tension. You ended up, like now, wondering where you were and why you were here and what you were doing with this other human being who had no idea whatsoever what she herself was doing. You sat stoic till your watch yelled "Time" so you could tell yourself that you were useful, while you bored each other senseless.

All right. She was forced to this but she would not feign a friendship.

Prudence said, "It is better you do not tell the sense to me." Prudence was wise, and firmly rude.

Agnes said "Oh" at the rebuff.

Prudence said, "I read aloud. It is better."

Agnes saw a rest. Her enthusiasm grew. She said, "I will not interrupt."

Prudence read, with rather heavy stumbling:

>The infernal serpent; he it was, whose guile,
>Stirr'd up with envy and revenge, deceived
>The mother of mankind. . . .

She could merely watch the girl, or not watch the girl. As she chose.

Prudence was shorter than a pure-blood Tutsi, but she had the long thin Tutsi nose and the gigantic droopy-lidded Tutsi eyes—

and the tortuous Tutsi deviousness. Her lips were full, sculpted like
Egyptian lips. Her skin was warmish brown. The smooth quarter-
inch of her hair fuzz was molded to her scalp. A Brancusi head. But
at the moment it was making incomprehensible sounds, which she
guessed as

> Hurled headlong flaming from th' ethereal sky
> With hideous ruin and combustion down
> To bottomless perdition . . .

She took her eyes off Prudence. She watched the middle of the
floor. Fuweesiky the cat was crouching torturing a tailless lizard.
The lizard was laboring to move. Its tail was a regurgitated heap, at
the edge of the mat. Fuweesiky pounced. Fuweesiky pawed at the
truncated creature, slapped it, bounded up and down in front of it,
behind it, over it, and on both sides of it. Fuweesiky was a stupid
cat. He could not digest lizards, but maybe he made some kind of
sense because lizards were easier to catch than birds. He could stay
inside, be lazy, stalk what he could torture.

Prudence stopped reading. She asked, "Please, Madam, what is
the time?"

Agnes began laughing—genuinely. Prudence laughed.

Agnes said, "We could perhaps abandon Milton temporarily—
Pilgrim's Progress is on your list. We could do some Bunyan."

Prudence giggled more. Agnes felt a flush of warmth toward
Prudence with this comprehending laugh. She had never quite
trusted Prudence: Prudence's ambition was too raw and pesky. But
Prudence was so bright that that itself was a pleasure. Prudence
picked up what was going on, like just now with her quick giggle
at herself.

Prudence said, "Let us do that, when we have completed this
Milton."

Abruptly the girl stood up, walked to the painting over the
bookshelf, stood in front of it, and reached her hand up.
Reverently she smoothed her hand across the gobs of inch-thick
paint, across the squatting woman in the picture. Agnes watched
from where she was. She did not say anything. She'd noticed

long ago, when Prudence first came into their house, at Mityana, that the girl looked at the paintings. She'd seen Prudence's eyes come back to this one over the bookcase. It was not usual. Africans came to this house every day, but she couldn't remember one person studying a painting as Prudence studied the paintings. But Prudence had never asked about the paintings.

Prudence said, "This is an animal?"

Agnes did not understand. She said, "Is what an animal?"

Prudence said, "This." She smoothed her hand across the squatting woman.

Agnes was baffled. But she did not let on she was baffled. She strained to see what Prudence was seeing. The painting was, yes, minimally expressionistic. But not unrecognizably. The woman in the painting was larger than life, in a monumental Mexican style. The woman's curves were ultra round. She was turned so you could not see her face, and colors were distorted. But no one could mistake the figure for an animal.

Agnes said, "It's a woman sitting. When a person makes a painting, they make things different from the way you see them every day."

Prudence did not turn around. She continued to stare up at the painting. She fingered the reds, yellows, oranges, and seemed to wonder at them. Agnes was realizing, Yes of course our seeing is learned. Where would Prudence have seen a Western painting? The painter is a pure Mugisu from a hundred miles away but he painted here, at Lubega College, under Western teachers. The man's force came from himself, but his technique came from the West— from Westerners bombarded with a thousand ways of seeing, who might wonder at nothing any longer. While here was Prudence seeing painting new.

The girl was rapt, her arm still up, her fingers still tracing the paint. For a moment Agnes felt something close to envy of this girl. Prudence was caught in a state of unselfconscious wonder. Which would not come pure like this again. Which was virginal.

Prudence might one day paint, find what she wanted, but this, in her face this moment—it would not come back.

Prudence said, "Why do they do such a thing?"

Agnes rubbed her lip. She knew it would matter, her answer. But before she spoke John was in the doorway—in his dark red shirt that framed his suntanned face, his dark hair and eyes and beard. The color showed him off brilliantly, as he was aware it did—making him a magnet for naive mystified women. Yes, Prudence had dropped her hand, lowered her head predictably, and smiled demurely up at John.

Agnes didn't like this shadow play. She did not want to watch.

Prudence had a crush on John. Crushes—certainly you had to put up with them if you managed as a teacher. She was a teacher. She was clear about that. And it wasn't that John liked Prudence. He did not. John did not like Tutsis and he did not trust Tutsis. John had no intention of getting caught in a Tutsi intrigue. The trouble was messier with Prudence.

Prudence's sickly amusements had come to a head at Mityana, one afternoon at teatime. Prudence was taking tea with them, with herself and John, out on their porch. Prudence sat with her cup and saucer on her knee and a plain white blouse on her bosom, only the blouse was as thin as gauze and nothing came between that gauze and Prudence's full black breasts and rosy-sweet perky fat nipples. And she herself, never mind her helpless husband, was paralyzed. Of course neither of them talked too rationally, over their biscuits and tea and bosoms—John kept actually biting his knuckle, as if he was suddenly starving. And neither of them could mention the reason they were flummoxed and tongue-tied. If she, Agnes, was affected by those bouncy nipple-bright bosoms, what were those breasts doing to her husband? And yet they were in Africa, she reasoned, and black bosoms lived in Africa. They watched black free-bouncing bosoms at the tribal dances. There still were tribes that didn't cover breasts, and those that did couldn't be expected to run and buy steeply priced brassieres. So here was an African student, for tea, her bosom covered by a sweet white blouse. And here two teachers sat in mortified excitement, not knowing how to lift a teacup around these full black rosy-nippled tits.

The shabby scene was monstrous. She knew it. It was so macabre she could never open her mouth about it, then or later. That lock-lipped silence was guaranteed. And the girl was quietly and fully conscious of her effect, and knew there would not be one word spoken, ever.

SEVEN

On Marriage

W HAT GOES ON IN A marriage. Suppose the man and the woman are both good-looking, young, bookish and idealistic, have children, live in a place that sparks their energy. Suppose those things. And suppose, in spite of those things, they use their energy destructively. Then does one look for reasons?

We're used to tracking faults—call them causes—in the West. But almost any fault will do; the tools for this pursuit are blunt. So blame mothers and stepmothers, or blame the permissive sixties or original sin—according to your ethics. It's also possible to blame the fifties, which is the time they were in college and neither one had touched the other sex and weren't quite certain what all those parts were for—they had to marry to figure those things out. But then if they were raised in the sixties or the seventies, you'd have to blame some opposite contingency.

Anyway, most probably nothing, fundamentally, was wrong with either of them. One dusk, sitting on the grass with the lightning bugs, they fished airily for talk about Paul Tillich and it felt like falling in love. The next day people thought her ditsy, she remembers, because her laugh was rippling all day long, over nothing at

all. So they started going out on dates and debating the philoso-
phies of God to entertain themselves. They married, and after
they'd figured out about the body parts, the sex worked out okay.
That it didn't rate the press it got was simply one of those perver-
sities that were anchored in the heart of things, she assumed. She
could compromise, and she could hope she'd change, or he'd
change, or both of them would change.

And suppose any explanation is a fundamental lie. Because this
fifties woman was not such an idiot as that. She'd halfway whispered to herself, sometime before they married, that she might not
genuinely love this man. And that mere hint served to terrorize
her—because she herself had chosen just as he had chosen. And
she would never find the courage to listen to this interloper,
truth—though from then on out she would somewhere know,
beyond her rationalizing, that the bewilderment and anguish of
their marriage grew from this one colossal cowardice of hers. But
she could rationalize back then that a whole vast structure had
been hammered up around them—by friends, by families, by their
own heady expectations. And he provided her a place, an escape
from parents who had dwindled, in her exacting eyes, to a heap of
dull conventions.

Everything supported their young marriage. Together they
could boast of children, of friends, of work and plans and hopes.
They had all they needed, one would certainly have hoped.

Depression is the bedrock. Accept it. The phrase erupted, not loud
enough for anyone to hear. She closed her mouth. But it didn't
stop her chewing on instructions to herself: Don't expect different.
You'll last if you grasp in your bowels that depression is the
bedrock, that depression is your eternal inescapable bedmate. You
start to like a person and the liking bites. You start to love a person
and the loving gnaws you raw. There is no escaping. Adore your
sweet depression and you might creep by somehow.

She'd waked with rotten dreams. Now she stood in the Penguin alcove, in the Uganda Bookshop. The shelf in front of her was gray with modern classics but out the window beside her, looking out on the alley, the sound was like her dream. She heard shouting in Acholi. She glimpsed a group of soldiers carrying machine guns—they were disappearing through a low back door a couple of squalid holes down. The sight of them left her queasy.

It was midmorning. The bookshop was shadowy. And now newly quiet, with the soldiers gone. She could hear the first fat raindrops hit banana leaves outside. This sound was companionable, like gray classics were companionable. Any book you reached for from where she was—*Notes from the Underground, The Sound and the Fury, Heart of Darkness, Death in Venice*—let you wallow in the comforting kind of depression. You were almost all right with these misanthropes; which meant, clearly, if you intended to be wise like them you had to get born with depression. Or maybe you simply holed up and wrote novels and let that kill your marriage—maybe that sank you low enough to belong with these gray Penguin books.

The flaw—she wasn't kin to these men. She wasn't writing at all. The play she'd promised to finish for the school only made her futilely guilty. But these gray Penguins were bound to give her something.

The Horse's Mouth. She'd long intended to read that book and never gotten to it. She pulled it out. She wouldn't start if there were many pages. The book fell open. A line leaped out: *Go love without the help of anything on earth.*

She didn't get farther. That line knocked something loose in her.

She looked up, out the window, not seeing out the window.

The line was strangely flat, *Go love without the help of anything on earth.* It was unpoetic, didactic. But her tongue held onto it. *Go love without the help of anything on earth.*

It grounded her. As if this person knew her own depression, and handed her at least a tiny outlet.

Her mood rebounded. As if she stood on something hard.

Something bleak and dependable, like she was looking for. *Without the help of anything on earth.* She spaced the words, and vacantly she watched the fat drops shake the leaves. She listened to the hypnotizing rhythm of the splats.

Of course—the line was Blake's. Odd that it should be Blake's.

Blake was symbols, idiosyncratic—and then he fired off pure didacticisms like this one. As if love were something you could *will*—whatever kind of will he meant. Maybe the line just acknowledged that whatever moves a person is never totally unconscious—that some kind of will is imbedded in the roots of things. It would have to be, or else *guilt* wouldn't make any sense. Yet still—a charge to love is a presumptuous charge: The shape of the words is biblical. But then, since Blake declared he never put a comma down without a good reason, he was conscious of the implications of a charge like this, that it takes you out of the normal range of the readily humanly possible. It means, if you're meant to obey that injunction, you have to burrow down into something deeper. You have to dive into unknown waters, draw on unknown forces, evolve not-yet-discovered capacities. But you're compelled to do so. You can't ignore this thing. It's commanded of you. Who knows where it's commanded from—but instinctively you know it's from a *where* that makes the highest form of sense. You are forced to live far out beyond the borders of your self.

Strange how Blake could be affecting her this moment. It was as if Blake himself could be looking out at this rain, and these banana trees. Because Blake's words were changing her right now, changing even the way she looked at the alley, and after all these many years since the man had died.

She reached to put the book back on its shelf, and she heard Megan's voice.

Not now. She might love—but not just now. Not yet. And certainly not yet people. Please. She stepped back farther in the shadows, and she heard Wulf's voice. Wulf was answering Megan.

Her breathing started having gaps, but she was hidden. The two of them, Megan and Wulf, were alcoves over from the spot where she was hiding out. She strained to hear them, but she couldn't quite.

She heard "Azande." Yes, Megan read anthropology.

But Megan did not need Wulf to study the Azande.

She had not suspected her depression could go deeper.

Two people she had loved (and she'd loved Megan, with passion. It had never come to physical passion—but from that time on she'd grasped how such a thing could be. It was years ago now. And Megan, with her instinctive wisdom, had calmly ignored the attraction).

She drew herself in tightly, leaned against the windowsill.

Two people she loved. She should have known that they'd be drawn together. She'd always known you had to love Megan—anybody did. And it was now clear everybody loved her Finn. Why was that always true—if you loved a person, of course it was a person everybody else loved too. If you felt it, everyone felt it. It didn't have to be commanded, this kind of love she knew.

She heard them leaving. Their backs would be turned. They would be heading to the counter and wouldn't see her so she moved to the edge of the bookcase to look out.

He was walking beside Megan, nodding, listening. The way he moved, the way he crossed his arms, the way he held his head down. She loved him. No matter what.

They were looking toward somebody. She couldn't see who. They were waiting. She saw it was for Piet.

Piet was coming up to meet his wife and Wulf. They were casual. They chatted. They had come to the bookshop together. They'd been in different sections. That was all this meant.

It was as if the toilet room had changed places with the living room. There was not a reason in creation she could not go over and speak.

She called "Megan" and came up to the three of them. Wulf was gracious and turned a little red, or she imagined it. They said the innocuous things—while what she said came out disjointed and maybe upside-down. And after the three of them left the shop, she kept on standing in the very same spot until the clerk said "Madam?" and she moved. And walked a few steps off. And in perhaps three minutes Wulf rushed back into the bookshop. He folded his umbrella, and he grinned at her while he was doing it, while she grinned back at him. He came up to her, and he asked her please would she go upstairs with him for coffee, to the Nile Café, and she said yes she would.

The stairs went up from the first floor between the Ladybird books and the cabinet of odds and ends. The staircase was mammoth, Victorian, darkwood paneled. It turned twice, at right angles. The banisters and newel posts were square. Everything was massive and at angles, and it made the two of them quite tiny. They went up step by step in unison, dwarfed by heavy wood and by all the things inside themselves. Her face was flushed. He held her elbow. They did not speak.

At the last bend in the stairs they were washed by rainy light from the veranda. They heard clicks of spoons and voices—English English and English spiced with accents strange as Wulf's. The sounds were muffled with the rain and the traffic. It was cozy, with all these people packed together with the smell of rain and coffee.

She didn't notice anyone. He was leading her toward a table by the rail. Their knees touched when they sat. He drew his back at once. They did not let on they noticed.

It seemed to her that they were closed in by the rain and it seemed to her his face was lighted by it. Between them was a red-checked tablecloth and a white hibiscus blossom in a bottle. The rain fell close enough to feel the sprinkles on her arm.

Primarily, they smiled, and at Erasmus the waiter too. Erasmus was attentive. Wulf surprised him—because Wulf spoke phrases in Luganda, which surprised her more, that Wulf had caught the tune you needed for Luganda quick as this. Wulf asked Erasmus words. She ordered scones and coffee, but Erasmus wouldn't leave. He leaned toward Wulf—talked softly, conspiratorially. He meant Wulf (this newcomer) to grasp how good this country had been until this Lango man, Obote, took charge; how the Lango'd tricked Buganda, ground the civilized people in the mud. That Lango couldn't trust his own people, said Erasmus. The man had to bribe his own army—hand over good money this country used to have. Wulf seemed to get Erasmus's drift.

They had a gap, when Erasmus moved away, of quite self-conscious quiet. They looked out through rain, over the rail, at people crushed in doorways waiting for the rain to stop. She couldn't see the tinsmith, but she could hear him faintly.

She noticed Wulf go still, abstracted, as if he were listening for something. For what?

He said softly, as if he were talking to himself, "Gujarati."

So he was listening to the men who were sitting behind him. She said, "Can you speak that, too?"

He shook his head.

She said, "But you can hear it?"

He said, "I know only bits of the languages of India. I can tell them apart, read Sanskrit. That is all."

She said, "Have you always been able to do this?"

He smiled at her mockingly, and he waited before he answered, "It is merely training."

She said, "It is not merely training. Were your parents like this?"

"My mother. In this I am like my mother, though I have had the opportunity to study. She had not the opportunity."

His mother, yes, all right. But she did not ask about his wife. When he talked about his mother she was looking at his arms a bit, in his rolled-up blue-checked shirt. Mostly she watched his finger move across his bottom lip. She rubbed her own lip, but all at once she thought what she was doing and she abruptly dropped her hand. He hadn't seemed to notice.

The sun came out. He said, "The rain here, it is strange."

She said, "Is it?"

He said, "Suddenly it starts—the streets empty. Just as suddenly it stops. The sun appears, just so, and the streets are crowded once again."

She said, "I forget that it is strange."

There were growing gaps between the things they thought to say. She dared, "Forgive me for my coldness."

He studied her before he said, "I do not find you cold."

She said, "But you did."

He did not answer. She had turned her head to the street in apprehension, but when he stayed quiet for so long she looked back, curious. His eyes were somewhat narrowed. They held the play that she had grown used to. But he was not answering her. He was waiting for her. She said "Never mind" and shook her head. She was embarrassed. She did not know where she was with him.

He said, "Of course I considered your change. Where had it come from, my offense. I search for the offense."

He seemed on the point of continuing. But he stopped himself. She said, "And did you find it?"

He said, "I keep my legs to myself, on my own space."

She laughed while she shook her head. He began laughing. She moved her leg so that it pressed against his leg, and he did not draw his away. Rather he drew his breath in audibly. She was looking down. His fingers moved to touch her fingers, and while the tremble lasted she did not look up.

EIGHT

On the Numinous

There are visitations stored as memories, or memories stored as visitations—it doesn't matter which. The earliest stay luminous, resurface, light other spots around the globe. You may never know the reason. In one you were swinging. Your mother was nearby. It was a sunken soft-grass patch on a mountainside, and the swing hung from a frame of rough-cut logs. On three sides of the grass was forest, but the sun got through. You were small. The swing and sunshine made you happy, and after that morning it was stuck in your head that this was what they meant when they said *heaven*—thick soft new-green grass, in a circle in the forest, with your mother and the sunshine and the swing.

It was Megan and Piet's house, late afternoon. Odinga was occupied in back—they'd made their *jambo* courtesies. In the front, it was a haphazard gathering for a visiting Nigerian who'd come as external examiner, grading examinations. They sat on the low veranda. Trellises of orange bougainvillea mixed with golden shower vine. The sweetness came from frangipani trees.

The spot was sunken thicknesses—the greens were thick and the smells were thick and the walls to the mud-brick house were thick. Megan's was books and music and children and whoever might show up. Hans, Megan's misanthropic German with the long and scraggly beard, had inhabited her thatched guest house for months.

Agnes had just arrived. But when she did—like she had before—she had a kind of déjà vu, as if she knew these sounds and smells from her own South, sometime when they'd sunk into her without her knowing. It could be she'd dreamed it. But whether she'd dreamed it or whether she hadn't, she had inhabited a spot like this where she had heard black voices under vines by a house with a porch around it.

She was in a deck chair. Beside her was the table where the Schofleurs ate their meals. That early morning when she'd rushed here about Odinga she'd stopped at this table, which was set for breakfast. It sat then in a checkerboard-leaf light with green-and-orange papaw on white cloth. For a minute she'd watched a spider hanging over the table—a banana spider, big and yellow and striped and hanging in leaf-shifting yellowish light. A wagtail bird had hopped up on the tablecloth, and when she jumped to shoo the bird little Maggie came out the door and announced her mother was on the bed crying. Which disoriented her. Lying on beds crying belonged to her own life. It did not belong to Megan's life. When Megan came out puffy-eyed she wanted to ask questions, like what could Piet have done to her. But Megan was English and she did not ask questions.

She still loved Megan, though now in a calm, domesticated fashion. But she'd been sure she would never have let Megan see the undomesticated side of her feelings—that time when she was young and clearly mad—if she hadn't felt some hint of reciprocation on the part of Megan. She guessed their past was part of the odd constraint that still held between them. Because something kept them from speaking of intimate things. That morning she'd merely settled with Megan about Odinga's work and left.

Today Wulf was here already, and so was John. Hans strolled over to the porch. He seemed interested in Wulf.

A commotion broke out across the garden by the guest house. All but John and herself and Hans scurried over to investigate. Even Wulf. Michael or Lumumba had found a snake and they were catching it or killing it or something. She didn't go see, because if Hans had chosen to leave his hut and come and sit beside her here then she would not jump up. It was rare for Hans to join them when Megan and Piet had guests, but now he was asking her how *The Potter* was coming (the play she was writing for school was called *The Potter and the Shadow of Death*). Hans had more invested in her play than she herself was managing, or so it seemed to her.

She knew Hans's story from Megan. Hans was here because he didn't need to work. His wife, in any case, lived with another man. He was the lifelong friend of Piet Schofleur—they'd lived in the same Dutch-German border town once upon a time but Hans's father had had to fight for Germany. Yet most of all Hans came and stayed out here because he loved Megan Schofleur. His love was unobtrusive and hopeless (like her own love for Megan had been hopeless), and Piet persisted in welcoming Hans because Hans had given up on life except for Megan and Piet. Hans watched birds and wrote "Lines on Death" in a rust-colored cloth-bound book and moved about obscurely—he didn't go places with Megan and Piet. It was comforting to her to think of Hans being here in Megan's hut—Hans didn't hope for anything at all, and vaguely she herself felt something solid when Hans was here at Megan's.

Hans stopped talking. She let him be, not saying anything either. It was one of those things about being with Hans—he managed with silences, so she had better manage as well. But John began speaking low, to her alone. He said, "Don't be angry—I haven't had a chance to tell you yet. I asked Wulf to Turi."

She covered her reaction. She said, "Why?" because that was as good as any other answer.

John said, "It's only for two days. He has a conference in

Nairobi. He's never seen the Highlands, and it seemed obvious. I assumed you wouldn't mind."

Irony was not John's nature. Once Megan tried to dissect John with her. Megan said, He has no irony, your husband, and when Megan said that thing she'd understood—she'd grasped years of their life together, why when she tried to track down her annoyance it swilled off into pettiness and left her standing with a load of guilt, because it was clear to everybody that John was the interesting one; John was who you needed at your party, what with his questions keeping you trawling for opinions on, say, what to do when your student gets possessed. And in spite of all that, Megan spotted why you bogged down sooner or later when you talked with John. It helped, what Megan said. Like now, there wasn't any doubt what John was saying—John meant it like he said it. Astoundingly.

She said the innocuous: "The children seem happy with him."

She could see Wulf across the grass, but barely. He was hidden in bushes and a scattering of shade. He held a pole. He was bending down, pointing something out to Lulu in the undergrowth.

Wulf liked her child (she wondered if he knew how Lulu mocked his lip-rubbing), and John liked Wulf. Wulf would come to Turi. Everything was good. So good she went lightheaded. Suddenly. As if—as if this spot had floated onto an undiscovered plane, and all that she could see was as it ought to be. As if all that she could see had reached what it was destined for, and that was here this moment, in this sunken garden, on this very afternoon with this sweet smell of grass and frangipani. It was as if each person's tiny gesture was ordained from the dawn of things, and for precisely these few minutes, when she herself in her rose dress and Hans and John and Wulf and Megan and bounding children black and white and birds and butterflies, when they all moved simply, in a honey-colored light.

The air was thin in Kenya, cold and clear. You breathed woodsmoke and cedar, and in the mornings you smelled dew like stiff cold hay. You needed a fire those mornings, and when the sun went down you needed fire as well. In between you were hot in the sun, but you escaped under bluegum trees. The fields were wheat fields, and the sun turned these to gold, and the gold and the black-green firs stood out against the deep wide blue of the sky.

They stayed at Turi, near Molo. Turi was a hill in the high wheat country, with a railway station and an English boarding school. The buildings at the school were simple—dark wood houses hooked together by stone walks. The walks had roofs, and the labyrinth of covered paths ran through lilies and daisies and hollyhocks. When the school was out for holidays vacationers could stay there if they wanted, and the ones from hotter Africa did want, if they couldn't get to Mombasa.

In the room they were sitting in just now, you smelled pipes and wood and horse-size dogs. It wasn't Africa. You sat in Morris reading chairs and one of the things you wondered at was the stonework in the chimney. The rough stones shifted colors and shapes and the rounded lines of their mortar sketched evocative abstract patterns. Italians had built it. It was a story you heard at Turi. The masons-artists had been prisoners of war out here, because Kenya was next to Ethiopia and Italians had not lasted in Ethiopia, but here in the Highlands you came across stone walls that were Italian walls. And Italians built the Tuscan chapel; only the Tuscan chapel sat up over the Great Rift Valley on the peak of the Mau Escarpment. And inside the Tuscan chapel was the mural of the black Madonna.

John had driven to the village to fetch the Sunday paper. Wulf was sitting on a low brown chair poking at the fire. She sat on a zebra-skin hassock and Anne was leaning on her. Anne had a cozy way of sucking her finger, sticking her elbow up in the air, and rolling a bit of her blouse in her other hand—three of these occupations at one time, while her mother was considering how to put some questions to Wulf. Like—will you tell me please why you're in Africa without your wife? Is it truly because you couldn't manage to get your wife out of Poland? You didn't have to come here, did you, if you knew your wife couldn't come? Is this maybe a divorce you want? Do you maybe not like your wife so well (I wouldn't blame you, you know; these things happen, you know) but then if you don't dislike your wife then what can I mean to you, or am I making all this up and how can I know if you don't speak, when you could, you know, have spoken. Like at the Nile Café, when you touched my hand. Like yesterday, when we walked to the railroad station and everybody else was ahead of us. It scares me you don't speak. It means you want to keep *will* out of this. Speaking means will, and will would make this human, and dangerous—if you brought will in, then you couldn't just think it was a quick little burning in passing. If you ever spoke. Which you will not.

They were quiet around the fire, where she did not ask her questions. Maybe because the rest of the room was noisy. Lulu and the dog were yelping. Michael was catching Lulu—it was a free-fall game in the midst of the floor, and in the middle of the commotion Wulf stood up and leaned close to the window. She knew this manner by now, this sudden quiet, this dropping into absorption and more or less disappearing—when he'd be picking up some language she had not heard at all because the languages around her were a background blur.

The *sais* was talking to someone, outside the window by the woodpile. It was not Swahili—she could tell that much. (*Sais* was what they said up here in Kenya, as if of course you knew a *sais* looked after the horses—all good Indian colonials knew *saises* looked after horses.) She could watch Wulf openly when he was turned away like this.

Anne was restless, monkeying with her pigtails, making faces, showing her gap tooth. Now she poked her mother's cheek. She said, "Sing, Mama. Sing about hot rooms."

Agnes said, "Shhhh."

Anne said, "Why shhh?"

Agnes nodded her head toward Wulf but Wulf had turned

around and said, "Do not shhhh. Sing, Agnes. I would like a song about hot rooms."

She frowned at Anne, "What hot rooms are you talking about?"

Anne sprawled on her mother's lap. Her arms stretched up, hit her mother's shoulder. Agnes looked down at Anne's red cheeks, red from the fire and from the Kenya cold. She liked her children sprawled on her.

Anne said, "Hot rooms, hot rooms—you know. Rings. Rings all over her."

She said, "Oh, that, but Mr. Kieslowski and I were talking."

Anne said, "You weren't talking. You weren't doing anything."

Wulf said, "We are waiting on hot rooms, you know, and rings all over her."

She said to Anne, "I am not sitting here in front of this fire and singing for no reason, not in front of a grown-up."

Wulf came back to his place, and sat, and bent his face down close to Anne. The top of his head was an inch from Agnes's face. She smelled the woodsmoke in his hair. He whispered to Anne, "Tell your mother I am leaving the room."

He stood up, and he held her eye while he leaned the poker on the chimney. Then without looking back he crossed the room and went out. Michael ran after him. The dog ran after Michael. Lulu tripped, got up, and limped more slowly after the dog. Anne got halfway to the door but changed her mind, came back to the chair Wulf left, brushed her hair back out of her face, tucked her arms under her thighs, and said, "Now you may sing." Anne was a very proper child.

She could hear Wulf outside with Michael and Lulu and the dog. They were just outside the door, at the bench on the covered walk.

She said loud enough for him to hear: "It's not worth the scramble. I've forgotten heated rooms."

He called, "Then it must be of the rings all over her."

His answer made her smile, so she sat up straight, and she sang, "I know where I'm going,/And I know who's going with me."

She tried to sing with a lilt and a sexy, mysterious voice but her voice cracked and she stopped singing. It might be she couldn't sing at all. It might be she could only sing for children—but she meant for him to be seduced now she'd started singing, and it would not work with a creaky voice.

She leaned to sip some liquid. It was his lukewarm coffee. She cleared her throat, started over, and her drawn-out not-quite-sexy notes competed with the train, which hooted and she knew it would keep on hooting till it reached the top of the escarpment. The fire began popping explosions. The cooks in the nearby kitchen started throwing pots against the metal. She laughed and closed her mouth. He came in with a fistful of daisies and dropped them in her lap.

Anne said, "I'm going to stick them in your plait." Anne did that sometimes, because her mother's plait was fat and long and good for holding flowers. She sat where she was while Anne snapped the stems of the daisies and poked them in her hair.

Wulf took out Anne's barrette. He fitted a daisy in it, and he laboriously closed her barrette while Anne held still for him. And then he took the child by her shoulders and held her away from him, admired her, brushed her hair back from her face and said to Anne, "Sometimes I have placed a flower in my little girl's hair, so now I pretend you are my little girl."

Anne said, "What is her name?"

Wulf said, "Her name is Thea."

"Where is your little girl?"

"She is in Poland."

"You didn't want to bring her here?"

"I wanted to bring her here. I tried hard to bring her here."

"*You* came here. How can it be hard?"

"We have funny rules in Poland."

Wulf spoke to Anne, but once he looked up at Agnes while he was speaking to Anne. So he was thinking of her hearing him while he was talking to Anne. So he was saying all these things quite consciously for her, informing her deliberately that he missed his family, which he had not said to her. He was meaning to be honest maybe, in his way. He was warning her maybe. Telling her—the naive, guileless American—telling her not to trust the way he acted. Words were what counted and—notice—he'd avoided words.

She felt the night-in-the-driveway mood come back. She should have listened to it. Of course John brought Wulf to Turi. John was aware of Wulf's lonely state, the way Wulf missed his wife. John knew European flirting and knew it was meaningless. John could be sophisticated when he wanted a friend.

She couldn't.

Already he must feel her rigidness again, because he was getting up and saying to Anne, "This last flower, your mother needs it in her hair." She felt the shock of his hand on her shoulder.

Heat shot through her body. She did not pull away. She felt him wedge the flower in, and then drop the plait. She felt him keep on stroking the plait, and the fingers of his other hand moved back and forth and back and forth, deep into her shoulder. She turned her head. Her face was at the level of his groin, a half an inch off from him. She closed her eyes at the movement she could see. It seemed to her he was circling her.

She heard the step. She glanced up. John was back. John was looking through the door glass.

NINE

On Banishing the Loneliness

THERE'S A DEEP LONELINESS IN Africa. You drive and drive and it doesn't seem to matter. You see bush and cows and flat-topped hills and no inbreak, no landmark you make sense of. You don't know how to think about an empty vastness. You've had no initiation into the spirits of the place.

Kenya now—you've read books about the Kenya Highlands. You think you'll recognize the land. But you don't seem to be any longer in the tropics. The sky is banked-up gray, the hills are straw, and the wind is cold. You see one figure only—a Kikuyu woman climbing a steep path. She is not the graceful, regal-strolling, hip-swaying caryatid of the easy-living Africa you left, the ones humming out their long-extended greetings. This woman is bent double. She's underneath the wood she's carrying. The wood is tied with a cord and the cord is looped across her skull. Her forehead is corrugated ridges from the weight, and through the black-green pines behind her, the light is very weak.

It wasn't long. But time is weighted oddly. When things collide—

or persons—with no warning, measurements don't hold. Seconds or minutes or hours make no difference.

Wulf did not see John. But between herself and John was merely glass. John had not touched the door handle. He stood in his brown Norwegian sweater. He held the *London Observer* over his chest. His face was in the shade but the auburn dog beside him and the yellow flowers in back of him were in the sun. He looked direct to where she looked at him from around their visitor's hip. It occurred to her—from John's angle her face would be against their visitor's groin. It might as well have been. And yet she didn't move. She gazed at her husband levelly and guiltless and he returned her gaze—no hint of a shifty eye. As if the door between them let them speak square on.

Her eyes, her stillness, would tell him she could not move, not with this man's hands on her. They would tell him it was impossible to move, that she had no will, that yes, this might affect him, John, but that was the way it was.

And what she expected in his face, she did not find in his face. What she read was rather: He was not surprised. And more complex than that: He was not unhappy. As if he had invited what he saw. A person rarely looks at someone else unguardedly. But now that it was so, now that they looked unguardedly, she saw what she had not grasped before: that she'd been thinking in the same clichés as everybody else.

But Anne and Wulf turned around and the lucidity was gone. Her shoulder went cold, and she felt merely exposed.

She spoke minimally, got up, and escaped with Anne to the kitchen.

In spite of odd-placed doors, to the woodpiles and sheds, the school kitchen was dark and the smell was fertile—coffee, and woodsmoke from the room-long woodburning stove. The *sais* and who-knew-who-the-others-were were hanging out by the woodpile. She spoke Swahili, mostly with the *sais* because she knew him best, while she collected cups and plates and knives and spoons, and sugar and jam from screened-in darkwood cabinets. She let Anne spoon up the cream.

The cream was a layer on top of the milk, which was still in the pail, which had come from Turi cows this morning. It smelled sweet and warm. It was yellow-clotted to a butter thickness and hung clumped and dripping over Anne's spoon. Anne plopped it in a yellow bowl. Anne stuck her finger in it, licked her finger, and stuck her finger in again and offered a lick to the *sais*. He shook his head. She offered the finger to her mother, who bent down to suck it. Her mother pointed out lumps to catch around the edges of the milk, lumps stuck to the sides of the milk pail.

Her Swahili was Uganda-bad and the *sais's* was the classic Indian-Ocean-style Swahili. But he got what she said and that was comforting right now, talking to him—she did not care to think about the room where she was headed. She discussed the weather. She discussed the horses. But the *sais* kept picking up the tray. He believed she had her duties. He was forcing her to get on with the serving of her men. He meant to carry the tray for her. Anne ran off with Lulu.

She held the door of the common room for the *sais,* said, "Put it by the fire."

Wulf and John didn't notice their coming, or they pretended not to. Wulf still clung to his poker. He was looking at the fire and listening to John. John was reading out loud from the paper. She heard "Czechoslovakia," saw Wulf nod.

She sensed these men were managing, and quite happily. As if she'd invented her shame. As if neither of them had noticed any need for shame. As if to them the things that mattered came in Sunday papers. As if sex infected things of course but only around the far, far edge. As if who except a woman cared to make an issue of the subject, find monstrous meanings in a simple fleeting attraction, blow it up, and spoil the things that mattered. As if sex popped up, yes, came and went. Wives or mistresses, both wives and mistresses—men didn't give them undue weight, and the world would run much smoother if women didn't give them undue weight.

That was her depressing sense.

Wulf turned around and looked up, seemed to merely see the *sais* and hopped up smiling broadly, as if he had a new-discovered friend.

The *sais* said, "*Jambo, Bwana.*"

Wulf said, "*Habari?*"

"*M'zuri sana, Bwana. Habari?*"

Wulf said, "*M'zuri.* What language do you speak?" He asked it in Swahili.

The *sais* looked mystified, said, "Swahili, *Bwana.* Same as you."

Wulf said, "*Hapana.* What language did I hear you speak an hour ago—out there?" He gestured toward the window.

"Kikuyu, *Bwana.*"

Wulf said, "*Hapana.* Another language."

"This day, *Bwana?* I do not know, *Bwana.* Somali?"

Wulf nodded vigorously. He said, "Somali. That's it. Somali. A moment I thought it was Arabic."

The *sais* said, "We are one people, *Bwana.*"

Wulf spoke a phrase she could not understand. The *sais* grinned and answered very rapidly.

Wulf looked around, apologized to John and her, and walked the *sais* to the door. She heard him arrange a meeting with the *sais.*

John was overplaying things. He brought her an extra pillow and her sweater. She rather thought they needed noise, any noise to diffuse things, or diffuse her own constraint if that was all it was. She searched the phonograph records, put on the *St. Paul's Suite.* They drank coffee, ate thick cream with scones, and quickly divided the thin-sheet airmail *Observer* and took refuge in that.

They knew farmers in the area. They were invited for the Sunday midday dinner. The farmer was actually a horticulturalist with the Kenya government, and the man, the woman, and a daughter (home for school holidays) played violins and a cello for Sunday dinner guests.

It was after Sunday dinner, three or so in the afternoon, and a truncated Trout Quintet.

The room was light-flooded, pale green, and open on all sides to the fields. A rain had come during dinner, and then the sun, and now the smell of grass, new-scythed, washed into the room with the light.

The listeners were sitting at odd angles. Wulf found her hand and held it, there in the middle of them all, but secretly, behind a chair.

She'd put the children to bed. She was leaving the san (the sanitarium, which was the school infirmary, which was where they slept) but she changed her direction. It was almost dark and someone was playing the piano. It was the old piano in the school refectory—she had never heard it played. The tune was halting but she recognized it. From this morning—the hot rooms and the rings.

She made no sound. She stood in the refectory doorway. He'd left the door open. The room was shadowy and bleak, a cavernous forest of upturned legs to chairs, which were all piled up on wooden tables. The piano was at the far end of the room so his back was turned. Slowly he was picking out the notes. The pond was near the refectory so the croak of frogs was loud and the crickets were louder than the frogs. His notes were hollow echoes in the empty room, and they mixed with frogs and crickets, which all made a lonely sound, with the chair-legs up on tables. As if each time he hit a key it was sucked into something remote, and vulnerable.

He let his hand drop in his lap, and seemed to curl inside himself. Then the sound was frogs and crickets alone. But he raised his head and twisted his stooped body around to the side, as if he'd known that she was there. He didn't hurry.

He wasn't smiling. His eyes were far from crinkly. She didn't smile either, and for a while she didn't move. She let the refectory be shadowy between them. But then she walked across the room and bent her head and kissed him.

TEN

On Building Love of Reading

COMMUNAL. SOLITARY. AFRICA IS COMMUNAL, you hear. It will work out structures that fit, that don't force Africans to counterfeit whites.

Is it white or black, or is it the climate?

African houses are shelter from rain, and from animals at night. Life takes place outdoors. Whites, who're living a second generation in the Kenya Highlands, no longer recognize their children. New generations live outdoors. They're good at sports. They don't read. They're a different kind of people, say their sleet-bred English parents. We don't understand them. So you hear.

It's striking to note the way the Scottish-Highland farmers took to farming the hills in the Kenya Highlands. Made electricity from a rusted lawn-mower motor. Fitted up pumps and irrigation out of wheels from defunct wagons and out of hubs from a burnt-out still. And sat on the lonesome hilltops, the craggy individualist and happy to be that way. They'd have to be, because the land isn't rich enough to support more people per acre.

It's not the skill, it's not the hard work, it's not even the reading and the know-how—it's the cultural image of the solitary person, or the lack of it, that makes the pattern unduplicatable. It's the African wanting more people around. It's some cultural assumption about how close people ought to be to each other, and how many of them ought to be close to each other. You see ten men in the middle of the road painting a single foot of a line—it's somewhat difficult for European funders. But for being human, it's comforting, and becomes hard to do without, for blacks who leave as well as for whites. The whites can fall into the warm seductive rhythms, and into the African spacing.

❦

Prudence was staggering out loud over:
> A dungeon horrible, on all sides round
> As one great furnace flam'd; . . .

Their arrangement bound them—no interference until asked. Prudence darted her eyes at her teacher's face and quickly back at the book.

This afternoon Prudence was emphasizing her determined new demureness. She deduced that from the girl's blouse—the same white gauzy see-through blouse of edgy Mityana memory. Only now an opaque undergarment masked her perky bright nipples.

The girls made a racket in the hall. Michael and Bernard (Bernie, along with Maggie and a four-year-old Annika, being Megan's children) and Jomo and Lumumba Baku were marching past the porch in cut-up cardboard boxes. They were shouting the Pete Seeger song. Michael had taught them. It was their marching song:

> Things to do—it's getting late,
> We're all brothers and we're only passing through.

Prudence giggled and went on:

> Regions of sorrow, doleful shades, where peace
> And rest can never dwell, hope never comes.

Prudence put the book down and tried to stop her giggling. It pried loose Agnes's laugh, till she couldn't stop. She got up holding her sides and stumbling over the floor for a handkerchief.

Lulu and Anne and Maggie dropped their objects and stared. They were dragging mammoth objects across the middle of the room.

Anne made a snaggle-toothed, lip-hiked-up frown at her doubled-up mother. She said "Did you hurt your stomach?"

Lulu said to Anne, "Don't be a bubble-headed booby. Can't you see she's laughing?"

Maggie said to Prudence, "Did you tickle her?"

Prudence said, "The book I read causes laughter."

Lulu said, "Will you read it to us?"

Prudence picked up the book and ran her finger down the page. Three girls stood in front of her and waited. She read:

As far removed from God and light of heav'n

As from the centre thrice to th' utmost pole.

Lulu was scratching her leg with one bare foot. She said, "It isn't sooo funny."

Maggie said to Lulu, "Maybe it's rice on the poles that's funny."

Lulu said "Maybe," and went back to dragging objects. The object she was dragging was three times taller than she was. She scraped it through the room. It tangled in mats. She bumped it down the step to the front porch. Then Maggie and Lulu and Anne marched back and forth along the trail between the porch and the kitchen sink, across the living room. They spilled water and splashed paint.

Prudence persisted: ". . . But O how fall'n! how changed. . . "

Agnes was not laughing any longer, but she was not absorbed in Milton either. She was merely rubbing her lip and staring out the window.

Wulf was in Zanzibar. He'd be in Tanzania for one whole month. He'd sent them a postcard of a narrow winding street. It was an Arab town, with balconies and donkeys and men in *kanzus* and fezzes and people selling balls of orange spices and bolts of purple cloth. The postcard said, "This place is red and white and black and orange and so heavy with cloves and Arabic and the sound of waves and sailors that I feel desire for the clear pure air of Uganda." The card was to both of them. And that was it. But it put her in a cool room bristling chair legs where the sound was frogs and crickets and notes on his piano, which she liked best when the piano hushed. She stayed with the minutes the piano hushed. When she crossed that room. When she didn't have a choice but to cross that room. When his eyes were clear about where they intended her to be. When his lips opened. When he waited. When his lips met hers, while the frogs and the crickets kept on with their croaking, droning, humming and his skin kept pouring out its sweetness. She hadn't smelled his sweetness quite so strong before. A natural sweetness soaked in deep. Low and rich and fertile like he was. Sweetly smoky, or woody, seeping out of his skin. She closed her eyes at the smell coming back, into the living room with Prudence and with Milton. She drifted off to lying in silk in a narrowing Zanzibar alley. It was violets and pinks and stones gone warm and sweet with sun and oil and a cinnamony spice and he was bursting the gate of the alley and he was leaping dates and cloves and coconuts and crashing through to where she lay in heaps of down-soft cushions with the filmy rosy gauzy cloth draped loose across her thighs and where her breasts lay naked open waiting . . .

Abruptly Prudence stopped reading. She said, "Madam, what is that object?"

Agnes started, opened her eyes, said, "What object?"

Prudence said, "What is the tall thin object which Lulu pulled?"

She said, "It is an easel, for painting."

Prudence said, "Why must the object be painted?"

She said, "Oh no no no. They don't paint the easel. The easel holds pictures they are painting."

Prudence looked doubtful, strained to see out the window.

Agnes said, "Shall we abandon Milton?"

Prudence pursed her lips and nodded. They smiled, and Agnes said, "Come watch."

Prudence followed her out to the porch.

Lulu was directing things. Lulu liked directing, when Michael left her free. Anne was setting out the tins of paints. Lulu was tacking up her paper to an easel board. Maggie smoothed her paper on the table. Anne settled on the floor for her own table.

Lulu said to Prudence, "Do you want to paint?"

Prudence said, "I want only to observe what you are painting."

Anne was occupied already. She had brown, inch-wide zigzags on her page. She stood up. She said, "What is that?" She meant her brown zigzags.

Prudence said, "That is a brown line which goes in many places."

Anne said, "I mean, what it really is."

Prudence said, "It is paint?"

Anne looked up confused and said, "But *really*, what it *really* is." She appealed to her mother with her eyes.

Agnes said, "It is mountains."

Anne shook her head.

Maggie said, "It is you and Michael and Bernie playing leapfrog. See—that little heap is you."

Anne grinned and shook her head. She was glad to keep her secret.

Lulu said, "Copycat. I told you not to copy what I do."

Anne winced as if she were caught out. She drew her lips between her teeth, stuck her paintbrush in the red and drew long lines from the points of all the zigzags. She stepped back, said, "It is not your stupid anthills. Now you tell me what it is."

Prudence repeated "anthills" with a question in her voice.

Anne said, "It is not anthills now."

Prudence pointed at the brown zigzag. She said, "I am seeing those anthills. I see them."

Anne nodded up at her, said "But what is it now?"

Lulu was absorbed in her own painting. She spun her head briefly to glance at Anne's. Immediately she said, not looking at Anne's any longer but making broad green strokes across her own big piece, "It is anthills in the tops of trees but the trees have turned red because a jackal came and ate the giraffe and the giraffes were

so tall that the blood spilled down over all the trees in the jungle."
Anne calmly shook her head and said, "Nope. I said it wasn't
anthills." She dipped her brush back in the paint. She made the
zigzag solid, turned it to a high triangle on top of the red lines.

Maggie said, "It's the *kabaka's* tomb."

Anne said, "Yes."

Prudence said, "May I put some paint onto your paint?"

Anne said, "If you don't mess up my tomb."

Prudence said, "It is a proper tomb. I know that it is the *kabaka's* tomb. I want people to see your paint is the *kabaka's* tomb."

Prudence took up a brush. She peered into the tins of paint.
She stuck her brush into the brown and she made the beams of
the roof come lower almost to the ground. She stuck her brush
into the black, into the gold, and she made the royal spears across
the entrance. She put her brush into the yellow. She made the
thatched enclosure. She made green banana trees and one blue
goat and an inky sky. She was wrapped up in her tombs. Anne
looked at her mother to protest. Prudence did not notice the
protest. Agnes set a paper out for Anne, a different one, and hushed
her fuss.

Prudence covered every white space on the paper. And then she
stopped, stepped back, and looked.

It was bold and vibrant. The strokes were rough and caked with
paint. The colors were bright and arbitrary, and around each
object-color was a thick black line. The girl's eyes were shining.
Agnes saw Rouault.

Anne pointed to the great brown roof and the forest of red
poles. She said, "I painted those."

Maggie said, "Look at Lulu's painting."

Lulu was looking at Prudence's. She said, "It's good. For being
the first time you've painted a picture, it is really good."

Michael and Bernie and Lumumba straggled up. Fuweesiky was
riding Michael's shoulder. Michael was talking ventriloquist style
in Fuweesiky's voice, Fuweesiky's African-English style of talking.

The boys were toting bamboo poles and elephant grass and sticks and baskets and mud. They were building a house.

Lumumba said, "Look, men. The *kabaka's* tomb. We can make our house like that."

Prudence said to Agnes, "I like painting, Madam."

Agnes said, "You may come here . . ." but the boys had started grabbing the pictures and taunting and the girls had started screaming and beating and chasing them away.

The noise was good. It meant Prudence had not heard what she'd said. It meant that she could edit what she said. Prudence was gifted, yes. Prudence should paint, yes. But not here in her house. She was glad that Prudence could not have heard that offer. It might be a bit too much to have Prudence in her house forever.

And of course she was not free to instruct this girl to study art and forget seventeenth-century Englishmen. The aunts had their minds made up—their Prudence would become Kampala's mayor or Obote's chief solicitor or Kizito's surgeon at Mulago—anything with honor, anything with heavy *ekitibwa*. Prudence was meant to grow rich for her aunts. As it should be. The aunts would be secure with Prudence's fame and fortune and they would not be robbed of their *shamba*. For a while. And apparently you got to fame and fortune through the seventeenth-century Englishmen, and not by painting.

ELEVEN

On Entebbe Picnics

Uganda was the haven. Refugees poured across its borders, from north, south, east, west. To escape the mau mau in Kenya, and after that in waves from Congo-Zaire, and barely after that in surges from Ruanda, and then from the South Sudan and then in still more floodings from Ruanda and from a few more Zaire Simba flare-ups. Uganda welcomed them, integrated them, gave them land, and educated them. Uganda was the pearl of peace, of dignity, prosperity. It had the ancient kingdom of Buganda with the roots of its kingship far away in Egypt, in the dynasties.

The river of blood was in the South Sudan. The South Sudan was black, the North Sudan was Arab. The South attracted missionaries (a feisty wing of them, who wore black ties and floor-length dresses at the dinner hour, took on the tested British mode of keeping the spirits up in underdesirable climates). And with the missionaries came the churches, the hospitals, and—most undermining to Khartoum—a literacy level which could, one day, mean power. So the North expunged the South, obliterated anybody who could read, who owned a bike, or shoes, or who could give inoculations, or merely anybody they saw. It fit the new word, *geno-cide*, but the world kept its lips tight shut—there were more vital negotiations going on with Middle Eastern peoples, over Arab oil.

❧

The rain stopped. The clouds, late morning, broke into chunks, so it was mostly sunny, and it was Saturday. The Peugeot was jammed and they had one more child to fetch—one of Megan's, whichever one ran out the fastest and jumped in the car the quickest.

John was driving. She was beside him and Anne was in her lap. The Peugeot was narrow, but Wulf and Abraham Lasu and Maggie and Lulu were squeezed in the middle seat (Abraham Lasu was the Sudanese student with the tribal markings down his cheeks). Lulu sat on Wulf's lap. Michael squatted in the trundle seat with balls and blankets and shoes and bananas and some useless inner tubes nobody knew what to do with.

Wulf was telling Lulu stories from his safaris—about the way the Masai smoothed their hair with mud. Agnes was bending around to listen when abruptly the car went cool. They'd turned into Megan's drive, which was damp and overhung with branches. She was laughing for no reason—or because it was the first time she'd seen Wulf for weeks, and John hadn't told her he'd invited Wulf to come with them to Entebbe. John forgot to tell her insignificant things.

Piet and Megan were coming to Entebbe as well. They would follow in their own car, with what children they rounded up.

John hopped out. She paid no attention. Wulf was describing palavers with the Masai and her eyes were bright with him, with Wulf. But she turned to wave to Megan and when she did she saw Odinga. Odinga standing mere yards off. Half hidden in the bush-es. Their car was pulling up the hill. Odinga was focused on her. Odinga was not smiling.

It disoriented her for a moment. Odinga'd been there watching her, and she hadn't seen him watching her. She went on laughing anyway, and in the middle of the laugh with Wulf, she nodded at Odinga—briefly and politely.

Odinga did not nod briefly and politely. He did not nod at all. He watched like a stone colossus until the car was hidden by the thicket, and when it was, she stopped talking, and turned back around to the front, and contracted in herself a bit.

She was a little put out with herself. Her laughing nod had been cheap somehow. And Odinga jogged her memory. Yesterday a student turned up at their house—the best-known student drummer at the college. He was looking for Odinga. She hadn't asked why he was looking for Odinga, or how the student drummer knew about Odinga. But it made her wonder. It made her realize she didn't know a thing about Odinga. She'd never talked to Odinga.

They sat underneath their jacaranda tree, with the same high-angled lookout on the water. They meant to try a different jacaranda tree, but they came back to this one, as if this spot held the shape of their bottoms. From here you watched sailboats, one or two, and you saw islands, one or two, and you saw the ramshackle pier down below them on the lake. Around the dock odd poles stuck up. Fish eagles sat on the poles. Downhill on their left a dark rainforest blocked the view, though it was actually botanical gardens rainforest. The smell of curry was a few trees off, which came from an Asian picnic, which meant pots and fires and steaming primus stoves. Women cooked. Boys and men played cricket.

They didn't cook and they didn't play cricket. They owned swaths of grass to the water, it felt like. But monkeys came screeching out of the rainforest and bounced tree to tree across the grass and weren't at all polite. They assumed this spot was theirs. They made faces at the humans and mocked them. They stared and pointed, sniggered and gossiped, and then begged bananas. And fought each other when they got the bananas.

The pack of children water-skied, which meant they slid down the slopes on banana leaves. Except the grass was only smooth a few yards at a time, so every now and then a head cracked on a root or on another head.

Grown-ups were lazy. They lounged on mats with wine and pushed aside the fruit and bread and Matchbox-toy Volkswagens. Wulf was next to her, his head propped on a basket and one knee up, listening to talk about Sudan. Piet was fresh back from the Sudan. Piet organized relief, ran medical supplies across the borders. The borders were closed and they were dangerous. The last man who went with Piet did not come back from that border.

Piet was saying to Abraham Lasu, "So you know that woman."

Abraham said, "All persons in the South Sudan know Miss Hilary Rainwater."

Piet nodded, chewed his stick, said, "Tell me your thoughts about Miss Hilary. About the work she used to do."

Abraham said, "You don't have thoughts about Miss Hilary Rainwater. She is the hill on the Juba plains. That hill on the Juba plains will raise itself up in your vision, any direction you approach."

Megan said, "Tell Wulf about this woman."

Piet said, "This woman, Wulf—my guess is she's late seventies—you think?"

Abraham shrugged.

Piet said, "This ancient woman has refused to leave. Crops burned, mass burials, and there she sits, Miss Hilary Rainwater. Her house burned. She moved into an outbuilding. The outbuilding burned. She built a hut herself. For right now the Arabs are leaving her alone. She distributes medicine we smuggle in to her. She passes the word about lost Sudanese—families come to her to find out news. Her place is thick with refugees. She writes their letters, gets their letters delivered in the pockets of somebody fleeing. Granted she's not meek. She has a healthy mustache."

John said, "A missionary. CMS. With the first ones into the Sudan."

Piet nodded.

Agnes kept her head down. They were all well aware Hilary

Rainwater was a missionary. All of them knew a fact like that—even Wulf would know that. John did not say this to Wulf. John was shooting his remark at Piet.

Piet was not disposed toward missionaries—he and John had their long-term sniping war (Piet was subtler than John): Do missionaries usurp people's spirits? Or (and these are questions John throws back at Piet) are missionaries the ones who stick things out, get to know the people, get to know their ways, master the languages that no one else will bother with? Are missionaries the last ones left in crises? Can Piet name a civil-servant/anthropologist who would still be hanging on in the ashes of the South Sudan? But Good Lord, John (she'd like to say), Piet did have the grace to bring the woman up and John might have the equal grace to forego jabbing taunts.

Piet neglected John's quibble. To Abraham, Piet said, "Miss Hilary's languages—is there a Sudanese one she doesn't know?"

Abraham said, "Let me consider." He banged on his head with his fist for a moment, looked up, said, "Her Bari is not every time modern. But her Dinka, her Nuer, her Shilluk, her Arabic—they are perfect. She speaks Acholi, Lango. No. There is not a Nubian language which is foreign to Miss Hilary. She employs them all."

Wulf said, "I believe this is the woman they talk of at the Institute." He looked at Piet and said, "Will you allow me to accompany you? On your next trip in?"

The question agitated her. The South Sudan was a funeral pyre. Only atheists like Piet took risks like that.

Piet said, "We will talk."

John held the bottle up and when no one responded, he poured himself the rest of the wine.

She said to Wulf, out of hearing of the others, "How will we ever know you, if you're never in Kampala?"

Wulf said, without looking up, "You may persuade me that I need to stay put in Kampala."

Megan was conscious of Wulf and her, and the men were not. Megan wasn't looking at them. Just conscious, it was clear. She wished that weren't the case, but at least she was safe with Megan—that was not the trouble.

They had to stir.

They packed the car and walked down toward the lake, toward the gardens. Children ran ahead of them. *Tarzan* was filmed in these botanical gardens.

They strolled along the vine-hung paths with tiny orchids dotted through the leaves. The smell was wet and heavy and the monkeys and the birds were noisy. She walked beside Wulf. They were out of hearing of the others. He said, "I do not like to be secretive, but quickly, before some creature interrupts us—I must talk with you alone. Tell me where we are able to do so. Tell me where I can write a letter to you, so that you alone can see my letter."

She started to say the Nile Café, or Christos. But it was all too public. She said, "I will think. I will tell you. I will put a note in your mailbox, and I'll tell you where to write to me."

He said, "Thank you." He touched her arm. They caught up with the others.

She felt his hint of urgency. He had not showed that before. It made her happy.

TWELVE

On Cows and Cathedrals

M OST PLACES IN THE WORLD, most times, you are born into religion and that's that. But you have to choose to be a priest, or a pastor or a deacon even, and the reasons for such a choice are quite idiosyncratic. That's certainly true in the churches in the West or in the Church of Uganda, which is the Protestant church in that country. You might hear a "calling" from God, or fake the calling if you like the songs and smells and vestments. You might need a job. You might feel a thirst for power, or enjoy social work. Or, not too oddly with Germanic Christians particularly, the choice might come through your head, purely through thinking. You read a lot. Your favorite professor pronounces: It all boils down to "God is Love." You see dead ends of lives around you, you are drawn to the mystery of things—but still you need a little money every now and then. You become a teacher and decide to be a deacon on the side. The spirit of the sixties comes along and you go out to Africa. And how you fit in there—with all the other brands of new convictions, which include a healthy sprinkling of the "saved" variety of Christian—is anybody's guess.

Anne was reading from a tombstone. She read haltingly, "'There is no content . . .'"

Lulu said, "'Constant.' That says 'constant.'"

Anne corrected herself, said, "'There is no constant ab . . . Abraham.'"

Lulu said, "No. 'Ab . . . Absent.' Like in school."

"It is not," and Anne called out, "Mama, what is $a - b - i - d - i - n - g$?"

Agnes said, "Abiding. It means living, staying."

Anne pronounced, suspiciously, "'There is no constant abiding.'"

Lulu said, "You die. So. That's the stupidest of all."

Agnes did not interrupt. She was sitting some distance away, on a backless wooden bench. She was leaning against the mango tree. It was the first time she'd been semi-alone since Entebbe and that was yesterday already. It took that long to follow up one thought. And she had to write him, tell him where to write her. It was crazy, all these steps. It would take years. Of course John didn't open her mail, but why wave a red flag under his nose.

It was Sunday morning at Namirembe Cathedral. Michael was at Megan's. John was helping with the service—it had never mattered that he was merely a Lutheran deacon—and Lulu'd taken to tickling Anne and giggling in the cathedral. It wasn't so important—babies slurped their mothers in the service noisily. But Lulu was a good excuse for all of them to go outside and sit.

Namirembe was the highest hill around, and it had the oldest trees and the thickest vines and it had the history of the country on its gravestones. Also the breeze up here never stopped, so outside was the best place to sit, especially if you liked to hear singing not preaching—the walls of the cathedral were one foot thick but the doors were open so you could hear. They sang in Luganda or Swahili or in English or whatever anybody felt like singing in so the sound was a lively jumble and the bouncing echo of the organ was extravagant. And that all reached the mango tree.

Poste Restante—all she could tell Wulf was Poste Restante. And that was not so sensible. Lots of times she didn't have a car. John left town for days and then she never had a car.

Lulu was reading: "'With the help of my God I shall leap over the wall.'" Anne and Lulu were giggling.

How could she still not know where Wulf's house was? It had to be easier to walk to his place than get to Poste Restante. Or maybe he could leave a letter somewhere, in a hollow tree somewhere. Or with his houseboy—unless he meant this thing to be ultra secretive.

The thought made her swallow, see the alley in Zanzibar on a dark and thick-warm night, see him leaping over walls, sense him pounding up the lane to where she waited halfway buried in her slipping down-soft silk . . .

She heard the rumbling lowing of the cattle. Down the hill— she could just see the bumps and the wavering horns. Long horns. Tick birds rode on the humps. They were a dazzling white. The bobbing top of a stick was all she could see of the herdboy. He must be a tiny little boy.

Megan, then. Megan was the only person she could ask to bring Wulf's letter.

No. Megan must not be in on this. Megan would do it, but she wouldn't be neutral about it. Or maybe she herself would not be neutral about the idea of Megan maybe not being neutral about it. And where were you supposed to find a person who was neutral?

The cattle lowing was a good sound. And now there was the muffled chanting coming out from the service. The lowing came under the chanting. It was lovely. It was as it should be. She smiled to listen to the lowing and the chanting both at once.

It was ludicrous, these absurd intrigues to get a single, innocent letter.

Megan didn't have to know who wrote the letter. Wulf could use a second envelope, sealed up, inside Megan's envelope, and neither one of them needed a return address. They could be carefully typed, innocuous. She'd merely swear to Megan it wasn't an affair—which was true and that was that. She didn't have to make some tiny simple thing so wildly complicated just to save Megan from being too jealous, and of who—herself or Wulf. As if Megan could be jealous. Which wouldn't be bad if she were.

Lulu was stumbling. She called out "Endure." Lulu read "'Heaviness may endure for a night, but joy cometh in the morning.'"

A woman and baby landed on the bench beside her. Without warning. Alexandra Baku, a year-old baby in her arms. Alexandra was large, tall, brown, regal, and elegant, but now Alexandra was breathing hard and mumbling. Her narrowed eyes glared straight in front on her. She said, "You will have to forgive me. I can't hold this in. I don't know where to turn. I don't know how to handle this. But I will. I will think of something. I won't put up with this. This is public humiliation, which is precisely what he meant. I could never have dreamed that he would go so far. This is Satan's work."

"What has happened?" She was frowning at Alexandra in bewilderment.

Alexandra turned and studied her a minute before she said, "Mwanga has had prayers said—in Namirembe Cathedral. Giving thanks for the birth of his daughter."

She wasn't sure what the woman was talking about—some child who died? She would've seen if Alexandra had been pregnant.

She frowned. She said, "John said that prayer?"

Alexandra shook her head, said, "No, the dean. I see you don't know what I mean. This is an illegitimate child." Alexandra gave her a look that said, Don't be a baby, woman. This is the way it is. I will face it but I will not be stamped on like this man is stamping.

She said, "I thought Mwanga didn't like the church."

Alexandra said, "He hates the church. That's what makes this— what do I say . . ." she dropped her head and shook it hard.

The baby was crying and struggling away. Agnes took the baby. In astonishment the baby hushed. Lulu and Anne had stopped to watch, from near the graves.

Agnes thought if she were half a woman she would put her arms around Alexandra and hold her. But she couldn't. She never acted that way. It would be false. Probably it would embarrass Alexandra. Why was she so bad at comforting?

Alexandra must have felt it. She straightened her back. She said, "This is war. There are no rules. I don't know what you know. You know Mwanga and know he means to resurrect the customs—as he defines the customs—I say the customs always changed. He makes them up to fit his lust. Africans are all polygamous, according to his rules. So he will treat each child he begets in a very public manner, all equally he says. He will not, he says, skulk around the edges, like the church has scared the Africans to doing. I, me, Alexandra, he tells me, am a pawn of whites. I won't put up with this. So what am I to do? You tell me what you'd do."

Agnes made appalled sounds and shook her head.

She knew bits of Alexandra's life. Mostly she was awed by this impressive woman. Alexandra was good. Alexandra looked after people. She was a Zulu from South Africa and a high-church Anglican. She and Mwanga were political refugees and now he was the art history professor at Lubega. Jomo and Lumumba and Nelson were their sons. Jomo and Lumumba played with Michael and Bernie, and Nelson sometimes played with Anne. The problem was a new one. Was Alexandra asking her to answer, in seriousness? She felt a flicker of relief it wasn't John who had read the prayers.

Agnes said, "I'm sure you can't leave him."

Alexandra said, "He would get my children. We are trapped, we women. I will not give up my children."

Agnes said, "I know. I was saying nothing. I can't think what I'd do."

Alexandra took the baby back, said, "But I want to know what you would do with rage. Tell me that. African women have their ways, but they don't fit with my religion. I need new ideas."

They were picking up the organ chords. Vaughn Williams— "For All the Saints." The hymn started rolling in her head even while she shook her head in ignorance at Alexandra's question, even while the things she was thinking of were greedily profane and no help at all about rage. She should reciprocate this trust somehow. By confessing her own crisis? By saying she also had a few problems with men? By saying there was an ex-Finn Pole that she had every intention of seducing but she couldn't figure how to get his letters so she could know if he ever even had the slightest intention of giving in to her. She should say, Alexandra, help me please—never mind Mwanga. Tell me how you get your own love letters and keep Mwanga from guessing.

She rattled the keys at the baby and let Alexandra do the talking.

THIRTEEN

On Living in a Crowd of Dreams

THERE ARE COLUMNS BESIDE MAIN Hall at Lubega College. Not columns holding up a roof. Free-standing columns, on a low foundation wall. The columns have no capitals. They are tall, but they simply change their minds before they get anywhere, break off at odd heights. They are vine-draped like the ruins of a temple, but there has never been a temple at Lubega so the columns are incomprehensible. They're now the backdrop for garden parties, in the country where the mountains are the Mountains of the Moon and the lakes and rivers are the long-sought sources of the Nile.

It was Ptolemy who named the Mountains of the Moon, but the place's mystery was old when he named them. Solomon tracked the Queen of Sheba in this direction and for millennia the spot was lost in mistiness. Then the English brought their engineers and artists. They told the artists, Tell us what this means (knowing the business of the artist is naming essences). So the artists built dream columns, because you float on dreams in this country, coming as you do from Poland or from England or from Samarkand. And you knock against the other person's dreams.

The air goes loud with dreams, like the wind in eucalyptus trees.

✳

She dropped her pen in the middle of a line. She left the house without a word, climbed the hill, and walked along the path through sun and shade and students to the Main Hall mailbox aisles. She could check.

But the mail was John's. It was brown Uganda envelopes. If he'd written, Megan would have brought it, but who knew.

If she hung around Main Hall, if she acted like she had some weighty project that had to be done in the mailbox aisles he was bound to show up eventually. Or she could go across to the library, then trundle back to the mailbox aisles as if she were checking for the very first time. Only just now she didn't want to go out there in the open by herself—two armed soldiers were ambling around for no reason. She'd never seen them on Lubega Hill.

John. Preoccupied. He was in the sun, about to reach the shadowy aisle where she was. She didn't move. He walked nearly into her and jumped. But his smile was quick. He said to come with him. She said okay. She liked the Senior Common Room.

It was crowded. John headed to the counter to order scones and coffee. She spotted a table by a window and crossed the room searching for a sign of Wulf. There was no sign of him.

She put her elbows on the table and waited. Out the window she could see the fake columns, and a hawk on top of one. Inside, the room was streaming dust-mote light because the windows were high and numerous and widely arched. The voices had a hollow muffled sound in the echo.

She thought, if you are American in here you feel a bit illegal, as if you're spying out the British secrets. Nothing is African in here. A trickle of black faces. That's it. Otherwise it's timbered-ceiling Oxford-like exclusivity.

She couldn't come in here by herself because she only taught two mornings a week at Lubega School and the law said you had to come with somebody who taught at Lubega College. John's category was legal—they had, since independence, to overlook that he was American. John could bring whoever he wanted in here, even wives or students.

John deposited the cups and plates and sat across from her. She noticed Piet coming in behind a group of Africans. And, Lord, it was Prudence with him. John nodded, but he made no comment.

She said, "Are you going to ask them to sit with us?"

He shook his head.

She said, "You don't want to?"

He said no, and stirred his coffee.

She waited minutes. And then she said, "Why not?" She meant not to say "Why not?" but she said it.

John said, "If you have to know, today Prudence has asked Piet to escort her into the Senior Common Room. Yesterday was her day to ask me to escort her into the Senior Common Room."

She said, "I see." In a minute she said, "It could be Piet asked her."

He said, "I think not."

She did not accept John's judgment. John never grasped what was going on between a man and a woman. John read C.G. Jung and he thought about things, but he didn't notice things. It was preposterous that he hadn't noted Piet's eyes following after Prudence. But then, it was that blindness of John's that kept him almost comforting—or in certain of her moods it did. John was tied to her—in spite of her orneriness—and that, oddly enough, appeared to be genuine in him. And he needed to be tied to her because he didn't care to complicate his life. Mostly he wanted to stay at home and read and have her in the room with him if he could manage that, she reading and maybe listening to music. He did like people who talked ideas, but he would like to overlook the sticky people who never talked ideas, and that included Prudence. She could safely trust he didn't notice Prudence's crush on him. The blatant bosoms yes, but those were far too messy for the thinker, which trait was halfway charming.

She said, "Prudence actually asked you to bring her to the Senior Common Room?"

"She came to my office and she asked me to bring her to the Senior Common Room."

"That's preposterous."

"Not for Prudence."

"You mean she's done it before?"

"Yes."

"And you bring her?"

"Yes."

"Why?"

"Because she asks."

"I see." She paused. She said, "And that happens frequently?"

He nodded across the room, said, "You see it's not confined to me."

She could see Piet from where she sat. Piet could not see anybody; he wasn't moving his eyes from Prudence. When he had to greet a colleague, he looked immediately back at Prudence.

She kept her observation to herself.

John let out a snigger. She never liked that sound, but she said, "What?"

He said, "I suspect she's asking Piet to be her 'spiritual adviser.'"

She scowled. If she thought John was visited by irony then she would have laughed. She knew him better than that.

He said, "That was her yesterday's plan."

She said, "You're teasing."

He said, "She wanted to talk—in here, in the Senior Common Room. She took a while getting around to it. She said she's in dire need of a 'spiritual adviser.' I would please be her spiritual adviser."

"I don't believe you. You're making this up. Prudence comes from born-again Uganda, and where would she come up with 'spiritual adviser'? It's the last thing Prudence has on her mind."

He said, "Don't worry. I told her I had a hard time with spiritual advice."

She said, "What a ruse. She's pure Tutsi. She hasn't got a drop of dilution."

He said, "She picked up the term from Father Waswa-Sentanda. He's full of English jargon now that he's back."

Mwanga Baku left the next table over, and he sidled up to theirs. He was a gruff-looking man. He was dressed today in something long and flowing and orange-black-red. He talked to John while she watched the hawk out the window, feeling vaguely guilty, as if she were betraying Alexandra by smiling at her Mwanga.

Prudence. You couldn't turn your back on Prudence. But. Prudence was a painter. She hadn't stopped thinking about that. Prudence had no idea she was a painter. Two nights ago in her dream she had found a room of Prudence's. Only it wasn't a room, it was a cave. A red cave. It was filled with magical black-and-white cow-and-buffalo-type drawings. Pure. Breathtaking. But she'd walked away and hadn't said a thing to Prudence because this girl frightened her. She ignored the girl.

The dream made sense. Obscurely she was guilty—she was the one lone soul who'd glimpsed down into Prudence, what Prudence could one day be—maybe, if she herself gave more time and energy to Prudence, which she was not about to do. And now it was not just she who meant to draw away from Prudence. Here was John turning Prudence down as well.

Still. John—a "spiritual adviser" to the gauzy bosoms. It was laughable. The term made her skin crawl—all these priests and deacons taking on their young and nubile "spiritual advisees," snuggling into deep-confessing intimacy in the name of sanctity.

Yet John was being more than good about Wulf—which of course he should be, because she would not, when it came to it, be unfaithful any more than he would be. Still, John had to keep on being good about Wulf, so she had to keep on being good about Prudence. They could not both throw out this girl, slam the door on her outright. What were they doing in Africa if they slammed every door on Africans?

Mwanga said good-bye to her—though he hadn't talked to her—and left.

She said to John, "Why did you turn her down?"

John said, "What?"

She said, "She's ridiculous, 'spiritual adviser.' But skip the jargon. What do you think she wants of you?"

John let his air out through his nose.

Her blood rose. His snigger always made her blood rise, never mind the reason. Nothing mattered anymore except his snigger.

She said, "All right, she's a beautiful woman and sneaky. But why does that mean she can't have a spiritual adviser? She's got some tremendous thing inside her. Young men—somewhere maybe—come up with spiritual advisers—or where did we get the term? Why shouldn't a woman have a spiritual adviser?"

John frowned, said, "Why is it you suddenly turn so perverse?"

She couldn't say, Because I hate your snigger. That wasn't even it, maybe. It was more like: Okay, you snigger and I become Prudence when I hear you snigger. I'm a woman with bosoms and hopes and ambitions and I'm burning to get someplace and do some things, like Prudence. So she has to yank at the hem of your garment because you're a man. Make herself a plague to get her way. Pester till Jesus responds. Getting places by being a scourge but getting places she means to go. So she's a woman. So she's beautiful. So why do you snigger if she wants a spiritual adviser? You didn't snigger when Abraham Lasu asked you to be his spiritual adviser.

She said, "Prudence is a woman, but she's got more in her than Abraham Lasu."

John kept frowning. He said, "I never have the faintest idea what's going on in you."

She said, "Are you ready to go? I have to go." She reached for her basket and fished for her sunglasses.

FOURTEEN

On Perversity

I T ' S   N O   U S E   A S K I N G   F O R motives. That would say a man could know himself, or a woman could recognize herself. Haven't philosophers and theologians and psychologists and psychiatrists tried, for millennia, to trace patterns, sketch maps? But they never weighed quite accurately the simple factor of getting tired of waiting, say, when a mosquito whined too long. Or it never occurred to them to measure your shabby reaction to his snigger at precisely the moment you would say your yes. And then, too, the maps they make of the psyche never print the footnotes—they don't record it was an impulse, an accident, that spun you closest to nirvana when the light fell at just that slant.

Prudence read, "Thick as autumnal leaves that strow the brooks . . ." Prudence read it with a heavy question in her voice. It was the signal her tutor could speak.

Agnes said, "*Autumnal*, it means the time of year the leaves drop off the trees . . ."

Prudence said, "That would never happen, Madam. The trees would not drop leaves one time of year."

Agnes said, "Not here, no. But in England where this story is happening . . . "

Prudence said, "But, Madam, I have understood that this story is happening in hell."

Agnes said, "There had been a lot of wars in England when Milton wrote this story and he was blind and he hated his wife and he had to force his daughters to sit and write for him so his daughters hated him, and I think Milton got hell confused with England."

Prudence frowned. She said, "I hope the man did not remain so afflicted and confused, Madam."

Agnes said, "Only sometimes" and went on sewing Lulu's underpants.

She could make this Prudence hour useful—she might even get to John's shirt and he'd stop pestering her about his gaping-open clothes and eventually she'd get to disentangling the safety pins from Michael's useless zipper. If Prudence could refuse to give up her afflicted Milton, then she could do her mending.

Prudence hung like a spider on demented ideas—Prudence was confident: In her mind, if she grasped these knots of sentences then she would master the whole of European culture, solidly, and then she could go anywhere, do anything she wanted. Everything would open up for her. Milton was the hurdle. Only ignorant people would escape John Milton. And Milton wrote Bible stories, so you could believe the man.

Agnes knew, too sadly, what had infected Prudence. The girl had listened to the pop-eyed Englishman Nigel Seth-Smith out at Mityana who meant to say—"All you women understand: Your way to God is through your man, and that is the order of things," but who'd snaked around a devious way, pronounced to his girl students: "No one claims Education until she masters Milton." Nigel Seth-Smith had the title of Provost. The Reverend Mr. Seth-Smith knew what was what, said Prudence.

Agnes held up the rotten cloth, Lulu's green-checked underpants. This kind of mending wasn't quick. Her thread pulled through the rot. Not even her triple knots would hold. She kept looking at the pigheaded Prudence and back at the rotten underpants. Once she stopped looking at either, and drew her breath in sharply.

Prudence glanced up at that. Agnes shook her head and said it was nothing.

It *was* nothing. She was folding herself sweetly in this chair and mending scurvy underpants when she meant to be shouting at Megan, "You *have* to have my letter. It's been a week! Wulf would not keep me waiting a week. Why are you eating my letters?"

Three times this week she'd started to Megan's. Once she got as far as the porch—when she knew Odinga would not be there—and Megan shook her head. Once she lied, said she was looking for Anne. Once she felt ashamed and turned back up the hill.

It made no sense. Or it was something to do with John.

John couldn't grasp when to leave things alone. John never got it that he wasn't wanted. John still assumed Wulf was his own friend and badgered the man for conversation. He drove Wulf to Mityana. He gave Wulf books and papers and took Wulf to meet the Kitale chief and the hodgepodge of people on the sugar estates. And Wulf was an honorable man, an obligated friend to John, which skidded her off in the lower circles of something.

Prudence said:

> In Vallombrosa, where th' Etrurian shades
> High over-arch'd imbower.

At these words Agnes dropped her sewing, gave up on Lulu's pants. She looked out the window and fished for something worthy. She said "Forget Vallombrosa and Etruria."

Prudence said, "But, Madam, I do not want to forget. I am able to learn, I hope you understand. I desire very much to learn."

Agnes stared at the set of Prudence's lips and wondered at the girl once more.

You didn't get it many places—a Nefertiti-looking girl yanking at your skirt for you to teach her Milton. And maybe it was genuine learning. At least it was a person to a person, and maybe nothing ever took, anywhere, unless it was a person to a person somewhere along the line. Perverse as it was, this girl was becoming important to her.

It all came down to time. It was time that was yoking them together, but then mostly you didn't choose companions anyway. People just happened up to you by chance and that was that.

Wulf was not happening to her, so here was Prudence. Prudence was it. So be it. Starting this minute. Wulf could go to hell and thank the Lord she learned that before she threw away the purpose of her life, before she tossed out anything good and right and honest—before her jealousy and lust had run rampage. This girl needed more than advisers for her spirit. This girl needed paints, and she would buy Prudence paints and she would take Prudence places and she would introduce the world to Prudence. Simply showing her things was the first step—and then the girl could choose. This girl had things to choose from and that was rare enough and thank God she, Agnes, saw this in time, saw what she herself was meant to do in Africa. Thank God she hadn't gotten sucked forever into the muck. If there was anything personal in Africa, anything with meaning in Africa, it had to be—for her—this girl. From now on it would be this girl.

She jumped up. She said, "Okay. It's time to see some painting. You're an artist and you need to see some art."

Prudence was puzzled.

Agnes said, "It's okay. Come with me, it won't take long. It's something I want you to see."

Prudence looked more hesitant.

Agnes said, "It's education, Prudence. It truly is education. You have to see things or you will never know that things exist and one day you will see and you will say, why didn't someone tell me because now it's too late."

Prudence said, "I don't understand, Madam. I am learning now."
Agnes said, "But you will see."

Agnes was in the doorway. She screamed, "Lulu, Michael, Anne."
Anne was in the mats-and-bushes house. She said to Anne, "If you
find Lulu and Michael we're going to the Nommo Gallery, and
Maggie and Lumumba can come too."

The street was almost busy, outside the hedge. Government buildings lined the street, but abruptly when you came through the
hedge the city went quiet and you were happily secluded. Only a
gardener was watching. His shirt had a gash across his shoulder. He
smiled and nodded. She thanked him for his work, *Webale nnyo
okukola.*

It was a one-story, white stucco, vaguely classical kind of house,
the Nommo Gallery. A drive circled up to the front steps, behind
the high hibiscus hedge. The flowering plots of an English garden
were spaced here and there across the green, around bottlebrush
and frangipani trees and mango and papaw and jacaranda trees.
Theirs was the only car.

Lulu ran to the steps. She looked back over her shoulder at
Prudence and called, "We'll show you what to look at."

A large fat man with glasses showed them in. The house was
quieter than the garden. Even the children stood still half a minute.
The light was reflecting off the red cement floor and off the blues
and greens and oranges along the wall. The paintings were large,
expressionist landscapes.

Lulu moved first. She didn't run, but she hurried into the other
room and called "Come" to Prudence.

Prudence was glued where she was, in the doorway. She was
eying the walls with a frown. Agnes watched her. She said, "Go
closer if you like." But Lulu was pulling at Prudence's arm.
Agnes said to Lulu, "You let Prudence go where she wants."

Lulu dropped her arm, but Prudence followed the child. The
children stood observing Prudence, who said, "Where do you
want me to go?" Children giggled, mumbled. Prudence wandered

into the room of figure paintings, came to the painting in the alcove, in the shadows, where you had to come on the painting by yourself. The children were in higher stages of poking at each other. Prudence's hand went up to cover her mouth.

The painting was red and orange and black, of a Karamojan man. He was leaning backward, with his spear drawn over his shoulder and his penis out in front of him about equal in length to his spear.

Prudence shook her head at the children and giggled for a minute and walked away from them.

The children ran out to the garden.

Prudence reached to touch a painting of a fig tree. She said, "Did a white man make this painting?"

Agnes showed her the name of William Mukebe.

Prudence knew of the Mukebes. She did not believe it. She said, "His paintings are in this white man's gallery. I do not understand."

Agnes said, "He is a famous painter. There are many in Uganda. We can go and see a place they paint."

She said, "Is that possible?" And she walked across the room to a painting of three figures. She said, "This is what I want to paint."

Agnes said, "When you paint it, it will be a different thing."

Prudence said, "I want to paint this one. I like this one very much."

Agnes said, "When you begin you will discover things to paint."

Outside she was looking down, talking to Prudence.

Prudence said, "Someone wants you, Madam."

Agnes looked up. Wulf was under the bottlebrush tree, watching her, smiling very slightly.

Anne said, "He told us not to tell you he was here."

Wulf pushed up and started toward her. She crossed the grass with Prudence, reached out her hand. She thought to say Prudence's name and in a minute he said, "Will you excuse us half a minute, Prudence?" and he led her over past the frangipani tree. Prudence and Michael and Lulu and Anne and Maggie stood in a phalanx watching them.

He said, "*Nnyabo*, I need to see you alone" (he used the word for *madam* in Luganda).

She said, "Yes, *Ssebo*" (it was the Luganda word for *sir*).

He said, "Can you come here tomorrow, *Nnyabo*?"

"What time, *Ssebo*?"

"Three?"

She said, "Three."

And they joined the curious observers.

FIFTEEN

On the Search for Culture

RELIGION RUNS DEEP IN UGANDA. There are more "Episcopalians"—if you prefer that term to "Anglicans"—in this small country of eight million than there are in the whole of the United States of America. And as many Catholics and Muslims (the British, when they had a say, outlawed the churches of the "sects." Lutherans and Presbyterians and Methodists and such got ecumenically dumped in with the Anglicans). But given the Bible to read on their own, one group of Ugandans uncovered what the British hid: The Jews with their straightforward Old Testament god were comprehensible heroes. The group would prefer to be Jews. So they established Judaism, obeyed the Talmud, and have followed it for generations now. They have invited foreign rabbis to inspect and certify.

Another student, a Uganda Protestant early this century, got loose in the seminary library. He uncovered the Orthodox Church. He studied the phenomenon, built his church in the Orthodox style, wore the robes, and founded—with the blessings of an Eastern patriarch—a congregation. Which endures.

❦

Early. Here she was at the Nommo and it was fifteen minutes before he said.

Another car and it wasn't his. That car changed her imaginings. She'd pictured this scene precisely—the Nommo was empty in her mind. There was him and there was her and there was an empty garden and an empty building filled with paintings. Misty sunbeams poured in over them.

She parked at the edge of the gravel and let her arms fall blankly, before she gathered herself and looked up. She greeted the gardener and she dropped her keys. She scratched around between the seats, found them, and dropped her sunglasses. Her aim was to hurry inside the building. She meant to see him by herself first, without the gardener scrutinizing them.

The same fat man with glasses was sitting on a stool. He said, "Good afternoon, Madam. You are alone today. I am happy you like our Nommo Gallery, Madam."

She said she was waiting for a foreign visitor.

She wished he'd go away. And she wished the other two Englishwomen would disappear. She walked outside again, ignored the gardener, sat under the bottlebrush tree and arranged her sundress, full and fluid and rose-colored, generously over her knees. She liked this dress because she liked the color and because she could move and she could sit just as she liked. Her arms were dangling over her knees. He might recognize the posture.

He was coming around the hedge. His walk was still odd but it had a grace, like the grace you quickly noted about everything in him. Her smile did not stay as small as she meant, not as cool as his smile yesterday. At least she didn't speak. He didn't either. It would have been redundant with the smiles.

He thanked the gardener for resting (Wulf had perfected his Luganda customs)—which sitting position the gardener had undertaken next tree over, so he could watch them better. Then Wulf folded himself down under the bottlebrush tree quite close beside her. He echoed her position, leaned his back and head against the tree but he angled himself away in the opposite direction from her. His shoulder pressed into hers. Their faces were inches apart and their smiles weren't much contained.

She said, "Would you like to see the art?"

He said, "No."

She said, "Shall we stay here?"

He looked around him slowly, at the wagtails hopping feet away, at the hanging nests of weaver birds that clumped in the mango tree, at the white house with the red tile roof. He said, "How did we get here?"

She smiled.

He said, "How did you get here—with a rose dress over your knees? Please keep that rose dress over your knees."

She said, "If that is what you want."

He caught her ankle, went still, looked down at what he held and seemed surprised. He drew his hand away, and he leaned back—newly quiet—against the tree. He nodded to the gardener, who seemed interested.

They sat silent for minutes. And then their heads, which both were against the tree, twisted toward each other all at once. Their faces were close, and they weren't smiling.

He looked away first, drew in his breath, put his hand back on her ankle and rubbed it gently. But he did not speak.

Or not until, without looking at her, he said, "You know I've grown quite close to your husband."

Stones rolled over her spirit. She hesitated, said, "I'm sorry."

His hand on her ankle went still. He was still looking at her ankle, took a while to say "Yes."

She'd told herself she expected this, but she had not. She knew from her collapsing she had not.

He said, still looking at her ankle, "I am paralyzed. I'm unmanned by what is happening. It is why I could not write to you. I am unable to betray your husband. I am unable to stop scheming to see you."

She breathed again. He'd said nothing really, but it was better than his start. She closed her eyes. She could not force him. She merely said, "I know."

His manner changed and he looked at her. He said, "I have to kiss you. Those Englishwomen are looking at us."

She said, "I don't know them."

He grinned, studied her, said, "And do you know the gardener?"

She said, "We have an understanding, the gardener and I."

He said, "And the museum man in the doorway?"

She said, "Him, too. He has to know what art's about."

He said, "Ah but. There it is. I am not an artist. So I must not love you."

She said, "I would not trust an artist as a lover."

He did not stop watching her face, nor she his. But his smile slowly faded out again.

She watched the kiss pass, unkissed. She knew when it passed. She knew it wouldn't come again.

He said, "That is what I don't know how to say." He was not finished. He was struggling.

She helped him. She looked away from him. She said, "That you don't intend to come any closer to me?"

He closed his eyes, frowning deeply. He said, "I am unable to say it. But I know that it is true."

Everything about her remained motionless. She could gauge, by the quickness of her fresh new chill, how much hope she had still perversely clung to, no matter what he'd said a bare ten minutes earlier.

She said, "I understand," without looking at him. Without understanding.

In a sudden movement he dropped his head on her shoulder. She bent her head to his. He said, "But I have got to kiss you at least, and the way I have to kiss you I cannot in front of this damned crowd. Where can we go?"

"The car—we'll find a place." She was getting quickly up.

They reached the car in silence and headed out the drive. She couldn't think the way to turn. She couldn't think where they could go. She couldn't think. She headed up the hill. She stopped at the side of the road, at the first small street that wasn't mobbed. He didn't seem to care where they had stopped. He pulled her over to him, and they kissed.

The afternoons would be good times, yes. They could steal an afternoon or so. Never mind it was hard to find spots to even hold each other a minute.

One afternoon they headed to the country. *Shambas* and cyclists and herdboys and goats and chickens and ants and mud filled up the countryside. They went farther into the bush. They stumbled onto the tiny church that looked Eastern Orthodox. It was white, with a circular dome, on the top of a high hill. And no one seemed to be there. They could wander in the graveyard—except the African priest in his beard and robe moved swiftly up and offered them a tour, gave them forty years of history, walked them down the weed path to the icon painter, who was a woman, who worked underneath a mango tree.

They thought it wise to stick to Kampala. The military convoys decided them—too many lorries running motorcars off roads. As if the army ran this country and not Obote.

In town they tried the Uganda Museum, which should be lonely on weekdays. Only they drove into it when all the high schools in town were gathered for a chorale, and a few dozen acquaintances nodded at them, including Hugh's Claudia, whose smile was a bit too knowing.

SIXTEEN

On the Deviousness of Certain Tribes

U GANDA, ROUGHLY, MARKS THE CENTER of Africa, measuring both from east to west and from north to south. The
northernmost border of the Bantu peoples crosses through
Uganda. Above that border, in Lango and Acholi and West Nile,
you have Nilotic peoples. The tribal organization of Nilotic
groups is relatively democratic. That is, the males sit around and
decide things by consensus. The people display a fresh straight-
forwardness. The kingdoms of the south, however—Bunyoro and
Buganda and, farther afield, Ruanda (the Banyaruanda edge into
Uganda) were never democratic in their structure. Theirs is a
rigid hierarchy. These are the peoples that the British understood—royalty means manners of the courtier, and leads to polite
duplicity. It means never disagreeing to a face, however one
intends to act. Warm, agreeable politeness—good practiced
politicians. But Americans have been known to be uncomfortable with the British choice, to find themselves more comfortable with aboveboard peoples of the north.

She said, "It was hare-brained to try Namirembe graveyard—I know everybody there."

Wulf said, "This looks good. Good breeze."

She said, "Wind," and pushed down her skirt.

He rooted for the blanket in his Land Rover.

They were on Kololo Hill, or in the meadow at the top, high above the red-tiled roofs. The Chinese built their glass-spiked walls up on Kololo Hill. It was the hill of foreigners, where Russians scowled and the Americans threw cocktail parties and the British, sundowners. The meadow had some scenic flaws, like a radio tower and a chain-link fence around it. But nobody came up here. So they could appraise the hills of Kampala—seven of them—and dream it was Jerusalem or Rome.

Which they did for a minute, sitting in the wind, surveying the city under them. During which activity Wulf abruptly said, "I love you."

Just as easily she said, "I love you, too."

They kept on looking at the hills. She did not care to risk a movement. It was as it should be, the hills and the wind and the easy way they kept on sitting, simply looking over city, on Kololo Hill.

And then she said, without looking at him, "I thought you wouldn't say it."

He said, "I thought I wouldn't either."

He looked at her out of the corner of his eye, until she turned, and they kissed, and kept on kissing, and lay back on the blanket, and kept right on kissing, until Wulf sat up.

She put one arm underneath her head and studied him. She could see his form against the sky, or the back of his head against the sky, the way he'd bounded up. She didn't like him far away as this. She pushed his legs out straight, put her head in his lap, and stretched herself out on the blanket. She could look up in his face and keep her head against him.

He rubbed the back of his hand along her cheek and down her plait. Then he propped a knee up (which left her head a bit bent), looked at the red-tiled roofs, and said, "So we meet with John's permission."

She bolted to sitting, scowled at him, said, "Of course not. Why do you say that?"

He looked at her closely, seemed to see what he wanted, drew his breath in, and more or less dropped in her lap, face down, and said, "Oh God."

She put her hands on his head, said, "Do I have to guess what you're talking about?"

He said, "It sounds as if you know."

She said, "I know you frighten me."

He went stiff, then slowly pushed himself to standing, said, "I didn't expect this." He jammed his hands in his pockets and walked up and down, stopped beside her, looked up, observed hawks circling the valley. She watched him, in fear.

He said, "So John knew where you were those days the last two weeks. And you didn't know he knew."

"No. He never asked. I told you I worried—all those people saw us. But who would mention it. Claudia—but then it was all so stupid—why would we go somewhere public if we were hiding something. Was that wrong?"

"Wrong? If we use that word, I have chosen our 'wrong.'" He sat down. She was sitting up now.

"So what are you saying?"

He said, "I want to tell you all of it. It will take long. You will wait?"

She nodded.

He said, "John took me to the bookshop—he meant the café. We chatted, and then his voice changed, went high and nervous. He said—pronounced I should say—that men need the friendship of women when they are away from their wives."

She dropped her head on her arms and muttered, "He did not."

Wulf kept talking. "He said he understood that better than most people and he wanted me to understand he trusted me completely even though he knew I 'admired'—that was his word . . ."

"He did not, he did not, he did not." She was intoning it with her eyes pressed shut.

"He said his wife and he would have been insulted if I did not 'admire' his wife. He himself compared his wife with other women he met and he thought he was objective—yes he said this—thought he was objective, when he concluded that his wife was the most interesting woman he knew in all the ways that mattered so how could he expect to keep other men from noticing that fact."

Now she was pushing at his arm, saying "Stop it, stop it, I do not believe you."

"He said at first he'd found her attractions somewhat troublesome but he realized in time it was a blessing. He said a few times he'd been worried, early on in his marriage. He named a couple of incidents, somebody called Piers, in England . . . "

She was storming at him now saying "Shut up, shut up" and he was saying "Wait. Wait. Wait. Don't interrupt me yet—someone named David out here—you see I was listening carefully." He was ducking her blows when he said it. "Both these men, he said, initially were friends of his, who he brought to his house and he'd been immature enough to worry. But—wait—but, but—it became quite clear it was all platonic on his wife's part and there was no way in the world he could prevent that kind of attraction between her and appealing men. His wife couldn't seem to help it. It was the way she was with men."

He stopped, said, "You said you would be quiet."

She slid back to stillness, with her head caught in her hands.

"He said in time he realized it was all a kind of game with his wife."

She pressed her head tighter and he went on in a monotone.

"He said she couldn't help loving certain men, and women show their love in a more diffuse, less concentrated way than men. He'd done a lot of reading in Jung, he said, talked of those things with analysts, learned to understand. He could see I knew exactly what he meant. And he had come to know at last, quite deeply—

his words—that it was him and him alone she was committed to."

She wailed out "Oh my god."

"He said in the end she loved him alone, and when it came to any final act of infidelity she would let another man go. That was the way it was. He himself, and her children, constituted her bona fide existence. He himself accepted and trusted that now. He knew these intense platonic attractions were an integral part of his wife's character and he wanted to warn me. He did not want me hurt and he did not want to lose my friendship. He had to say all this before anything blew up and became irreparable and it was, he felt, the time to say it now. He would be too guilty if he did not have the courage to say these difficult things to me, at the time they might be heard. But it in no way meant that he intended to try to control the friendship between his wife and me."

Her noise now was merely moans.

"He said he understood that you and I wanted to go places, see things together occasionally, without him. And that when I did that I was not to feel guilty. He was aware of it, he was not insulted or hurt by it. It was one of those things he accepted because he loved, and finally he trusted, his wife. And he would not let this kind of inevitable and harmless attraction ruin the genuine friendships of his life. He knew he was being potentially embarrassing. But he had to risk that, and he hoped I understood."

She stopped moaning, and the silence stretched out. She kept her head down on her arms. She was aware of the cicadas, and the crows.

He said, "Please speak."

She said, "I feel too sick."

He said, "I know."

In a minute she raised her head. She said, "Does that mean you feel sick?"

"Of course it does."

"Why?"

"Why?"

"Yes. Why?"

"For the reason you do."

"But it's a lie. It's all one gigantic lie—that's why I feel sick. You could think it's true—how do I know? You haven't said."

He said, "All these words are your husband's words. You cannot think I do not consider all that that implies, all that your husband means, by saying these things—all he means to let me know."

"I don't know. I know—I know you miss your wife. I know I'm your help for missing your wife."

"You don't think that."

She said, "And I don't see myself in anything he says."

"I am reporting. You asked me and I tell you exactly."

She hushed. In a minute she leaned her forehead on his knee. She said, "Will you tell me your reaction?"

He said, "I think about it. You are not a game to me."

She drew away. "Then you do believe what he said. You do believe my life's a game."

She jumped up, marched up and down. He watched her, until she sat back down beside him, until she said quietly, "Forgive me," and then burst out. "It's what I hate—how can he know what goes on in me? He couldn't live if he knew what goes on in me. It's best he thinks my life's a game. All right. But he has no idea. It's true I've never been unfaithful. It's true I loved the two men he mentioned. It's true I respect him. But he can't begin to know what I have paid—he doesn't believe in feelings. And if he says I play with men—my god, he's the one who says 'flirting' is the accepted game. Look at Prudence right now—we'll go into that some other time. To think like that, as far as I'm concerned—all I can say is, it's as far from me as I can dream. Oh, good Lord—he's succeeded hasn't he? He's laid everything out on the table. He's demystified us—he studies demystification, you know. He studies the theories of religion, I suppose you know."

He said, "Please, darling. Let's lie here quietly. We're late. We can't leave this way. Please."

She lay down. She put her head on his shoulder. But her spirit was not calmed.

SEVENTEEN

On Living Houses

T HERE ARE PERSONS COMMITTED TO the functional. They search for neat houses with outlets and gadgets, built-in closets and windows that shut. New-constructed European houses in Africa are functional houses. And then there are the persons who blossom with the unexpectedness of things, and with the simple feel and smell of things. They prefer the houses that the early Europeans built, from mud, in the thick-walled mud-brick style. These are whitewashed inside and outside. They have big square rooms with high timbered ceilings. They have breezeways separating roofs and walls and they have a door leading out of every room straight onto a veranda; and the veranda circles three sides of the house. There are no closets, there's one outlet here and there and the wires run over the walls. These mud palaces are cool and living. Life flows in and out of their pores. They are flooded with shadowy movements, snaps and creaks and scratches and sudden gusts of breeze. All unpredictable.

She was restless. She couldn't listen to Prudence. Her mind was not controllable.

She set off with the girl up to the art building. Anne came with them. They walked up the hill and through the copse of eucalyptus trees. The light fell breezily through sparse and rattling leaves and it smelled like roasted lemon.

Three pairs of rubber flipflops slapped against their soles, but not quite simultaneously. Anne held Prudence's hand, swung their hands high, and sang their marching song in Michael's boisterous style:

> I was at Franklin Roosevelt's side
> Just a while before he died.
> He said, One world must come out of World War Two.
> Yankee, Russian, white or tan,
> Lord, a man is just a man.
> We're all brothers and we're only passing through. . . .
> I saw Adam leave the garden
> With an apple in his hand . . .

Prudence said, "Those words are not intelligible."

Anne said, "What words?"

Prudence said, "I believe Franklin Roosevelt is an American. No one can see Adam and the American as well."

Anne said, "It's a song, so it doesn't matter what it says."

Wulf was in Fort Portal and she was high-strung this afternoon—dumbstruck by John's trick, her anger still boiling. And she couldn't let it out. Lots of things about her husband she wished she could obliterate. But she had never thought him a worm like this. She had never suspected he manipulated her behind her back.

And who was it running up to John with gossip? If Prudence told John about all their meetings, then that was it. But how could Prudence know—except that once at the Nommo? And if she asked Prudence what she'd said to John, if she asked anybody—of course that was impossible.

Claudia (Hugh's Claudia) had seen them a couple of times. But Claudia wouldn't run to John.

It could be anybody who saw them. Innocently saw them. Or it could be the children—so forget it.

People saw her with Wulf, so what. They weren't about to sleep together—that was clear. Especially now that John had changed Wulf's thinking. Especially now that Wulf believed he was a game to her, whatever he might say.

John was abominably slimy. And he got away with injecting Wulf with doubt because he seemed a reasonable creature. John talked tolerance. Wulf respected John. So now between herself and Wulf there was a thorny subverting suspicion before there even was a *them* to be between.

Wulf *had* to see John's reason was a superficial kind of ratiocination, if he assumed people ran on reason. Which of course they didn't.

She would not start searching out spies. That way she would crush herself.

And she couldn't tell the children to shut up, but goddammit there was hardly anything undercover anyway unless they perversely counted his announcing he had no intention of coming anywhere near her. Was that supposed to make her an adulteress?

John's maneuver was the criminal act. Which of course she couldn't mention. Which of course made it fester like a swamp of snakes and eels and worms and slugs anytime she thought about her husband. She couldn't look at him. He told Wulf outright lies. He could never have stooped to this kind of thing if he truly thought she loved him, or if he genuinely thought that men were games to her. He couldn't do this if he were certain about anything: If he were convinced she were safely predictable like a puppet he'd created, he wouldn't have bothered with this convoluted trick. She was scowling and yelling in her head, *God damn, if he's going to play this way he'll see how predictable I am.* His puppet. So that's what he thinks of me—he'll see. Okay, he will see.

Prudence said, "Madam. A man is looking at you. It is the drummer. I believe he knows you."

Agnes looked up toward Odinga.

Odinga was walking up the road, which disconcerted her, brought back a quick bit of her dream. It was a dream of Wulf, but of course Wulf had turned up black again with glistening muscular arms.

She nodded to Odinga.

He spoke Swahili. He said, "*Memsahib*, may I speak with you?"

She said, "*Ndiyo*" (yes), and they stopped.

He said, "*Memsahib*, I wish to speak with you alone."

It troubled her. In a minute she said, "Now?"

Odinga said, "I can wait, *Memsahib*. It concerns Tabula."

She said, "Tabula is doing all right, Odinga. Now is not good."

He nodded and he turned away.

Anne and Prudence were talking to her. She answered them automatically.

She said to Prudence, "Why did you call that man the drummer?"

Prudence said, "I see him play the drums. He plays at Wandegeya—in the Sputnik Bar—but, Madam, I have only been told. Of course I do not go to Sputnik Bar."

She said, "I believe you have that man confused. That man works in the Schofleur's house."

Prudence said, "It could be, Madam." She could hear it in Prudence's voice—that Tutsi diplomacy.

Agnes looked around. Odinga was watching her.

Anne poked her arm and said, "Is it?"

She said, "Is it what?"

"Is it far?"

She looked at the child, while Anne forgot what she had asked because she'd stopped walking and bent down to scratch. Anne didn't stoop. She poked her fanny in the air and flopped her head down and scratched hard, unthinking, her pigtails flopping wrong-way up. No self-consciousness.

Her mood lightened, looking at Anne—that breezy unselfconsciousness. She leaned and caught the bundle of Anne up in her arms in one big swoop, Anne laughing, Anne still intent on scratching.

She said, "Shall I throw you in the pond? Shall I drown the bugs so they won't eat you up?" Anne squirmed down and ran ahead of them.

She called, "That's the wrong way. We're not going to the Bakus' house."

Anne yelled, "But I'll play with Nelson while you go" and spun down the other path.

Now Agnes had to stop at the Bakus'. Now she had to ask Alexandra if Anne could play with Nelson for a minute.

The Bakus' was hidden by hedges. You saw bits of the corrugated roof through the branchy tangles of trees.

The hedge-break led to the back of the house. The *beat beat beat* of a mortar and pestle. A goat. Women laughing. Clothes draped over bushes to dry. Chickens running free. A bare-bottomed baby was sitting on a mat, by the woman pounding groundnuts. Not Alexandra's baby.

She was thinking, No one is lonely in this house. It used to be an English garden, but now it's full and noisy.

Alexandra called out, took broad strides down the steps from her front veranda, and crossed the lawn to them. She forced the two of them to sit with her for tea, out on the grass, while children and other unknown figures passed in and out of the house.

But it was not long before Prudence stood up, said she must honor an appointment, and excused herself.

Agnes was aware: No one had appointments at this time of day, except with spiritual advisers. John preferred advising at this time of day, when the building was emptied and quiet.

So John had taken her complaint to heart—he was checking up on Prudence's soul. She couldn't think easily about that scene. It was one more absurdity intensifying her connection with this girl, her inexplicable connection.

EIGHTEEN

On Reasons for Being Faithful

TOURISTS LOOK FOR GAME PARKS. In Uganda there's Murchison Falls, Queen Elizabeth, Semliki, Lake Albert, Lake George. You see elephants and crocodiles, rhino and hippopotami, baboons and lions and odd-striped curly-horned deer. But amazements are closer than the game parks. On any tarmac or dirt road you see them. They aren't mere cows. They're fabulous top-heavy beasts. Their heads hang down since they lug horns eight feet across from tip to tip. They're useless as food, the horns take up the food. A white man is put out: Cows can be useful, he instructs; they're a way to live well, he declares; there's no sense in herding horns for the sake of herding horns.

But there are values and there are values. And these are the valued cattle here. These are the ones that call out faithfulness. And anyone who sees these beasts—unless their soul is dead—feels the wonder that a soul obscurely craves.

She'd stayed in the country an hour too long, with Wulf, at the icon painter's. Now driving up Kironde Heights she was concentrated on willing: Don't let John be home. Don't let John be home. She didn't care to feel him watching her, with his forgiveness plastered on shakily.

She shifted to grind up the drive, stopped the car, and was mystified. No sound. Nothing from the garden and nothing from the house. The only sounds were distant. A baby crying. The thump of a mortar and pestle.

The door was locked. The house door was never locked—there was always somebody here.

The door was glass. She could see a sheet of paper on the floor inside. John's handwriting—"Don't worry." A slug hid the next words. She unlocked the door, stooped, grabbed the paper, and turned to the grass to scrape away the slug. She read, "At Mengo Hospital. Michael. He'll mend. Hesita's with me. Others at Megan's."

She shot back to the car and headed toward Namirembe Hill. Guilt was quickly edging out her fear. What had happened and what might happen when she was away from home. Hesita wouldn't know what to do and what did Hesita do anyway and what if Megan had not been home and could Lulu find John's office—and people were coming for drinks at six o'clock.

She sped up the Indian hill—sun on the pink-wall houses. The smell of coriander. Gujarati voices. She circled Lugard's fort and turned off onto the murram—a pack of soldiers trotting double time, calling rhythmic noises. More coming, up the side road. What was going on?

She drew up at the hospital. Now which building?

A scruffy cluster of women by the open ward, cooking over primuses. She turned up the hill toward the labs. She was sent elsewhere. Hesita came puffing up to her. Hesita bent her arm up crazily—showing how Michael's arm got twisted. Michael fell out of the treehouse.

She stood outside the recovery room.

Her child would feel like she'd abandoned him. He would not want her near him.

The nurse said, "Go in now."

Hesitant, she looked around the door. John had his back turned, was leaning out the open window talking with somebody. Michael was lying in a strange white gown. His arm was in a plaster cast but his eyes were on the doorway waiting. He smiled with his lips pressed together. His eyes had an almost teasing flash of triumph. It released her. She bent to kiss him. He said, "I *can* keep going to the treehouse. It wasn't my fault—the branch broke off."

John was brusque. He said, "We've got company coming, I'll take Hesita and we'll take care of people. You bring Michael. I've got Megan's car so I'll get the girls."

She said, "Nobody will expect drinks now. Forget about the company."

John said, "There's no reason, Michael is fine."

She said, "Are you fine, Michael?"

Michael sat up, said, "See?" His face was drained and defiant.

At home children crowded up to Michael. They ran their hands along the cast. Michael rode Fuweesiky on his shoulder and let them ask him questions.

A handful of people were in the garden already. Hugh kissed her hand. Wulf arrived and they nodded.

They were down the terrace from the porch, below the bougainvillea bank. The spot was halfway hidden from the road and big enough for a circle of chairs. You had to carry things up and down the hill, but it was worth the effort—at this hour the light around the leaves was turning the color of honey. Her spirits went lighter. It could be all right.

She didn't look his way. Megan was watching her, smiling at her, but she felt safer talking with Claudia.

Claudia said, "John told us you were showing Wulf around— John said he'd asked you to show Wulf around. But you must have been frightened when you got home."

So John had made an announcement. When John need not

have said one thing. So John intended to keep it clear that Wulf was *his* friend first of all. His wife was merely helping out with entertaining *his* friend Wulf. John was making a fool of himself as well as of her and Wulf. John had to charge like a bull, pretend he held the reins. Announce nothing would take place without his instigation.

Then let John entertain. She wanted nothing to do with this tortuous psychology of his. She would ask Claudia about her children and pass the food and hush.

Better if she went checking on Michael.

But Hugh was getting things going. Blessed Hugh was drawing John out about his talk on Jung to the psychology students—what the psychoanalyst was up to on Mount Elgon. Good. The archaeology of psyches. Dreams and shadows and possession. Amnon Ogwal—Hugh and Claudia had brought Amnon Ogwal, who'd been their visitor some weeks—took exception to John's notion, John's saying the same archetypes cropped up in dreams all over the globe. Not so, swore Amnon—no way was anything the same in Tesot dreams as in white Bazungu dreams. Good. They all had something to say about dreams. Even Wulf. Fine that John had set them arguing. It meant she could listen to Wulf—she never seemed to get to Jung on dreams when she had Wulf by herself, but now Wulf was saying, Yes dreams are freedom, paramount freedom. In the end, he said, it's dreams that pull down tyrannies. A people turn back to dreams in time and then turn up with art. Dreams sprout, the crack in the state gets bigger, and dreams smash through the megalith.

Yes, they said. But. But but but. But the mosquitoes, said John—mosquitoes are biting and they must move inside. Nobody else felt mosquitoes biting. But everybody else now hushed and left. Wulf left. She was left with cooking supper.

She was in the girls' room, and the door was closed. The room was dark. The dark was outside as well as inside except for light streaks over the grass. She was singing:

Time, like an ever-rolling stream,
Bears all its sons away;
They fly, forgotten, as a dream
Dies at the opening day.

It seemed to her—when singing streamed out into the dark, it touched what you only guessed at in the light. When it was dark, and when no one was watching and no one was asking what you meant, then things you couldn't name slipped out and took you off with them. As if, caught up in those distances, it was actually possible to love without the help of anything on earth.

Anne was asleep. Lulu was fingering her mother's skirt, very very drowsily. Agnes stopped singing, sat listening to insect drone.

Michael was safe once more. But she couldn't keep pressing her luck. The thought made her halfway resigned to the way things had to be.

NINETEEN

On the Need for a Nile Hotel

THE HUT IS A WOMB, a cave, a shell, a nest, a tomb. It warms, surrounds, and nourishes. Make it circular, thatch it, and it's primal mother-warmth. The mansion is a regal loneliness. The hut is the shape of our dreams.

❧

She was at her desk in the bedroom. She had a stack of papers before she could get to *The Potter and the Shadow of Death,* which she'd been picking at forever. What she was actually doing was learning games from butterflies. The butterflies were flying in twos, but they kept twosomes interesting. They'd dart away from each other, each try their own sweet bushes, and then they'd flutter back and touch. And it was all by instinct, that variety, all that faithfulness.

Her chin was propped on her fist. She was trying to watch three pairs at once until she dropped her fist in shock. Wulf, leaping down her bank. Wulf, passing her window and not looking. Wulf did not come to her house in the morning. She leapt up. Half her excitement was terror. Something was happening. He was knocking. Hesita was going. She reached the living room. Hesita stopped halfway across the floor.

She did not forget Hesita—she did not touch Wulf. But neither of them glanced at Hesita. Wulf was prancing. He had to show her something. Would she come for a drive?

He was driving. She was crouched on the floor of his Land Rover.

She said, "I'm staying here till you're off Lubega grounds."

He said, "When I am so chaste and innocuous?"

She said, "When who cares about details."

He said, "My guess would be John does."

She said, "John announces to himself what he'll believe, and then John proceeds to believe it."

He said, "So say he's the one who has it right."

She said, "He does not have it right—Lord, you did believe him! Can I get up—where are we?"

"Bat Valley."

"But it doesn't matter where we are. We're guilty anywhere we are. We're guilty because we're innocent."

He said, "I won't try to follow your labyrinth."

She said, "If we were guilty we wouldn't be so open, everywhere. Nobody would see us. It wouldn't enter anybody's head we were guilty. But since we parade around in the daylight we are guilty. Anyway, where are you taking me?"

"You will see."

She said, "How did you get mysterious—dropping from the sky like this in the morning?" Because happiness had dropped from nowhere. With no preparation. She said, "When you passed my window you didn't look. Don't you know in Africa you come straight up to a bedroom window and stare in?"

He said, "I trusted you were watching for me."

She leaned to kiss his cheek but it was far away in a Land Rover. She had to keep to her distant bucket seat. She did not like to be so far from him. She slipped her hand on his thigh. His hand caught hers. He rubbed her hand back and forth along his thigh.

She went silent, looked out her own window.

They were below Kampala Road. The teeming African section of town beside the taxi park. People as well as cars all over the street. Clots of wooden wheelbarrows. The hot thick smell of fumes and sweat and cattle dung. She felt watched. Even here, with scarcely a European she could see. She glanced up at a tall Luo—Odinga. She turned away quickly and, when they had passed, guardedly looked back. But the man was a stranger. She sank in the seat. She was deflated with relief that Odinga wasn't watching. Wulf looked curious. She said, "Any African you know, you always see them here."

He said, "Anybody I might know?"

She said, "I didn't see anybody" and they began to laugh. They did not need a reason to laugh.

They were headed out the Port Bell Road. She said, "What in heaven are you taking me to?"

"To the Nile Hotel." He smiled and did not look at her.

She could tell it was a joke but she could not tell what it meant. She said, "They need a little advertising, this phantom Nile Hotel."

They had turned off the tarmac, were on a murram road passing *shambas* and banana groves and heading toward the rainforest. They turned onto a smaller rutted trail through a patch of forest, into a partial clearing where the forest opened out. A hut, once-whitewashed mud with a corrugated roof and a rain tank. Shriek-red canna lilies strewn in weeds and in overgrown grass and one huge bougainvillea—a rangy gold, and slatternly—as if once upon a time there had been a true garden. Now there was the rhythmic sound of pounding from the forest.

A round-faced woman in a faded *basuti* was filling her *debbie* at the rain tank. The woman stared up at the car and kept on filling up her *debbie*.

Agnes said, "And where'd you find this Nile Hotel?"

He said, "A kindly gift."

She frowned at him.

He said, "For only the time being, not for eternity—alas."

She had turned to listen to the pounding from the forest. She said, "It sounds like somebody's hollowing a dugout. I know that sound from Navugabo."

He said, "It's what I'm told."

They greeted the woman at the tank. The woman placed the ring of fiber on her head, and bent to attempt the *debbie*. Wulf stepped up to her, lifted the *debbie*, and placed it on the fiber ring on top of the woman's head. The woman walked off swaying, humming out her thanks.

Wulf led her to the front. There was a tiny porch. Wet grass stretched down to the lake, under patches of trees and vines that made the sunlight green. She stopped at a rough-wood sign. It was stuck in the grass by the porch. The letters were scrawled out childishly in black—THE ROYAL INSTITUTE FOR SOCIAL RESEARCH. She began laughing and gasping, "Did you do this?"

He did not look at her or answer her. He merely smiled down at his keys, which he was fumbling with, trying out in the keyhole, which meant his arms were directly under her eyes, which meant she smiled a minute longer but not much more, what with arm hair curling down his wrists and his wristbones jutting and a rippling chain of little muscles running down along his arm and underneath his skin, and what with the way his hands twisted bony and hard, and all of which said she'd soon be rubbing her hands along those arms and wrists and chest and thighs and there wouldn't be a soul arresting her for rubbing his arms and wrists and chest and thighs and all of which said her own fat breasts would soon be rounded in those hands and she closed her eyes just briefly at her picture.

The key turned. He pushed the door. He held the door open for her but her eyes stayed on his arm, until she had to look where she was going. Abruptly, when she stepped inside the hut, she was afraid. It was going to happen.

But she could only touch his arms. He'd said so. She knew it herself. She could only touch his arms.

The Nile Hotel was stark. It was one room. It was dark except for the door light. He pushed open shutters. Curtains puffed out in the breeze. They were flowered rust-stained curtains. There was no screen in the windows, but it was a livable cabin. A bed, a table, straight chairs, a faded straw *kiganda* mat across the floor. A sink, shelves with a book or two. A primus stove, kerosene lamps, half-used candles here and there. Tackle and buckets and fishing rods were propped up in a corner. The *kabaka's* photo hung on the wall—Mutesa the Second in a naval uniform and Ethiopian good looks. The picture was illegal, under Obote.

She said, "I don't understand."

He said, "Cranshaw brought me—said I should rent it. It's the Institute's."

She said, "So your colleagues know of me."

He said, "Who knows?" He smiled, added, "He thought I liked lake men perhaps."

She sat on the bed to take this in. He sat beside her, began to rub her neck. She put her hand on his arm, back and forth on his arm, and then they were kissing, and then they weren't sitting any longer. Until she opened her eyes and let out a raucous gasp.

Two heads were holding the curtains back, peering at them. Wulf looked up and did not move. From where he lay he began the Luganda greeting. The men answered. Back and forth with the greeting. The men were smiling. They were friendly and welcoming.

Wulf said, "Excuse me a moment."

She thought he was closing the shutters. He wasn't closing the shutters. He was opening the door, walking outside. She heard him speaking with the men. Explaining—in Luganda—that he would be "working" here from time to time. The men were pleased. Wulf told them the water from the tank was theirs, just as it had been before he came. The men were very pleased. He walked them along the path, and he came back in to her. They laughed and he locked the shutters and came back to the bed in the shadows.

This time she sprang up, walked around the table, pulled a chair up to the table, sat and looked at him still on the bed. He said, "You like it better so far off?"

She held still for a minute, then shook her head and came back to the bed and sat beside him. She said, "Michael's accident. I don't know if you knew how guilty I felt."

He said, "It is why I came in the morning—I took my chance. The children are safely at school right now. I can't give up seeing you."

"That wouldn't be my plan."

He said, "The children are at school in the morning—you wouldn't have that guilt. How's the morning plan?"

She said, "It's okay—on mornings I don't teach. But how can you?"

"I don't mean often."

She didn't answer.

He said, "Then why are you sad?"

She said, "I'm afraid."

"Of me?"

"Of—maybe—what you said on Kololo."

"Which was?"

"You remember."

He didn't answer.

She said, "You've forgotten—but I have understood you. We can't be lovers."

He was silent. Before he said, "Anything I said was a temporary shield against myself."

She turned to look at him.

He was watching her, his hand held her arm lightly. But he began nodding at her slowly, saying nothing.

She lay down in his arms.

He said, "I will wait." He accepted her, passively and gently.

She had her head on his shoulder, her face in his neck.

It was not John—any longer—that was holding her back. The pictures that wouldn't leave her—they were pictures of Michael. And of Anne and Lulu sleeping.

She began to feel that she was sinking. In sadness yes but in something more. As if, right now, she were in the process of uncovering all that she'd been homesick for as long as she remembered. Whose absence left a vacuum, which came between herself and John. Which came between herself and any other person, or any other thing. Which came, most of all, between her self and her own self. She hadn't known the reason she had been so hollow. She hadn't known—not fully—what she'd been homesick for.

She thought of Hans, the misanthrope in love with Megan. Hans lived the way she'd have to live. If she pushed Wulf away.

Wulf pulled her very tight.

Somewhere around them she could hear deep throbbing from the dugout makers, and the rush of leaves and drone of insects and the splash of water and, once or twice, the cry of a lone fish eagle.

TWENTY

On Disseminating Whiteness
and John Bunyan

It's midafternoon. A group of women sit under a flamboyant tree, on mats. They're wives of teachers, and they're studying languages because they must go forward as their husbands have gone forward. The white wife helps the black wives with their English. The black wives help the white wife with Luganda. But all of them are giggling like children. One of the women has learned she'll go to England, study home management. Another one hops up to issue warnings. She pulls herself up stiff, scowls, sloughs off any trace of feminine sway, and speeds bullet-quick across the grass. "This," she warns, "is what you'll turn into."

It was afternoon, overcast and cool. Somewhere outside was the sound of dogs and children and gardenboys and drumming. The drumming was the one strange sound. She didn't actually hear drumming, but she could feel it. As if the bed she was sitting on were picking it up through the ground. She sat absorbing this odd underground drumming, rubbing her lips with one hand and holding a mouse head with the other. She wasn't aware she was

holding a mouse head. She was on Anne's bed and she was looking for things. Her life was looking for things. The mouse head
was a gray felt one but it wasn't what she was looking for. She
had forgotten what she was looking for because the drumming
was disturbing and also because she was actually in the Nile
Hotel and Wulf was smoothing back her hair and saying, not asking, "We will come back to our place," and she sprang up saying
"It's time," and he was saying, "It is not possible to not love you—
you forget transitions. But you can't forget we have this moldy
home."

His words were making her lose things.

She heard "*Nnyabo.*" Prudence. That was what she was losing—
Prudence. Somehow her energy had gotten turned aside in a more
compelling channel than this girl. And anyway the girl persisted in
begging for Milton in spite of the spurt of hope she'd had for
Prudence's painting. And Prudence wasn't having much trouble
these days finding herself advisers.

This was it. She would not do Milton one more day.

She would take Prudence to the Orthodox place. That was
made for Prudence—the woman icon painter. Combine her religion and painting. Make her forget the asinine new ambition the
girl had recently let slip—that she intended to become the first
female archdeacon. Mityana's doing, this new goal. It was at
Mityana Prudence discovered she was cleverer than men she studied with, and that she could not become a priest.

No. She did not want to be at the Orthodox place when Wulf
could not be there. She wouldn't mention it.

She handed Prudence the book, said, "Today we begin John
Bunyan. He is on your list. You will like John Bunyan. I will tell
you about him."

Prudence did not protest. Or not convincingly.

She told Prudence of the simple man, the tinker. She told about
the times John Bunyan lived in, about the outlawed preachers and
churches and the way the man believed he heard God's call and

had to be a preacher on his own. Different from Milton. But Bunyan was thrown in prison just like Milton was thrown in prison. It was illegal for Bunyan to be a preacher on his own. She told Prudence about dream writing, like Dante and Piers Plowman, and she told Prudence how writing out of dreams gave us what we wanted most, like the road, the way; like the gate and the light and the guide; like the slough of despond and Vanity Fair and the black Apollyon creature; the hill and the heavenly city. She told Prudence about allegory and . . .

Prudence said "It is best to read it, Madam." But she had a few more things that Prudence had to know.

Prudence said, "I will read now, Madam."

John Bunyan came easily to Prudence. She had reached: "I looked and saw him open the book and read therein; and, as he read, he wept, and trembled; and not being able longer to contain, he brake out with a lamentable cry, saying 'What shall I do?'"

Prudence put the book down in her lap. Her eyes were wide. She said, "This is Omwami Ssegawa who has left his home and wife. This is Omukyala Nakafero. This is Samson Serubidde. Madam, this is like the people here. This is the question they ask. All the time. All around us. They ask, "What shall I do to be saved?"

She said, "It is the very same question. It is the very same kind of Christianity. You know the word *evangelist*. You see it is the same word here."

Prudence said, "You said this man wrote this book three hundred years ago. Can that be true, Madam?"

"It is true."

"I am happy that you made me read this book, Madam. I want to know what happens next."

"Go on."

Prudence read on and on and on. She reached Pliable: "At that Pliable began to be offended, and angrily said to his fellow, Is this the happiness you have told me all this while of? If we have such ill speed at our first setting out, what may we expect 'twixt this and our journey's end?"

She put the book down once again. She said, "It is so, Madam. I believe this book is saying things that people understand. I believe the man called Milton is for another kind of people, a kind of people I don't know."

"Many people think what you are thinking."

Prudence read. And every few minutes she dropped the book and exclaimed.

Once Agnes said, "Keep reading. I must tell Tabula something."

Tabula's silence, all afternoon, had been seeping through to her. He wasn't in the kitchen. She went out in the yard and walked from back to front to side. Jomo and Lumumba were in the jacaranda trees. They had devised a basket pulley. Michael couldn't climb because he had his cast. Fuweesiky was sitting on Michael's shoulder and Michael was talking his Fuweesiky voice, Fuweesiky gearing up to ride up to heaven in the pulley. Fuweesiky did not think he wanted to ride up to heaven in the pulley.

She asked where Tabula had gone. Michael made Fuweesiky squeak in his African English, "Tabula, he tired, Madam. Tabula he sleeping somewhere else this afternoon."

She ignored Fuweesiky and went back in, suspicious. She had not forgotten Odinga mumbling about Tabula.

Was Odinga intending to take Tabula's place? And then what? Since it stank of Odinga's careful engineering.

Prudence was reading to herself. Prudence didn't seem to need her watching her read to herself. A change was coming over Prudence, and that was very good.

TWENTY-ONE

On Being Honest with Friends

YOU APPROACH KAMPALA, AND FOR a disconcerting moment you suspect the travel agent sent you wrong. You said Africa, not India. But here you're looking at a maze of cement courtyards with pink and purple steps. A mosque, its minarets so white against the dark-mud railroad yard you think it's just been scrubbed. Two more mosques along the road. A Hindu temple, pink and phallic and jutting with animal-heads in vivid fuchsia and in shades of lavender. You pass the cinemas—gigantic heads of women with red drops on their foreheads. Stop for supplies at the Diamond Bakery and you're waited on by a girl with sleek and long black hair. She checks the price in Gujarati (so you're told) with the man up on the ladder. The streets are bright with men in turbans, women ballooning pantaloons underneath sheath dresses, girls in filmy golden-threaded saris.

❦

Elizabeth and Essex. It was the title she pulled out, in wonder. A Ladybird children's book. Mysterious stories the English handed children. Ladybird books were infinite and they only cost a shilling seventy-five. She bought at least one every week because she bought a book a week to give each child. Michael wanted Enid Blyton and she didn't argue with Michael. Lulu only read fairy tales and she was trying her damnedest to unglue Anne from *Mamie's Magic Mongoose.*

No wonder English children knew history, even if the history was wonky. Michael told her the English invented the motorcar and the cinema and the phonograph.

She flipped the pages. She scanned for bedroom scenes with Essex. She heard, "No need to read it—it's all about conspiracies."

She grinned and said, "You've checked?"

Megan said, "Of course." She was meeting Megan for coffee.

There wasn't a seat in the place. Half the tables were Asian-filled, a couple of tables of Africans. Erasmus caught her eye. He led them to the table by the tree and by the rail. Mr. Nelsadry, of the grocery store on Kololo Hill, was abandoning the spot. It was elevenses time, which meant crowds at the Nile Café. She didn't bring Wulf any longer to the overpopulated Nile Café.

Megan said, "Do you know what's happened to Odinga?"

Agnes had prepared for this, but now she shrank. She did not like to ask herself why it was she shrank. What did she actually know? Nothing. She actually knew nothing.

What could Megan have seen or what could Megan have heard? Odinga watching her? Crazy. That was all there was.

She said, "What do you mean what's happened?

Megan said, "He's left with no notice. He didn't show up this morning."

She said, "Maybe he's ill."

Megan said, "The quarters are empty. I even owed him money. Apparently he doesn't care about money."

She shook her head at Megan, said she didn't know, said he was always faithful or she wouldn't have recommended him. That much was true. She didn't add—because it was irrelevant— she'd heard he beat his wife. It was not worth remarking in this country and besides it was pure hearsay from an Englishwoman Odinga once worked for and now his wife was in Kenya anyway—if he'd ever caught his wife. None of that had anything to do with Megan. It hadn't had anything to do with her. About the money, she passed on what she'd learned—that he must pick up a few shillings from his drumming at the Sputnik Bar. That activity of his made sense to Megan—some of the characters she'd seen around Odinga.

Megan said, "But he was never surly with you?"

She said, "Odinga's kind of surly. I guess I got used to it. He was so bright I never had to tell him anything. I really did think he would be good with you. I'm sorry."

"It could be I expect too much."

"I don't think—no, you don't, you don't. But then I guess I left him on his own—I mean his standards were higher than mine, so I know the whole thing is my fault."

"How so?"

"It was my fault. I discovered my shabby southern heritage when I read Carson McCullers—do you know her?—*Reflections in a Golden Eye*. There was a line about the layer of dirt on the top of the refrigerator—this was in the South—and suddenly I understood where I was raised. My midwestern husband once cleaned off the top of my mother's refrigerator and he never quite got her odd reaction. So maybe Odinga came with high standards, and maybe it was me who ruined them."

Megan was smiling. She said, "I doubt that's it, but it doesn't matter. You haven't told me what happened about your letters."

She was confused for a minute.

Megan said, "I know, it's been so long—but did you get your letters from Wulf some other way?"

"Oh, those."

She hesitated. She wanted to tell Megan. But she only halfway wanted to tell Megan. The ground between them kept its prickliness, in her mind, because of that ancient craziness of hers—that she'd loved Megan Schofleur.

It was from the first time she saw Megan, and that was at the *kabaka's* garden party.

John had led her by the arm, up to this Englishwoman. She'd heard of the Englishwoman married to a Piet Schofleur—she'd rolled that name around her tongue. Now she looked at the wife of Piet Schofleur and went a little strange. No explaining it. It had happened on the instant, the way those things happen on the instant who knows why. Some unknown trick of the brain etches the shape of a face in you and a shadow of that face dooms you, wherever you see it, no matter who or where or what the sex. Something like that happened then—with the quiet directness in those arresting eyes. And maybe a bit with Megan it had been the easy British voice, as if there were always distances wrapped up in her voice. Whatever it was, she'd spent that afternoon (which she remembered as pastels and whites) craning over shoulders at the English wife of Piet Schofleur. And once, when Megan was a group or so away, she'd caught Megan watching her. Or she suspected that—it was hard to know across the sun—she suspected Megan's eyes were narrowed with watching her.

One day, she'd vowed, she would know this woman. She intended to be good enough one day to know this woman, though she couldn't take that for granted, because Englishwomen's lives were closed and organized. And when, after all, Megan's life was anything but closed off and organized, her attraction to Megan grew to obsession with Megan, which led to letters to Megan. The kind of letters which, mercifully, went unanswered and unmentioned; though, she always suspected, not forgotten on Megan's part.

She'd kept right on seeing Megan in domesticated daylight, each of them packed in sardine-tight with children and husbands and Hanses. The bald and undomesticated all stayed darkly undercover between the two of them, forever unacknowledged in words or deeds.

She and Megan talked books instead of personal subjects. It used to be Van der Post and Murdoch till Megan uncovered Duras and Jean Rhys—Agnes counted on Megan for her reading. She was also aware that Megan got up early and played with poetry, but she didn't talk about that. Only once, when it was safely in the context of something else, Megan spoke a line without looking at her—"When we woke, it was day; we went on weeping." It was the closest Megan had ever come to her. The line belonged to Auden, not to her.

Now she said to Megan, "He never wrote. I'm sorry I got so carried away. It was all in my head."

Megan said, "I don't believe that and you don't either. I wish that much were in my head."

She said, "But it was. Okay, it's obvious Wulf and I have gotten to be friends, but I promise you it's not an affair. You have to believe it's not an affair."

Megan said, "I believe what you say, but you needn't think I'm standing in judgment."

She said, "I know it looks like an affair because I've taken him places. But that's the irony—it is not. Not at all. I would not and he would not."

Megan said, "Look, I'm hardly indifferent to the man's appeal. Tragic intensity thrown in with wit. Looking like him. You can't think I'm judging you."

"It doesn't make any difference. It's true. I would not do that to my family."

Megan said, "No," but she was smiling as if that was not quite what she was meaning. It struck her Megan's attitude was vaguely influenced by her unsympathetic attitude toward John.

She said, "All right, maybe I would have slept with Wulf. But he won't. It's the way things are."

Megan said, "If you say so."

They began laughing.

She said, "All right, I lied."

Megan nodded. But she looked too knowing again.

Agnes said "About his writing I lied."

Megan said, "About his writing." Her voice was flat.

"Yes. About his letter writing. He wrote me through John. Now you see what I'm talking about. Wulf will not do anything behind John's back. So you are right not to trust me in the least—but I'm having to endure Wulf's fidelity to friendship and that's the way it is. I will never have an affair with Wulf. Now do you believe me?"

They changed the subject. She said to Megan, "You are sad," and Megan said that it would pass. She left two shillings for Erasmus but when they rose from their chairs some ruckus started up. On the street again. They could see soldiers on the street.

It was at the next-door offices. Soldiers were forcing a hand-cuffed African into a camouflage-painted van. They recognized the man—Erisa Kibuka-Musoke, the minister of finance. Deborah's father. She knew him. Erisa Kibuka-Musoke was the last Muganda minister in Obote's cabinet—two other arrests had come in this past month.

They sat back down. Megan clapped her hands across her mouth and her eyes went wide. The hubbub of voices circled them—"Obote has gone too far. . . . The last honest man in the cabinet. . . . The country won't survive this one. . . . What does Obote think he's doing? This is it. The man has nothing but the army. . . . Nothing but Amin you want to say—Amin *is* the army. . . . And who is it controls Amin?" Erasmus stood motionless, shaking his huge head and muttering.

They left. They said little because the mood was heavy.

But they had both lived through upheavals. They had learned—independent Uganda had resources. Independent Uganda was resilient, and they were resilient. The fear at the moment was for the Kibuka-Musokes. Erisa Kibuka-Musoke was an honest, fearless man, beautifully educated. And his kind was being winnowed rapidly.

TWENTY-TWO

On the Green Sunlight

To step into a rainforest is to step into a cloister. You are enclosed, above you and on all sides of you. You hear the shrieks of birds and the wall of pulsing insects, but you hear them as if from muffled distances, through spraying points of green and gauzy sun. The air is dark, and charged with flashing reds. You breathe earth and wetness and a rotting sweetness. Your foot sinks in a spongy mass and everything is damp and slippery, fat and moist and glistening.

John was in Nairobi. He would be away ten days. The children were in school this morning and she was leaving her car at the Nommo. It was windy and the clouds and her red skirt were blowing but the sun was shining. You had to step up high to get in his Land Rover. She was watching the Nommo gardener and he was watching her, until his shirt blew over his head and he had to fight it down and then they laughed, she and the gardener, from across the lawn. Or the gardener assumed she was laughing with him and she was, she was, only Wulf also was talking—of the "social research" at the Nile Hotel that was getting backed up on them.

The road dipped into rainforest, and the wind was stronger there. The sun still shone but clouds were banking. It was exhilarating. They could hear the dugout pounding, trees swishing, birds crying. They walked under vines, over the bright deep green to the water and they stood at the edge of the lake. Waves were lapping. The surface, to the horizon, was dotted with whitecaps. Birds were shrieking and plunging and skimming the water and everywhere was noisy.

And then as suddenly there wasn't any noise, and almost not a movement. They stood as still as everything around them stood. As if everything were pausing, before some kind of change, they and the birds and the butterflies.

The fishermen were down the shore a way. They were standing knee-deep in the lake. Then the fishermen began to call, back and forth across the water. For a moment the drawn-out humming of Luganda seemed to be the solitary sound, echoing on water, and then abruptly, fast and faster, fat rain splats were hitting them and the water and the leaves and they ran. They stood a minute dripping, breathing fast in the closed-up hut before they kissed, took off their shoes, lay on the bed, and held each other chastely.

She put her nose in the hollow of his neck, where she could breathe his smell the most. They themselves were still, but the motion was everywhere around them. The rain was beating on the corrugated roof. Frogs were croaking. Doves were moaning. Geckos were scattering across the walls and slipping in cracks and his hand was slipping in the crack in her blouse and then was pressing sweetly all around her breast. But he went still. He quietly drew his hand away. He lay with his hands withdrawn and said, in a minute, "Forgive me." She could guess he said that, though she could not quite hear a thing but rain and trees and wind. The noise protected her. She sat up. She unbuttoned her blouse. She slipped off her blouse and slid down her straps until her breasts popped free and she picked up his hands, one of his hands in each one of her hands, and she cupped his hands on her breasts and she held them there, looking at him, with the tiniest of smiles. In a moment he moved to raise one breast and take it in his mouth, and in a minute or so he raised her other breast and took it in his mouth, and she shifted her position. She leaned against the wall and cradled his head while he cocked his head not letting go but looking up at her face the way her babies once had cocked their heads and looked up at her face and she this time reached over for his belt. He leaned back and put his own hand over hers. He stopped her. He said, "Are you sure?" Or he said something of the sort but all she saw was the silent moving of his lips because a fusillade was hammering the roof and the shutters and was machine-gunning the metal car outside and she did not attempt to speak and then his hands moved from her breast up to her neck and one hand held her neck in back and one hand kneaded at her neck in front and he pressed her down and the rainstorm took them up in it, the rainstorm let them think that it dictated everything and even if they screamed they could not hear themselves.

Until the rain subsided, and they fell apart, and the sounds came slowly back. The *lap lap lap* of water, and the birds—one chirp, and then two chirps, and three, and one long line of calls and high-pitched fluting trilling.

He shifted her head, till she could see his face. Their eyes played on each other, smiling. She said, "What have you done to make me feel this way?"

He stroked her face and body.

She said, "Americans have never learned your secrets."

He said, "I like Americans."

She said, "How do Poles know things Americans don't know?"

He smiled.

She raised her head up, resting on an elbow, and studied his face, in a frowning smile.

He checked his watch, said, "You have to be at home for lunch."

She jumped.

In the car she said, "I smell like you. It's so strong it's dizzying, and I will not wash you away."

He said, "It is fortunate John is not at home."

She said, "Tell me what you said you would tell me."

He said, "I said—I lived a free life. That was understatement."

She said, "Stop understating."

He said, "I mean not sexual—but of course yes of course a sexual thing but I mean not *merely* sexual. My apprehension in saying—I believe it is so much Eastern Bloc, this life of mine, it will be incomprehensible to you."

She said, "You are not incomprehensible to me."

He said, "You cannot have a way of imagining—the suicidal boredom of a communist state. You hear about alcoholism, yes. But among the intellectuals—I was known as intellectual in Poland . . ."

They laughed.

He continued. "It was a defiance, at its worst a suicide, all degrees of suicide. It became an absurdist way of playing with life, sex did. In Poland it was exhilarating, and chaotic. Among the intellectuals, especially among the intellectuals."

She said, "If that is what made you, Lordie, why didn't communism ever reach the South."

He said, "Darling, darling, you are wiser than that. No one comes out of such extremes quite whole. That is not all of my story. My life has gone in lurches—and that means you never know where you will land. I said, you may remember, that I could not sleep with you. . . "

They laughed.

"My reason—I said because of your husband, what your husband appeared to feel for me. And I thought—in some way I believed myself. If my life had any pattern—I suspected once it was a Tolstoyan pattern, without Tolstoy's Christian props. Because I turned completely from my past. I married a woman I loved. We swore fidelity, in full knowledge. Both of us."

She felt the crack down her middle. Again. She did not speak. It wouldn't go away.

This man loved his wife. Now this man would be tortured by his guilt. And would hate her, the woman who seduced him. And there was nothing she could say or do about it. He would be guilty because he genuinely loved another woman. She would be guilty but because of her children—and now, yes—more than she had known she'd feel—because she'd snapped the trust that she and John at the very least still had, when she could not imagine what she'd do if John had cracked her trust. But still—even that was a world apart from what she'd feel if she'd trespassed against love. In the way Wulf had just done. While she herself had always been afraid she'd die before she ever loved the way she now loved Wulf.

And yet here she was, turning herself away from him, looking out the window at the taxi park. He kept leaning to see her face.

He said, "I was slow to speak these things. For this reason."

Tears were running down her cheeks. She said, "It isn't what you said."

They approached the Nommo. He caught her arm before she got away. He said, "Please, you have to give me half an hour later in the day."

She said, "Come at nine tonight, when the children are asleep."

She hurried. Her face was streaked. She was wet and her clothes were crumpled. She was shaky. She was fishy smelling. She wouldn't get by them—Hesita, Michael, Lulu, Anne. She couldn't get back to her room without them knowing all.

TWENTY-THREE

On Flying, Creeping, Burrowing Things

W HEN YOU READ IN THE Bible "Forty days in the wilderness" you might have a forest in mind, but you'd be wrong. It's best to think "desert," because around thick green you're not at all cast out. You are twined with living things. You smell them and watch them and taste them and feel them crawling up your neck. The moles, the weasels, the rabbits; the wagtails, the barbels, the hawks; the butterflies and bats and dragonflies and most of all the ants, ticks, spiders, mosquitoes, wasps, bees, locusts, beetles, worms, slugs, crickets, grasshoppers, centipedes, scorpions, and all the million nameless creeping beasties. You hear them whine and buzz and whir and it's like you're hearing soil made just where you are sitting. The mating and biting and burrowing and gorging and foraging. The turning the flesh to good rich dirt so the weeds and grass can sprout through bricks and through the wee cracks in cement. You can't mistake that you've got company, and when you stop scratching and slapping and bending to inspect, you feel some kind of underground connectedness you never would feel in the desert, which is the genuine "wilderness."

She'd left the children with Hesita. It was dark. And still she asked, "Shouldn't I even duck?"

Wulf said, "Roll yourself in a ball on the floor—I say it is useless."

She said, "There are *some* people on Lubega Hill . . ."

He said, "You are an optimistic little girl."

She did not duck. She sat straight up, next to him in a tall Land Rover seat, past Lubega Main Hall. She did not look at who they passed. She carried her destiny stoically. He eyed her with ironic gleams.

She said, "Akhmatova says, 'Who would refuse to live the life they're given?'"

He said, "Who is it that refuses?"

She said, "Will you?"

He said, "Am I ducking?"

She said, "You'll go back to ducking."

He said, "We'll see." And in a minute he added, "I'll try disguise—how about cross-dressing?"

She was laughing and running her hand along his thigh. No one could see that. His hand caught hers and it took their concentration, and they went out quietly through the gates and past the Wandegeya Mosques, and along the eucalyptus trees that lined Bat Valley, past Uganda Provisions and Diamond Bakery and the Norman Cinema where the picture-poster woman with the red tear on her forehead went on weeping. They drove past Cristos and National and Grindley's and the Ottoman Bank and Patel Press and Savji's and turned at Bombay Traders, toward the clock tower, down the hill to the warrens of open-front *ddukas*. The stench of urine—even from in the car, the streetlights disappearing, the people thickening to crowds. A wrangle in the taxi park. Soldiers—ordering people out of taxis. It looked as if they were commandeering taxis—was it? They couldn't see clearly. They turned past the temple phallus and the mosque in the railroad yard.

Approached the clocktower roundabout where the Entebbe road skirted Mutubende slum. It was a flying-ant night. When you fried flying ants they were sweet. They swarmed streetlights some nights and then the word fanned out that this was the night to catch ants.

Wulf slowed, leaned forward, peered into the chaos. He slowed further. He had to stop. Figures were leaping with nets in their hands. They were blocking the road. They were yelling to each other. They spilled off the dirt-weeds in the middle. Their jumping was erratic, wild. One boy landed on the side of the car, and then another. The faces, the figures, were distorted in gleams. The dust was churning around them. The air was whites of eyes and noses sprinkled with shoulders and splayed-out toes and arms and calves. Each body piece was shining out, discrete, caught in dusty glitter, disappearing. Nets arched toward light and spinning wings. Men landed on each other, sprawled, leaped up again and flashed the net in crazy reeling air.

Wulf said, "There's a man with a drum who's watching you."

She looked around, saw Odinga, and started. He wasn't jumping. He was observing her, through the eerie leaping shapes. He was standing with a long thin drum under one of his arms.

She held his eyes just long enough to bob her head. He did not bob his of course. He moved his eyes, pointedly, to Wulf.

Wulf was saying, "I've seen that man somewhere."

She said, "At the Schofleurs. Can we move, do you think?"

He navigated the roundabout.

The road beyond was darker, emptier.

In a while he said, "He looks threatening."

She said, "He's not dangerous."

"No, but . . ." He hesitated.

She said, "He used to work for us."

Wulf said, "That makes more sense. He wanted to know who was driving you. Perhaps he recognized me."

"Of course he recognized you."

"You say that categorically. I would not have recognized him."

"That's different," she said.

Wulf said, "He was not happy with me."

"He's a good man," she said.

She contemplated how to say this. To tell Wulf, maybe, that Odinga'd walked out on Megan. But then it could be—what she thought she should say was merely in her mind. What was there to tell Wulf? Odinga had not come back to her, so there was no need to complicate this by bringing Wulf into it when she—it just might be—was making it all up. She had no way of knowing what was on Odinga's mind.

They had turned onto the side dirt road. There was only one faint light, from a *shamba* window, like kerosene flickering. And beyond that nothing. On the Port Bell trail it was only their fragile headlights. The rest was black. They neared the rainforest. The insects came at them, louder and louder until it was a wall of sound. She pushed Odinga out of her head. This was not Odinga's place.

Wulf stopped, turned off the carlights. They sat unmoving, listening to the forest roar, waiting till their eyes adjusted to the dark. They smelled water, jungle, sweet smells tangled with rot.

She began seeing specks of light dotting the forest wall. Perhaps fireflies. Perhaps eyes. Now she made out glimmers of water. She began to hear the splashes over insect shriek.

Wulf found his torch. They slammed their car doors and both instinctively went still, silent, as if they'd hear an answer, a resurgence, from their audacity.

The torch beam was sucked up in the black. The air was a jolt of oxygen.

She said, "Do we dare to open shutters?" The Nile Hotel was stuffy.

He said, "I'll turn off the torch. Perhaps the bugs won't know."

"You think?"

They leaned, strained, stood on chairs, unlatched the shutters and pushed them open. The air swam through the hut, fresh from the water and forest. And then he undressed her, and she undressed him, and in the streaks of moonlight through the gaping holes of the windows, they could see the white of the mosquito net. It hung from a fixture in the center of the bed. It was pulled to the side, twisted together, stuck in a clump to the wall. It felt as if that was the way that it had stayed for years. She had to tear it open. It smelled musty, spidery, dusty. She said, "You think maybe the mosquitoes might be better?"

Wulf was slapping at something. She said, "We need the net." They pulled the net carefully around the edges of the bed. She felt things crawling up her arm. She jumped, swiped. He said, "It might be—I think perhaps that I must check for scorpions."

His understated manner made her laugh. He began laughing. She swiped at something on her legs and on her fanny. She stepped on something spiky, jumped up on a chair. He switched on the torch. She stood naked on the chair but she jumped down and shouted, "Turn that off. They've seen me. They're out there watching. I know they are."

He turned the torch to the mosquito net, began inspecting. It was filled with crawling spots of black.

He said, "Darling, I'm crazy. I should have thought of this before. I'm going to get this washed. I'm going to bring gauze."

She said "*Gauze*?"

He said, "Never mind—come with me" and he pulled her toward the door.

She fought back. She said, "In the moonlight—they will see me running naked."

He said, "I won't let them see you running naked."

They held their clothes on loosely. They ran through moonlight to the car. He shoved things. They climbed in the back of the Land Rover, onto the mattress.

He said, "You see—this car belonged to an American. You see it has gauze on the windows. Here, feel."

She did not feel *gauze*. She buried her nose in his neck. She mumbled rapidly, "It's dark enough to ask you—educate me, please. Please. Like your intellectuals educated you."

He said, "I scarcely sense the innocence you claim. In fact, I have come to see your deacon of a husband in a somewhat different light."

Her laugh was throttled because the places he was kissing were disturbing her and then he took her neck in both his hands and she was helpless.

They lay folded, clamped against each other. In a while she rolled on her back, said, "Do you hear what I hear? They are right outside the car. They've been listening—or maybe they could smell. They are lined up waiting."

He said, "The jackals?"

She reached for him brusquely. By mistake she hit his head. They could not see at all. She said, "I ignored that sound. It can't be jackals so close, can it?"

He said, "What can they do to a car?"

They lay listening to noises all around them. And then she was rubbing her hands over all his limbs and body and saying, "I've never felt this kind of happiness in touching a little toe. I can't stop touching every inch of you. I want to taste every half a centimeter of your body." And she was kissing underneath his arm and he was kissing her knee that was somehow close up on his chest.

She said, "There's something funny. It must be the same for any woman who has been near you. It wouldn't make a difference what you are, what you say, how you look, how you act—it wouldn't make any difference about anything because there's something about your smell that no one could resist. I can't keep my nose away from you."

He said, "Perhaps I need your American de-smeller."

"Deodorant. Try it—I'll be free of you. We won't have any worry anymore."

He said, "Perhaps I shan't."

They struggled in the dark to find the tangle of their clothes. He locked up the hut. She heard the lapping, pulled him toward the water. But they stopped. Against the gleam of the lake were silhouettes. Two fisherman were in a dugout, pulling something. They watched in silence, before they walked back through the orchestra of sound.

TWENTY-FOUR

On Textures

Y OU COULD BE A PERSON who finds her happiness in textures. In handmade paper, in the knots of rough-weave linen, in the unpredicted warp of pottery or the dips and peaks of stucco. Maybe for a change you hold a flesh-warm chicken egg, or you are happy when you rub your fingertips along the soft inside of leather gloves. These textures of the world possess a rarely mentioned joy.

The children were safely in Nakasero School. The morning was sparkling and the car wind flapped his collar. He slowed, turned onto the trail, where the air went cool and shadowy. He said, "Do you smell that change?"

She smelled wetness, saw aqua flashing through trees and the women at the water tank. The women stopped their movements, stared openly.

She recognized one woman from before. The other one was older, thinner, and had a homemade pipe in her mouth. That one took the pipe out, greeted briefly, stuck it back in, and walked away. The other was left with the politenesses.

They carried squares of screens, the kind you propped in open windows. You could get them six inches tall or eight inches tall or a foot or even two feet tall and the best ones you could pull apart or snap up tight to make them the width you wanted. Mostly you had to crawl around the *ddukas* to find such things but she had found them in the garage. Left over from Mityana. None of them were quite the height they needed but maybe they could wire a couple together. Something.

Wulf had hold on one song line. He'd picked it up from her and he was worrying it like a puppydog, "I saw Adam leave the garden, with an apple in his hand . . ."

He stopped carrying objects and abruptly closed the door. That put them in a dark and stuffy space. No opening the shutters. They could hear Luganda coming closer. Bigger, more jovial gatherings—the water tank as fresh new entertainment. Wulf was whispering, "We need not renovate the whole hotel this minute." His lips were on her lips while he was whispering. His hand was spread across her neck. Carefully he unbuttoned the front of her dress.

The bed sounded like it cracked. She clapped her hand over her mouth, would not laugh out loud. The Luganda broke off and they held deadly still. Until they heard the laughing and Luganda starting up a foot or so from them, from just beyond their shutter.

The nearness of the women at the rain tank—and the way the bed kept whining—made their touches very quiet. When the talking outside the window grew more distant, they creaked the bed to screaming, ignored the shrieking springs, and fought off sleep.

The sounds seemed far away. It was playing in her mind that she had got to force herself to move, that she had to be somewhere. But the motions of her limbs stayed watery, and she couldn't make it matter where it was she had to be.

He was the one who dressed her. She helped him as she could, and she admired his will. But she admired it smilingly, and very languidly.

TWENTY-FIVE

On Banana Plants

A STEM OF GREEN BANANAS soaks up heat, arches low. The fat green leaves around it are longer than your arm and broader than your neck. In a breeze they twist. They rattle; they gesture; they beckon. They wave like arms beside the roads and on the hills and in the valleys.

Lunch was on the table. She was sitting on the porch. Fuweesiky was sleeping in her lap. It looked as if she were waiting for her children because it was the time when children came, at one o'clock, but as a matter of fact she was sitting because she was sitting and everything around her spot was plump and sweet. Her nerves had changed. She was at peace with things. She looked as if she dozed, in a low-slung garden chair. But she wasn't in a low-slung garden chair but rather in an amniotic sea.

Her eyes were on the valley. The sky was gray and foaming now but the sun spilt through a slit and slashed the leaves, banana arms, the Enyanju's floppy banana trees which now were flaming yellow-green while other things were gray. Yellow-green against a grey-black sky. She thought the sight was very strange and very beautiful.

The children were coming—she couldn't see them yet but she could hear. They trudged up the hill in a pack. Michael first, you saw his white—his badge-of-war—sling through the hibiscus hedge. He was looking down at something. He did not see her and she liked that. She liked to see her son absorbed. Michael had a perfect nose. If she were in his class she would have a crush on Michael.

Lulu was running up past Michael. Lulu was dragging her satchel and her books and papers and cups and pens were bouncing and spilling and rolling. Anne was squatting. Anne picked up Lulu's objects and Lulu kept on running.

They were beautiful. There was no explaining them. How could her children be climbing up this road, under these flamboyant trees, past yellow-green leaves and grey-black skies. None of which they noticed.

Fuweesiky bounded off her lap and leapt across the grass to Michael. Michael made Fuweesiky noises—his African English voices—and stooped for Fuweesiky to hop up on his shoulder, his sling shoulder.

She stayed where she was and she smiled, while they crossed the grass and stopped and looked at her. As if they were puzzled. All three of them. There was no reason for them to be puzzled but it didn't so much matter. She felt her front, but she was buttoned up. She glanced down at her breasts, but they weren't showing either.

Michael said in his Fuweesiky voice, "Have you got lunch ready?"

Lulu said, "Why are you sitting here?" but Lulu didn't wait to hear and her mother didn't stop what she was thinking. She was thinking: It is all one body, love. It is one colossal over-arching body and the flowing is what holds it all together. One thing flows into another, and then out again, and things keep flowing in and out and all around and if they don't they blow away and die—and how did she not know it, that this was what was holding them in one gigantic body, keeping them from blowing off in dust. And it never had been clear to her till now.

Anne was leaning on her shoulder, sucking her finger, her other finger rolling on her mother's blouse. As if the child were sensing the distance of her mother, as if the child would do away with the disconcerting space.

Agnes pulled Anne onto her lap and made some faces. It was enough. Anne hopped up and tugged her mother into the house for lunch.

She drove them back to school. Odinga was waiting when she returned, at the bottom of the drive. She'd expected him. Their talk about Tabula had never taken place. It merely hung miasmalike above her head, while Hesita shook her head unhelpfully over Tabula's disappearance. Agnes didn't care to think about it. It was not her fault, and in any case she didn't have a choice about Odinga. Odinga would come back, whatever she might want. That was how it was. Only she vaguely hoped that Megan would not hear about how it was. She hoped Megan would have the grace to pretend she didn't see.

She said "*Jambo*, Odinga" and smiled.

Odinga said, "*Jambo, Memsahib,*" and he did not smile.

She spoke in Swahili. She said, "Let me park and I'll come talk with you."

He was keeping well clear of the house. She was aware of that. Though it was somewhat pointless when Hesita followed any step Odinga made. And how long could Odinga keep clear of Hesita when he now intended to come back.

She was newly conscious of her skirt. It swished too much when she was walking down the drive to meet Odinga. But it was the feel she liked. It was Indian and it wrapped close around her hips and flapped out loosely on her calves. It was thin and soft and red-figured cotton, but it was all right if Odinga watched because that was the way things were. Indian skirts could flap on calves and anyone who wanted to could watch.

Odinga said, "When shall I return, *Memsahib*?"

She said "Tomorrow. I have to tell Hesita."

Now Odinga smiled.

And when he turned away, and she was halfway up the drive, she stopped. She called back, on the spur of the moment, "But you must tell the other *memsahib*—Megan, Madam Schofleur."

He watched her impassively a minute, and went back down the hill. Saying nothing.

Anyway, she'd said it.

TWENTY-SIX

On Keeping Abreast of the News

Y OU CARRY A MAT IN Buganda, one you've woven out of reeds or someone's woven for you out of reeds. It could be plain or it could be brightly dyed. You get together to exchange the news. You sit on the mat, if you're a woman, in a highly prescribed manner, your legs both pulled to one side like an Englishwoman's side saddle. So a grassy spot at a college or a school is splashed with brilliant colors, women in reds and blues and yellows, and, in town, with little white children sitting with their *ayahs* on mats, mysteriously proper, under jacaranda trees. The air around hums with the musical calls.

It was early afternoon and the shadows were sharp-cut and the air was still. She was working. A bright red dragonfly was buzzing at her papers. It was long and narrow and had black stripes that spiraled round the red.

Open books and papers were on the window sill and floor and on her lap. She had to give a class on *The African Child* since

Chekhov hadn't worked too well. But her mind had slipped into social research, his hands . . .

"*Memsahib.*"

Odinga. At the bedroom door. Quickly she looked down, inspected her blouse. She always expected milk was streaking her blouse but she was almost all-right looking. Hoarsely she said, "Yes?"

"*Memsahib*, you have a visitor."

Already! He was feeling like she was! She said, "I'm coming," and went quickly to the mirror.

At the living room, she sank. Prudence. She looked down at her watch.

Prudence said, "Good afternoon, Madam." She said it from where she was sitting, said it as if she knew the madam had forgotten.

Agnes said "Just a minute" and spun around to where she'd come from. She would get her sewing.

She scratched in her basket for scissors, which were tangled in wads of thread. Prudence did not start reading. Odinga slapping down the iron, the girls whispering—those were the sounds in the room. Until she said to Prudence, "I think you don't need me for Bunyan." She let it hang as half a question.

Prudence stiffened her posture. She said, "Madam, you have been kind to me. You have aided me greatly. I have made a gift for you."

Prudence was reaching into her own basket. She was pulling up a package, holding the package out to her. A large, flat object carefully swaddled in banana leaves—many, overlapping, vari-colored greens of leaves. It was tied with fiber from banana trees.

Agnes pushed away her sewing and took the package in her lap. The girls—Lulu, Maggie, Anne—came up to watch. Their expressions were knowing, and sly. Lulu said "Open it, open it."

She looked at their faces. She said, "Do you know what this is?"

Anne said, "We're not telling."

Odinga put his head around the door.

She pulled at the fiber, then carefully unwound the leaves. She turned the object over and over, unwinding long green leaves.

She held a painting up. It was a watercolor, fixed to the cardboard from a box. She looked at it in silence. It was of a *shamba*. It showed a hut in a courtyard in a circle of banana trees. A woman with a baby, a goat, chickens. The golds, greens, browns were deep and rich. The sky was a dark gray, but a sun streak broke through the clouds, and in the strip hit by the sun the banana leaves turned yellow and the brown courtyard turned rusty gold. It was vibrant and startling. But most arresting were the wide black Rouault lines. Prudence used the lines around each object, and around the sunbeam. Like in her first painting, as if Prudence had known her distinctive style from the time she picked up a brush. When no one told her what style was. The picture had the flatness of the children's tempera paint but the images were potent and alive.

She looked at Prudence and nodded her head and smiled her admiration, and looked back at the painting.

Anne was grinning at Prudence and nodding in the way her mother had.

Odinga came into the room. Odinga did not come in when she had visitors. He greeted Prudence. They seemed to know each other. Lulu held the painting up for Odinga to inspect. He looked at it carefully. But he simply nodded to Prudence and said, "Good, *m'zuri*," and left them.

Agnes said, "Prudence, why are you giving this to me?"

Anne said, "I know when she painted it."

Lulu said, "Daddy knew when she painted it."

Maggie put her finger on her lips and said "Shhh" to Lulu.

Prudence said, "Madam, you have showed me things that are beautiful."

Agnes said, "Now this will be a beautiful thing that other people see." She looked at the children. She said, "Where shall we hang it?"

Anne said, "Over your bed, where you took down Daddy's cats."

She made a face at Anne. Maggie whispered something and they giggled.

Prudence said, "Madam, I have painted it for you because you and the *omwami* are my parents. I know now that I have parents. Always I shall know that I have a mother and a father."

Anne frowned.

This was heavy. Agnes was uncomfortable. Why, right now, was this girl doing this thing? She said, "You honor us, Prudence. But it is your own talent that will take you where you want."

Prudence had not said what she meant, or what she wanted. She might never hear what Prudence meant—it would not help to ask. She knew better than to ask.

She asked, "What are you planning, Prudence?"

Prudence said, "I beg your pardon, madam?"

She said, "Shall we read some Bunyan?"

Prudence dropped her eyes. She said, "No, Madam."

The girls abandoned them.

After a minute Prudence said, "Madam, there is a person who has requested to become my tutor. I am having my hope strengthened—one day I can become archdeacon. It is possible. And the tutor has studied things that I must learn. I know that you are very occupied."

Agnes mind raced. The insult was coolly placed, but was this tutor John? Her spiritual adviser would take this on as well? And let his own wife discover it this way?

No. John would not. But this girl did not intend to name her newer better-model tutor for her ludicrous ambition—to be the first female archdeacon.

Perhaps Piet was this newer, finer tutor. Of course. It would be. Poor Megan. But she didn't have a reason to think Poor Megan just because Piet enjoyed his flirting with Prudence. If she were suspicious of Piet's intentions then there wasn't a soul she would trust around this place.

And when she said that to herself, she knew it wasn't true. She knew she trusted John, sexually, far more than Piet. Piet after all was European. John was a rigidly Protestant American. And, as guilty as she herself was now, that was still one thing that bound her firmly to John. John adhered to principles. John, in sexual matters, was trustable.

She said, "I am glad you have a tutor that can help you. It could be I am jealous." Prudence giggled. Prudence did not volunteer her tutor's name.

Voices on the drive. Michael with Piet it sounded like. They looked up. Piet was coming round the bushes. He called *hodi*. She called *karibu* and stood up.

He stopped in the doorway, looking first at Prudence. He would not sit, said he was aware that John was in Nairobi and had she heard the news?

She had heard no news. She heard more commotion out the door.

Wulf! With the girls—they were coming down from the directions of the commons.

Wulf would not sit either. He said, "I see Piet has come with news."

She said, "What news?"

Prudence said, "We do not know news."

Piet said, "Have you a wireless?"

Lulu said, "It's broken."

Piet said the borders had been closed. Wulf said the airport had been closed but no one knew what was happening. Obote was in Singapore. Rumors were virulent, but they were all conflicting. No one knew. Piet said just stay put—or come to them if she felt they'd be safer. He had no time to stay just now.

Prudence disappeared with Piet. Wulf lingered. Would she meet him at nine o'clock? Just up the bank a way?

She would.

Anne was whining. Odinga was hovering. Wulf left.

Michael read out loud, *The Lord of the Rings,* about dark passes through treacherous hills. They were crowded on one bed, around one lamp. When the reading stopped the insect drone became a high-pitched pulse that seemed to take them over.

It occurred to her—she lay here every evening listening to insect drone, and always she could count on it. On the very same sound every evening. It was dependable. Predictable. Comforting.

And now something was changing. Ominously. It could be—this insect drone was the closest to changeless things—which might as well mean to eternity—that they would ever touch. And somehow it gave all things a common grounding. It pulled humankind together, over time and over space. This same drone united them with every age and every place and every person who had been. Sophocles heard this very same sound—maybe when his world was turning over. And that was twenty-four hundred years ago.

She tried to tell her insight to her children. But they thought insects were a pretty low-grade heaven.

TWENTY-SEVEN

On Storms

I T'S POSSIBLE TO BE SITTING at tea, inside, at the dining-room table by a wall of windows. It's possible that when you pour your tea it's sunny. While you sip, you begin to note it's overcast outside. And when you're on your second cup you hop up quick to slam the windows shut before you calmly sit back down. It's possible you keep drinking, though you can't hear your companion for some minutes in the flooding pounding water and the *crack flash crack* of the ear-splitting too-close lightning strikes. It's possible that by the end of tea it's quiet again, and merely dripping when you step outside, though the ground as far as you can see is yanked-off limbs and shredded-up wood and heaps and tangles and hillocks of leaves piled everywhere you look.

The children were in their own beds. It was nearly nine. She was restless, eager to run up the hill, but Hesita intended her to listen to her moans.

Hesita'd been sighing all day. Agnes was aware it was the same old tension—Odinga. So she would not ask. Hesita told her anyway. Odinga got "saved." Odinga wanted to "forgive" her for taking his job. That man meaning to "save" her from her sins—to save her baby Emma from her sins!

A gross absurdity. She commiserated on this one. She trusted such weird shape-shifting would quickly disappear.

She wouldn't let in the more sinister suspicions—that Odinga had hit on a diabolical method of driving off Hesita. After he'd finished off Tabula already? Had Odinga driven off Tabula by threatening salvation?

Now it was Emma fussing. Emma did not fuss. Hesita must have read Emma's fussing as some sign because Hesita said, "You must not go off, *Nnyabo*. It is a bad night, *Nnyabo*." She said the Luganda word for *bad* over and over, and she shook her head at Agnes.

Agnes said, "*Kale*(okay). But you wait here a minute. I will come right back."

She left the house. She crossed the porch and went out in the thick gardenia dark. It was a moonless black. She saw her way by the yellow streaks from the windows. At the bank she jumped, but it didn't gain her anything because her flipflop disappeared. She skidded down, backward. She squatted. No light beam hit the bottom of the bank. She felt around the grass but she couldn't find her thong and then it left her mind and she went still, conscious of the pool of dark, and cicadas, and the viscous-sweet gardenia, and that he was waiting for her one hill-curve away. And unknown things were coming—she would not go off this hill tonight. Hesita need not worry. She was not mad. But she could be with him just where she was. There was dark to hide them.

She stiffened and looked around. Something was happening somewhere in this dark. It could be every person would be torn from every other person. Who knew what could be.

Her drifting, sitting shoeless in dark grass, had only been for seconds. Quickly now she twisted. She flapped her hand around the grass. She couldn't feel her flipflop. How could it have vanished? She crawled along the bottom of the bank until her hand hit rubber. She jammed the thong between her toes, pushed up, and climbed the bank more carefully.

She walked across the commons under jacaranda trees. The window streaks sufficed for her to make out obstacles, but it was dead black when she turned into the path under eucalyptus trees. The wall of insect sound closed in on her. She breathed the lemony sweetness, stood still until her eyes adjusted to the path.

The woods opened out around a bend, behind the wooden houses, and there he was. Leaning on his Land Rover in white—of all the crazy colors to conceal himself. She stood and closed her eyes at the sight and when she did—she saw him not himself. She saw his form pressed new inside her eyelids—his white turned to black and all the night around him turned to white. Black and white flipped over when she shut her eyes. She opened her eyes. He was white again, and he was coming quickly toward her.

They held each other tight and silent for a very long time. As if he, too, was frightened now by whatever this thing was.

She pulled back. She said, "I can't leave this hill."

He said, "I would not take you off this hill."

His eyes were hidden, but he seemed to be studying her face.

She said, "There's no reason you can't come to my house." She had not thought of it before.

He said, "Perhaps there is a reason."

"But there isn't. I have to go back to the children. With these rumors, and with me by myself with the children, of course it's right that you be there. John would want you there. We are being crazy thinking we can't act like friends."

"I think we're wise knowing we can't act like friends." But he said, "I will come stay—a little while—in your living room."

She hadn't known how much she'd been afraid, until he said he'd come.

They walked quickly, and then stood dawdling.

He said, "I'll wait out here until Hesita has gone home."

She said, "Hesita is my friend. Hesita would never say a thing

and anyway of course Hesita knows and anyway you're supposed
to be here. You are helping us."

He would not budge.

She said, "When she's gone I'll come sit on the bank. Come
when you see me."

She ran. She sent Hesita home.

He would not come into her bedroom. They played Schubert
low—until the power went off. She found candles, but they did
not want a light. They lay on the sofa, almost chastely. Happy. It was
all right being chaste if she could have him close and she could
breathe his smell.

She did not sleep. She stayed conscious of him sleeping, of the
way he would start and come a bit awake, find her there and pull
her closer to him. It was happiness that kept her from sleeping. It
was the amazement of it, that happiness was such a modest thing.
Once she'd thought the world was sad, but this was all it took to
make it new, complete, like it was meant to be, and she wondered
at it. All night long she wondered at it, that happiness was such a
very simple thing.

And when—she didn't know what time, two or three in the
morning she guessed—she heard shelling not far off, maybe at
Wandegeya, she'd been expecting it. She'd heard it other nights. It
wasn't as bad as it might be, or if it was she couldn't know it yet
and what she knew was happiness existed and maybe it would last
if she stayed absolutely still and did not move a finger or a toe.

It was better than rambunctious love. That kind ended, and this
kind did not need to end if she stayed still and silent and did not
stir this thing, which was as it ought to be.

She half wished he'd wake up, but she didn't really wish it. There
was nothing he could do. And she would not jar this happiness.

TWENTY-EIGHT

On the Comfort of Greetings

Y OU SPEAK WHEN YOU PASS somebody. That's the custom.
Cities mess up customs, shorten greetings. But in the Buganda
countryside you halt whatever you are doing and shuttlecock
the greeting—a rather lengthy formula—back and forth and
back and forth for minutes. And when you pass somebody anywhere you thank them for their work—*Webale okukola*. But suppose you happen on a person when he's lying in the shade—that
eventuality also has been coded for. You say *Webale okuwumula*,
thank you for resting. It keeps you both in touch. Loneliness
seeps in around the edges of all things, but Baganda keep the
loneliness from taking deeper root.

Light and dread—the curtains were closed but she could feel them
coming, light and dread.

He had to go. She had to move. She had to wake him, peel away
from him. Hesita would be here. Lulu got up early and Lulu would
bound out in the living room and see her twined with Wulf.

She did not move. Her head stayed on his shoulder. As deeply and as slowly as she could she breathed his woody smell and let it soak through her. It made her swallow. She thought the sound of swallowing would wake him up, but he breathed more deeply still.

Morning was demonic here. It did not creep out, it blasted everything.

She shifted her head—almost imperceptibly—so she could see his face. His eyes popped open. The light was dusky but she could feel his smile spill over, quivering and brimming to her face—until he bolted up whispering "My God," flinging off covers and fighting for shoes while she tripped up in blankets and yanked the bolts on doors. He shot out into fog and disappeared. While she stood barefoot in the doorway, hugged her arms against the chill and stared at fog.

The silence was uncanny. The air was foaming white. White swallowed houses, trees, bushes. Billowing puffs curled up her legs. She made out only ghostlike hulks and a smothered soggy quiet. No birds. No motors. No barking, humming, calling. No shots. White, and silence, and that was all.

And then a brusque voice. Odinga's. Swahili. Barking at Wulf: "The *bwana* is not on this compound. You are a bad man—you come on this compound. I protect this compound. You do not come on this compound." The words echoed. All the houses on the row would have heard. This man was deranged.

She strained to hear an answer. She couldn't.

Of course Wulf wouldn't answer. Of course Wulf had to be silent. He would not announce himself like Odinga announced himself. The fog hid him if he stayed quiet.

She heard Hesita calling her. She leapt back across the grass and through the house. The hall was filled with children sliding in a tangle, and calling at once, and Michael—maybe it was Michael—said Odinga was out his window yelling, and Lulu—it may have been Lulu—said where was she, and Michael said why was she dressed and why wasn't her bed messed up and Anne said It's snowing it's snowing and Lulu said It isn't but Lulu wasn't sure it wasn't snowing.

Her own thought was louder: Thank God not one of you can understand Swahili. Thank God not one of you can see in fog. Not one of you saw Wulf—you don't know why Odinga yelled. While other thoughts rolled in on top of these: Wulf could not take Odinga seriously. He would not buckle under to this absurdity. Of course he wouldn't. And: Odinga does not come at daybreak. Odinga has been watching us all night. Crouching. Waiting to spring. Odinga's mad—but what has he made Wulf think? It's preposterous—Odinga in some drummed-up bond to John. Odinga's got no use for John, but what does it make Wulf think?

The noise was from the kitchen. She was abandoned in the hall, which was a cave of shadows. She turned around vaguely, came to life, and hurried out. The living-dining room was milky light. She had to find her flipflops somewhere round the sofa. She got down on her knees. She saw one flipflop underneath a table. The other one was nowhere. She scattered the sofa pillows, found one flipflop in a crack between the cushions. She stood on one foot, then the other, jamming on her thongs. She straightened the sofa cover pulled all out of whack, smoothed her dress. She looked up to see Hesita eying her activity. Amused.

But Hesita had news. Hesita sat at the dining room table. Excited. When Hesita sat, it meant for her to sit down, too, and talk. It happened when John was away. They didn't sit this way when John was here. It wasn't anything spoken. It was the way it happened.

She sat. Hesita said Omwami Lubega said Omukyala Kivengere said the *kabaka* would come back—the *kabaka* was not dead at all, that was all Obote's rumor, and now the *kabaka* would come back. Hesita said Omwami Ssegawa said that the country would be Buganda again now, only for Baganda, and no more Obote and no more other tribes and everything was going to be peaceful now and good and there wouldn't be taxes or soldiers or cheating. Odinga announced quite loudly from the kitchen "The *kabaka* is dead. The *kabaka* will not come back."

Who was this man declaiming from her kitchen?

She had to confront Odinga. She had to demand something—
something about his yelling on the commons this morning. Their
guests were none of his business. How? She hadn't even managed
to keep the man fired when he was fired already and now he was
bloated hippo-size and thinking he had some power over her and
over their "compound" as he called it. He did not play by anybody's rules and how did he think that he could lounge his fanny
in her door?

The rest of this was just below admitting—that in some godaw-
ful madness Odinga believed he was responsible for her. Which was
halfway moving, if you overlooked its sheer perversity.

Hesita was saying, low, in Luganda, "That man knows nothing.
That man comes humping back in here thinking he is Lord. There
is no living with the Lord, *Nnyabo*. I don't know how we going to
manage. No telling what that man going to do. But *Nnyabo*, don't
you be worried. Things are going to be good now with the *kabaka* back. Today, you all right sending those children to school.
Everybody on the hill is acting like they always act. Shooting has
stopped. People are happy. That *kabaka* is coming back. No reason
at all to keep those children home. Already I saw those Megan
children in those uniforms."

The noise was mounting, around the hill and house. The fog was
lighter but voices and shouts and slams got louder. Paulo from next
door—just out the window—talked machine-gun-like to a
Muganda woman. Other women in *basutis* were gathering outside.
A man was calling across the road. Somebody shouted out across
the commons.

All right. Of course the children would go to school. If Megan
was sending hers, no question. She hated the way Americans were
so afraid out here. If the school was open then of course the school
knew it was okay to be open. The school had to know what was
happening. They wouldn't open if it was bad. She was not cowering even if she was American. There was no reason to be out here
if you were cowering, and anyway Wulf would come if they needed somebody.

A motor. A car coming up to the front. She looked quickly out to see if it was Wulf—Wulf would overlook Odinga's threats now that they might need him. Now that things were changing fast.

It was Hugh's car—and Piet walking up the drive. Hugh hopped out and banged the car door, said, "Don't send the children." Piet said, "Keep the children close to you. Kampala is a mass of troops." And they were off and Wulf was coming, trotting over the commons. Wulf leapt down the bank and said, "The fighting is worsening. None of you must go into the town." Odinga was poised listening, but of course Wulf would not pay attention to Odinga. Still, Wulf turned back across the commons, and children bounded round the porch and grass and drive and yelled in glee about no school. Except Anne, who leaned on her mother, reached to finger her mother's skirt, and watched her mother's face to see how much was wrong.

TWENTY-NINE

On Accepting Invitations

SMELLS. THEY ELUDE THE MASSIVE degradation that sight and sound have undergone in our wired-up, high-tech world. No media—not radio, not television, not computers—has yet exploited smell. Smells persist in being yoked, in something close to purity, to our bodily experience. The path they travel is silent, and unpredictable. They hoard their primal power. They transport you instantly. You walk by a rain-wet cedar tree, or woodsmoke startles you—and you're in the grass on Kironde Heights in the very early morning; or in a shadowy doorway, at dusk, in the Kenya Highlands; or in a hut on Lake Victoria. Your body is tied, obscurely, to the Africa you left.

She'd come into the bedroom for something but she stood at the window thinking about Megan. Megan had come to check on her, and left, and now it was Beryl her neighbor waiting in the living room.

The fog was gone. The smell of the grass was sharp and sweet. Kite-hawks were circling, sluggish and lingering and torpid. They hovered so slowly you felt eerie, as if clocks had stopped, but the air was so clear blue that you saw everything—banana leaves, and a dead-white tree from way across the valley. A shrine to death, in the midst of flopping yellow-green. The arms of the tree each held a creature, dark and hideous. Dead still. Vultures. The birds were bloated, shoulder-fat, and each with a sharp-bent ugly neck. The sight held her at the window—until Anne scraped on the screen. Anne was grinning gap-toothed, saying "No school—Maggie can come play." She kissed the air toward Anne, turned around, and tried to remember what she was looking for.

For something. Beryl her neighbor was waiting for something—oh, a map for some reason, and she began to root around in piles.

Back in the living room she handed the map to Beryl. Beryl asked what she had heard. She had not heard. Beryl said they had better hear. Somebody on Kironde Heights had better hear.

There'd been intermittent firing—she'd heard that—and tanks somewhere. Pockets of people were gathered along Kironde Heights, asking, wondering, speculating. She hardly knew Beryl her neighbor. Now she and Beryl were intimates. She didn't know the Yugoslav chemist a few houses down. Now the Yugoslav chemist was a close and chatty friend. She hugged the new Ghanaian from a couple of houses behind. The woman wore a beautiful silk-pink tight-wrapped skirt. Each of them told a different terrifying rumor. None of their rumors fit each other's.

She walked with Beryl to the next group by the ditch. One woman ran back to her house, said they had to stay inside. She herself would stay outside after that—since that word came from skittish Americans. Yugoslavs ought to know better about how to act in coups. Or maybe Poles knew best of all about the ins and outs of coups.

Frank Callahan came running. He said Amin had seized the wireless station—those were the last explosions they had heard. Absurd "news" was starting to come through. Turn on the wireless, he said.

Who had a wireless?

She strayed back up the hill.

Apprehension, at the moment, was weaker than excitement, with everybody outside everywhere you looked, with everybody pressing up to you to see if you were scared, asking what you knew. Now she was bound to the strangers no matter what might happen.

And you couldn't do anything about anything, so it was as if you were freed. From something. From routine maybe. As if suddenly you were opened up to whatever was to be—you couldn't guess what, but something. And things could not go horribly wrong if people came together like they were doing now.

Nobody trusted Obote. So who knew. Maybe this was the way things had to change.

She might as well write her play since she couldn't teach today. Out the window she could keep an eye on things. She could see, hear, smell if she needed to do something. Wulf would come back and the hill was swarming with children who were sorting out explosions, turning themselves into foreign correspondents because they ran the fastest and got the update news. Michael raced by, said he was Double O Seven. Jomo and Lumumba and Bernie and Lulu and Anne and Maggie ran after him and yelled some contradictory names.

She was pulling out her chair.

A blur of him—almost trotting, crossing the grass with his head down. She shot out to the porch in joy.

A message, he said, and stayed a foot or so from her. He would not come in. They sat in the deck chairs on the porch while he leaned on his knees to talk but she did not hear him yet because of an explosion somewhere, and then heavy shelling, and her standing and yelling for her children to stay where she could see them. Now she could hear Wulf say, "John is wrecked with worry. He can't get to Uganda. Flights, trains, buses, roads—everything is blocked and canceled."

"How do you know?"

"I talked with him."

"What do you mean you talked with him?"

"He managed to make a telephone call, through the American Embassy to the Institute, said it took him hours. He made me promise to look after his family . . ."

He stopped talking and looked away. He held his lips together. She did not smile either. This kind of irony was scarcely fit to speak. It made her chest go tight. It made her afraid, before she could say why it made her afraid. The way Wulf turned and looked at her perhaps. Which was too heavily perhaps. Perhaps because Wulf's loyalties would now be stretched as thin as a thread of gold. A new hook-up had clanged, ghastly loud, like the coupling of trains reversing their direction, and she did not want to hear these clanging new directions.

He said, in a lower voice, "As if he had to ask me."

She said, "He could have gotten the department—Hugh or Piet."

He said, "Perhaps he tried."

She said, "He did not try."

Wulf said, "No, he didn't."

They watched each other, and in the thick new lump of her confusion she closed her eyes, her head bent his direction.

They held still that way, until he shifted, pulled out a handkerchief, and gave it to her.

She said sorry.

She wasn't sure he knew why she was crying. Maybe she didn't know herself why she was crying. Maybe it was her imagination, this sudden feeling she was caught in an elephantine trap that she would never never never climb out of. And how could Wulf know that. And yet she thought he knew that. He knew why she was crying.

He started talking again, but even lower. "Look," he said. "It's bad. Other countries know more than we do. It's all over the BBC."

"What is?"

"Amin is gaining control. It's very bloody. Obote can't get back from Singapore."

"And what if Amin takes control?"

"I don't like to think."

"Frank Callahan was saying that it might be better than Obote."

"He's British. Obote thumbed his nose at the British. The British aren't thinking straight on this one. Except people like Cranshaw. He knows better."

"But whites aren't involved."

"If whites keep out of the way. What about your food? Your water?"

"We have tins. The tub is full of water."

"I suspect you know about these things better than I do."

"We've been through it. I should be helping you. So you will have to come stay here—for your protection."

He paused a minute before he said, "I had come to that conclusion. I believe I must stay here."

It surprised her. They looked at each other in the shock. She could see he felt it like she did.

Slowly she began to smile.

He got up. He said, "I'll keep checking. I have to get back to the Institute. Send someone if you need me."

She said, "I'll send Odinga."

He grinned. He said, "Yes, I have to think about Odinga."

She said, "I hope you write John's orders in Swahili—so you can show Odinga you're legitimate. Your orders are to stick to this compound."

He glanced back over his shoulder as he leapt up the bank. His grin was as broad as hers. The no-school-today exuberance had caught them both up in it.

THIRTY

On Candelight

CANDLELIGHT IS LIKE THE HUT. It takes us to the origins of things. The light is fragile, the dark envelops it, and the feel of that sits deep in us. The frail light draws us to its circle and it dreams for us, shifts and stirs, tries out shapes and colors, gleams off lips and cheeks and hands, glistens off foreheads. The candle leaves a space we don't forget—because imaginings have soaked up vacantness, and dark.

She hadn't moved. She was in the deck chair, not yet grasping what was opening. Or closing. Not yet knowing what to do. Not yet believing it was possible, him staying in her house. She had to stay still and let her turmoil settle. But there were strange loud noises all around and children were running and so was some grown man. Lulu and Anne were jumping up and down saying Michael said Lumumba said there was a man with his arm blown off just near the Wandegeya fence, and Beryl came hurtling through the hedge and said she thought she could still get some charcoal because the electricity had gone and she was saying yes she wanted some, that was very very kind of her and just one second, she would get some money.

She hurried. A racket was coming from Anne's room. The room was alive with boys and the floor was chaos. Michael was tossing out teddy bears and doll's heads and Slinky toys and she heard "Here it is" but she didn't stop to see what he had found because she was looking for her pocketbook, and then she saw it was the two-inch broken radio—the wireless radio—they'd uncovered under plasticine and wheelless wooden trains. Her mother'd sent that two-inch radio—she'd had to pay three times its worth in duty when it got out here so she remembered this radio. She heard Bernie: "All it needs is batteries." Michael said, "I know that." Beryl said she had some batteries, they kept a pile of batteries, but Lulu was calling "I've found some" from the kitchen. Michael sat and focused on what one did with batteries.

She followed Beryl out the door. The shelling seemed distant, but a burst of raucous squawking, from inside, made them turn around. A rapid, breathless announcement. Too fast to hear, in very broken English. Michael held the instrument up high, in front of a procession. He held it like it was the Ark of the Covenant. He bore it to the porch. Ceremoniously he set it down on the cement. The children squatted round it. She stood with Beryl. They strained to make out sounds. Hesita and Odinga and Paulo and a couple of Baganda came up around the fringes, listening intently. The announcement had a few words here and there between refrains. The refrain was coming clear, gobbling the time, over and over and over: "His Excellency Uganda's Military Head of State Major General Idi Amin Dada, blah blah Glorious Emancipator of the people of Uganda on this blah blah crackle crackle squawk, His Excellency Uganda's Military Head of State Major General Idi Amin Dada, incomprehensible blah blah blah blah blah, His Excellency Uganda's Military Head of State Major General Idi Amin Dada."

She was conscious: Odinga was a megalith two feet back of her. Silent. Daring Wulf to come to this house. Wulf would come to this house. Wulf would come to her bed. The curfew would protect them. During curfew Odinga could come nowhere near this house.

It wouldn't happen. Wulf wouldn't come to her bed. Wulf wouldn't have one thing to do with what was on Odinga's mind. She need not consider Odinga. She might, though, consider Kironde Heights—all Kironde Heights would know Wulf was at her house all night. But then what difference did it make? They all could go to hell—Odinga first of all.

Now she heard from Maggie: Her father had not come back from Namirembe. With Anne she walked down the hill to see Megan. Twice people stopped her on the way. Somebody asked if she had any water in her house. Frank Callahan asked if she'd had word from John. They seemed more subdued than they had been hours earlier. She was more subdued herself.

There was a crowd at Megan's. Someone had seen Piet at the archdeacon's house, gathering information. He was all right. She had coffee on Megan's veranda with Anne sitting in her lap, Annika on Megan's lap.

It was dusk. It was the golden light come suddenly. They'd eaten. Michael and Lulu and Anne were in pajamas. They'd been freed from baths—water had to last for who could know how long. Michael was reading *The Lord of the Rings* to Lulu and Anne and her, on the bed, and she was tense. The light was dying—and there was a curfew at sunset. After dark anybody still outside would be summarily executed. If Wulf was coming he would have to be here now.

So he wasn't coming after all. So he'd better not come now.

Hesita was gone. It was getting too late to move outside. Wulf had thought better than to spend the night with her.

She heard his car—up the drive. Lulu jumped up to the window, said, "It's Wulf" and ran to the front door. Anne ran after her. Michael put the book down. He looked at her and said, "Why is Wulf here?"

She did not like the way Michael asked why Wulf was here. She said, "Your father told Wulf to come. Your father thought we needed a man with us, just in case."

Michael said, "When did he say that?"

She said, "He got a telephone call through to Wulf. I told you he called Wulf—when he said he couldn't get a plane."

Michael didn't answer. She left him on the bed. He made her uneasy. She went with a tight chest down the hall, toward the living room. She walked very slowly, conscious of Michael.

She could hear from the living room: Anne and Lulu were happy Wulf was staying.

She came around the corner of the dining room. He was sitting on the sofa. Anne and Lulu were standing in front of him, grinning at him. He was talking to them and over their heads he was looking at her. He did not smile but it was better than a smile.

She said, "Anne, Daddy asked Wulf to stay here until he gets back, just in case anything happens. You sleep in Lulu's room, okay?" Anne was used to sleeping in Lulu's room, whenever they had company.

She moved quickly. It was getting hard to see with no electricity. Still the toys were scattered. She was stooping, throwing trains in boxes. Michael came up. He squatted and tossed the toys with her. It was unusual, his helping without saying anything, without her asking him. So he'd decided he was being silly? She smiled a thank you at him. She stood up and yanked the sheets and the blankets off Anne's bed and left to find clean sheets.

Wulf was on the rug with Anne and Lulu. They'd lighted candles all around them. Lulu and Anne were teaching Wulf to play pounce. Pounce was a quick card game. Hundreds of cards flew everywhere at once—every person had a deck of their own and the speed was cutthroat speed. Wulf was stopping them, asking what they were doing. Lulu spouted explanations. Anne said "See?" every now and then. Michael attempted to ignore them. Michael was sitting in a chair and reading his book by candlelight.

Lulu endeavored to explain to Wulf he couldn't move till she had moved. She kept starting over in her explanations. Wulf said, "Then I'll only move it on the other pile." Anne said, "No no no." Lulu once more struggled to set out the rules, stopped to make long sighs, tried to show him with her cards. Michael couldn't put up any longer with this sheer incompetence. He threw down his book, said, "What she means is you have to hold your deck in this hand and . . . "

She walked around the living room and the dining room and pulled the curtains closed. She got two more card decks out of the card drawer. She handed one to Michael. She moved Anne over and sat down with her own deck. Michael sighed "All right" and sat and crossed his legs. They started over. They sat, concentrated, and didn't talk for some minutes. They shuffled decks, set out the rows of cards, said "On your mark. Get set. Go." Now everybody watched each other's cards and scrambled over other people's arms to slap down cards on the card piles in the middle. They could hear shelling outside, but they had curtains closed around them, in every direction. They were in a circle, and they had candlelight.

Streaks of candlelight began to bounce chaotically off flailing arms or Michael's cast or arbitrary noses. You had to guess at any shape because weird shadows were looming up the wall.

Now all the shadows jumped. Now, in a sudden flurry, the space was a swirl of flopping hair and jutting elbows, Anne bouncing up and down on squatting heels and squealing Stop stop stop and waving cards while Michael swung his cast like a Flight-of-the-Bumblebee conductor. Lulu was darting arms in a *slap slap slap* card-fury and Fuweesiky was clawing to hold on tight to Michael's shoulder while Michael was firing gunshot African English in his ventriloquist Fuweesiky voice about that cheating Lulu and where that nine had gone.

She, Agnes, said "Hey wait" rather pitifully. And then she thought to pull herself away. She leaned herself back against a chair and let the melee pass. Wulf said "Coward" and stayed in the circle, and she was glad he stayed in the circle. She still sat cross-legged just like him, but across the circle from him.

She wondered what it felt like to him this minute, his being on her floor in this wild light with noise as lunatic as this with who knew what outside. Was he thinking what was going on outside? Was he thinking of their research? Or was he thinking he missed his child and was that why he was happy with these children?

Her eyes locked on his hands. His hands hovered out in front of him, near the scuffle of cards in the circle, as if he still were in this game when he was not at all still in this game. Only from time to time he made a feeble venture toward this game. He'd hold out a card—his manner was not certain he should be holding out a card. He was a sorry pounce player, but his hands weren't sorry at all. They were far too male to be looked at. His hands were so audacious that she forced her eyes away and her eyes kept drifting back and she had to keep prying her eyes off them because his hands were too exposed, because the current was too blatant in his hands, even in commotion, because she had to damp that current down but when he dangled his hands in front of her in this spurious eccentric light in the middle of her rug with hairs curling down his wrists then how was she supposed to damp that current down. His hands short circuited her efforts.

The fear of his hands was her sweet fear, while around their circle was dark fear. The walls and corners of the living room, and behind Wulf in the dining room, and through the black hole of the kitchen door and then the hall abyss—all back there was black, and around their puddle of light was black except for ceiling glimmers bouncing spookily. The curtains were closed, and miles and miles of dark was outside of that cloth. They were huddled in a cave. And suppose Wulf had not come. Suppose she had the children by herself, in the black. Suppose they didn't have the circle in the cave and suppose from now on out there wouldn't be a circle or a shelter.

She listened to the insect screech and hyrax screams—the hyrax seemed louder. You couldn't hear a motor. No one was driving, and maybe not even walking. All God's creatures were huddled in caves. There were these circles and there was dark.

She tried to see Wulf's face, but he was frowning, concentrating on his cards not her.

He was a little boy just now. He had to be in on the game. He had no interest in her just now. His eyes were darting toward one card pile and then quick to another card pile while Michael and Lulu *slap slap slapped*. His eyes were straying to a little bit behind the spot where any commotion had taken place, but sweet Wulf thought he was playing. He saw a jack. He fumbled to get his queen on top of that jack but by the time he got his queen picked up and slapped down on that jack the demon-Michael-hands shot cards down under his queen and his queen landed on top of that king and all their screams made him take his red queen back. He sputtered in confusion. His movements went erratic. But he was committed. He wasn't giving up like she gave up.

She grinned. He looked up straight at her this time and her grin turned happier, him keeping his eyes quite still a minute ignoring the brouhaha—and then Lulu poked her mother's arm and said "Put your eight of spades up there," and Michael shouted over her quick, "Don't be a bubble-headed booby, you see she's not playing." Agnes dropped her eyes—the flicker of Michael's glance said Michael knew exactly where she'd drifted to.

They hushed, at once. They stopped moving. Even Michael and Lulu and Anne. Someone was banging. The back door. The children looked at her and did not try to speak. Their eyes were scared. She looked at Wulf, and then she began to get up.

Wulf said, "Stay where you are." He got up. He picked up a candle.

Anne said, "Don't go. Somebody will shoot you."

Agnes said, "Nobody wants to shoot us. Somebody might need us."

She followed Wulf, and Anne held on to her skirt. She picked Anne up. She stayed in the dining room where she could see Wulf's form in candlelight.

He held his candle toward the door. The door was glass. He said, "It's a man, an African."

She said, "Don't open. You can talk through the window without unlocking the door."

He said, "It's Odinga."

She breathed more easily. Her fear flipped over to new fear, but already Wulf was unbolting the door. Wulf was speaking in Swahili.

Odinga did not come in.

Wulf said, "The mosquitoes are entering. Come inside."

Odinga stepped into the dark of the kitchen.

She watched with the children. From the dining room. Odinga must have sensed them there in the dark but he did not turn his head to them or speak to them. She could tell from Wulf's candle.

She put Anne down. She made herself ready, but she did not know for what. Odinga could not be dangerous.

Neither man was speaking. The tension was thick. Wulf broke it. Wulf said, "Come into the living room," and himself turned toward the living room.

Odinga said, "*Hapana*" (no). He did not say *Bwana*. She noticed he did not say *Bwana*. But Wulf was in the living room and Odinga followed him. Odinga mumbled "*Jambo, Memsahib*" when he came near her. She smelled *waragi*. She'd never smelled *waragi* on Odinga's breath.

Michael raced to the sofa. Lulu chased him, pressed up close to him. Anne padded over to the sofa in her foot pajamas.

Wulf said, "Please sit down."

Odinga said, "It is not my custom to sit in this room."

They both talked in Swahili.

Wulf said, "I am aware. Things are strange. You have come out after curfew and that is strange. It is also dangerous. Sit down."

Odinga perched on the edge of a chair. He stayed unbending as he always did. Wulf placed the candle on the coffee table and perched himself as precariously as Odinga, near Odinga. She sat at a distance.

Wulf said, "What is it?"

Odinga said, "The *bwana* is away. I protect this compound."

Silence. The silence held on. No child understood Swahili but all three children kept quiet. They began to whisper. She should get them to bed. But she would not leave Wulf.

Wulf said, "Odinga, I understand your fear—I not only understand—I admire your sense of duty."

He paused. Odinga said nothing.

Wulf went on. "But I received a telephone call this morning. From the *bwana* in Nairobi. He cannot reach the country. The airport and the roads and trains are blocked. He has requested that I stay overnight in this house and that I look after his family. I am doing that. That is all I am doing. I honor the *bwana*. You must believe this. I am merely protecting this family. We do not know what will happen. It is not safe that the woman and children be here alone."

Odinga did not answer. He seemed to her not to move a muscle of his face or of his body. He made the air go stiff around them all.

She broke the silence. She could not help herself. She said, "Odinga, the *bwana* is sleeping in Anne's room, where guests sleep. You may check. The bed is made up for him there. You see we are playing with the children." She waved her hand down at the cards. She stood up. "Come here, I'll show you."

Odinga stood up. He did not look at her but she said "Come" and started toward the hall.

Odinga said, "*Hapana, Memsahib.*"

She stopped short. She felt ludicrous. She felt the tone of pleading in her voice.

Odinga faced Wulf. He ignored her. Wulf was standing. The candle was between the two.

Now she was afraid. The *waragi*—how could she predict the *waragi*? She could see he had not budged in what he meant.

She walked up to Odinga. She put a hand on each of Odinga's arms, above his elbows but where his skin shone bare. She felt Odinga's shock. She had rarely touched Odinga. When it happened in the kitchen they had both drawn back. Now she kept her hands on him. She let the blow of her hands sink in. Odinga was not looking at her. He was looking at the wall above her head. She repeated his name and when she did he looked at her. Directly. It was her turn for the blow. His glance was fire. It frightened her. It told her he was misinterpreting. It told her he was taking her touch as something that she never meant. As a pact. As a promise. As a bond she never intended.

She dropped her hands. She had made a mistake. It took her what seemed minutes before she could say what she had meant. She said, "Odinga, this man is here at the *bwana's* request."

Odinga did not look at her or answer her. But she could feel that he had changed. She spoke quietly. She said, "This man and I will sleep apart. You must leave us, Odinga."

She was dimly conscious of Lulu coming up, stopping somewhere behind her. Lulu was not saying anything. But Odinga looked at Lulu. Lulu had smiled at him—she could read that in Odinga's face.

She said, "It is all right, Odinga . . . " She started to say *I promise you,* and stopped. She could not say *promise.*

Odinga heard her hesitation. He glanced at her, and when she said nothing more he nodded formally to Wulf and went out toward the kitchen. Lulu followed him. She heard Lulu talking to Odinga. She heard Lulu say, "You must not let anybody see you, Odinga."

Wulf moved to lock the door.

Anne said to Michael, "I was scared of Odinga."

Michael did not answer. Michael sat playing with the candle wax as if he had his mind elsewhere.

She sat down. Something had happened that she had not meant to happen. It would come back at her.

THIRTY-ONE

On the Noises of the Earth

T HERE ARE SPOTS WHERE THE rainforest touches Lake Victoria. If you're nearby on a moonless night you'll hear what sounds like peace. The lap of water in a breeze, the splash of a solitary fish, or of something bigger than a fish. The pulse of insects, the croaks of frogs, the mysterious cracklings of the underbrush. From time to time, the low roar of a hippo, or a hyrax crying like a wounded child. And holding steady under it you hear a throbbing moan, which might be bird or beast or man, or the voice of earth itself.

"Yes it was funny, him coming. No, of course Odinga would not hurt us." She said it to Anne. "Odinga came to see that we were all all right." She said it to Lulu, and she turned back to Anne, "No, Odinga would not hurt Wulf. It's all right. Odinga is looking after us. No, Odinga did not know that Wulf was looking after us."

Michael did not ask. Michael took the candle he was playing with and went to bed, on his own.

She sang to Anne and Lulu. Wulf stayed in the living room. She sang Bach, "Oh Sacred Head Sore Wounded" because that was the most heartbreaking music she knew and she knew he could hear her singing it. When she stopped singing she sat a minute longer. And after she kissed the little girls, and untangled Lulu's arms from around her neck, and got up, and carried the candle down the hall, she sat beside Wulf on the sofa.

But a kind of heaviness came in the room with her. She wanted to apologize to Wulf. She tried to start, and began considering why it was she needed to apologize to Wulf. Perhaps she didn't need to apologize for Odinga's being deranged—because he was born-again, was that the reason he was acting this way?

Wulf was thinking about it, that was clear. She said to him that Odinga had a madman's notion of his job. Wulf's eyes crinkled at her. He was still considering Odinga, or perhaps the dreaded sleeping arrangements. They did not mention it.

The subduedness of the mood had cracks—like explaining how he had to tilt the bucket if he had to flush the toilet which oughtn't often to have to happen because they had to save the water but just in case.

She couldn't sleep. She left the door to her bedroom open. Down the hall his door was open and the children's doors were open.

She lay on her back. She wouldn't switch to her side, which might let her sleep but wouldn't let her hear, what with a pillow in her ear. She had to hear his bed creak. She had to hear when he got up. She might not hear him walk unless the door squeaked or unless he bumped into something because cement floors didn't warn you, but she could see enough to know when he had reached her room, and then she would lie silent. She would let him grope his way to her.

He would come. He couldn't help but come. They would both say Go to hell to this bizarre and grotesque groveling—and to Odinga, when there was nothing to be seen and not a soul could be awake and they were twenty feet apart.

The shelling was very near. And her tossing was as noisy as she could make it—he would know she was awake. But it seemed to make no difference. When she stopped flopping to listen, when the shelling quieted, she heard merely insect hum.

At dawn he left. He would come back at dark and before that if need be, or she would send for him.

Hesita appeared. And Odinga. Odinga she ignored. Piet and Megan and Hugh and Claudia and Beryl and Alexandra and Frank Callahan came. They all knew Wulf was staying in her house and she wanted to announce—"Think exactly what you will, you'll never know how wrong you are. You have never been so virtuous as Wulf and I are virtuous." But nobody brought up the subject. Only Anne chatted about Wulf, while her mother tried to turn the subject in other directions.

Wulf stayed one more night, and it was just as sleepless.

Word came through from John a couple of days later—to Wulf. John had gotten a seat on a plane—the first flight into Entebbe. Amin was in control enough, it seemed, to make the effort toward a surface normalcy. John would be at Entebbe at noon on Saturday.

Hesita would keep the children. She would drive to the airport with Wulf. She said she would do it alone, but Wulf would not allow her to. The roadblocks—there was no predicting. The soldiers were erratic. They left hours early.

They approached the turn to the Nile Hotel. She felt it and was quiet. It was all she'd thought of since the call. But he wasn't mentioning it now. He was going to pass it by. And that would be it, when he kept on driving past their hut. Not because she decided that would be it, not even because he decided. But it would be. What they had would have slipped away, and not because of anything that had to do with them.

He took the turn to the hut. Only after that, in seconds after that, did he look at her. And everything pooled over, wet and warm and living.

She saw now—in new strange vividness—all the spots they

passed. The elephant grass. The papaw trees on the hillock. The woman halting with a *debbie* on her head, the woman twisting back to look at them. She saw mysteriously clearly the woman's scar across her forehead. The woman was Nilotic. She wondered why a Nilotic was fetching water in Buganda. She heard army trucks, back on the highway they had left. She watched clouds of smoke from somewhere beyond the Port Bell Road. She heard women humming. A chicken flutter-squawked beside the car, and all of it was quietly beautiful.

Their lovemaking was violent, as if they'd waited for so long that this was the way that they were screaming back. And after they spent themselves, after they lay damp and limp, they listened to cicadas and the *drum drum drum* of dugouts and to a single muffled shot. They lay with stirring leaves and lapping waves. She halfway drifted with the sounds and with the sweet smell of his skin and she wondered about the pulsing things that were surrounding them, because the waves and leaves and insects kept right on pulsing around them. The waves were ignoring the coup. The cicadas were ignoring her and they were ignoring him. But the two of them were here, in the middle of it all, still and spent and heavy. They lay against each other naked and dozing and warmed in wet sweet newborn smells. They were stretching out their waiting, as long as they could dare stretch out their waiting, on a rough iron bed that belonged to an institute while waves and leaves and insects seeped in cracks around their nakedness. Took them for granted. Assumed they all—the man and the woman and the insects—were the sole things going on and on in spite of coups and terrors and killings. The waves and the leaves and the man and the woman, love-wet in a tin-roof hut, were the lone predictable things.

For minutes she accepted this. For minutes she would swear that Wulf accepted this. But the clock on the Entebbe road kept ticking. There was a husband coming from somewhere. There were roadblocks to get through. There were *waragi*-stumbling soldiers to aim guns. There were skirts and shoes and underpants to find.

THIRTY-TWO

On the Usefulness of Anthills

DRIVE OR WALK AROUND THE countryside. You come on heaps of mud, highly irregular pyramids, a few with extra peaks, some taller than you are. You learn they're anthills. But then you ask about the scaffolding, the structure of bent sticks you see tied carefully around the edifice. For catching the flying ants, you're told. Oh. You know the ants are food. But still. You contemplate the mystery for years—can there be something gooey on the sticks? Something in the genes of flying ants that tells them not to pass through stick-built scaffolding?

In time the veil is lifted. You learn. When ants swarm, and it's at night they swarm, you drape a cloth around the structure and there you have the ants, safely trapped for cooking. Or you can, if the process catches your interest, continue building scenes inside your head—of herding flying ants from cloth to pot.

John grumbled about a lout named Duncaster. He shook his head, muttered the British all had grown brain tumors. The outburst was to Wulf and not to her. She was leaning forward, but she couldn't hear the answer. Her face was between the two front seats. Her gaze was out the windscreen.

Wulf was driving. John was beside Wulf and she was in the back. Her leaning put her nearer the men but it didn't help her hearing because wind swallowed their words.

Her gaze fell on two hawks, and vaguely on some hides standing stretched on stakes in a field. The observation was a vacant one— she paid no attention to what it was she was seeing. The field of weeds and cow skins merely told her they were closer to Kampala than Entebbe but then she saw Wulf twist his head to look closely, so her own head bent in the direction his head bent. She meant to see the way he saw, because she didn't take things in any longer— she'd had these things around her forever and they were blank wall-paper to her mind. She'd forgotten what seemed odd.

Wulf was looking across the moth-eaten patches of cassava. He was studying the cow-legs straddled in the sun and the cow-arms stretched high up on sticks. Suddenly they looked to her like car-toon-terrified cats—which must be making him wonder. The pelts were still here, undisturbed by Amin thugs. The pelts had reared up among the cassava stalks all the way through the coup.

They were approaching a curve in the road. The tarmac skirted a hillside. The hill was planted to the top with coffee trees. Two bicycles rounded the bend, headed in their direction. The men were barefoot and they pedaled jerkily, straining themselves, because the bicycles were overweighted with head-high loads of bananas. The green banana stems were roped precariously onto the narrow wheels of the bicycles.

An army lorry showed its bully face. It was coming round the bend overtaking the bicycles—on their Land Rover's side of the road. The lorry was colossal and camouflage-painted and it was not pulling back to its side of the road. It hurtled down on them. She gasped "God" and saw an abyss, saw her children screaming. John threw his arm out to hold her back.

The Land Rover bounded crazily, jumped the ruts on their side of the road. Her head hit the roof of the car as they crashed to a halt in an anthill, and shuddered to a stillness.

Wulf dropped his arms. For seconds they sat silent. Drained and shaking.

Slowly Wulf turned round and looked at her. John had his hand on her lap. Wulf said "Are you hurt?" and she shook her head.

She felt odd, but she did not say she felt odd—they would all be feeling odd. She was curiously conscious of herself: She was underneath Wulf's eyes and underneath John's hand. They had passed through something primal. Together. And they were all alive. And the fact that they were alive was raw. They were trembling with that fact. And it would burn them to this spot. The anthill; the cassava stalks; the petrified skins; the hill of coffee trees. In the vast and empty light with two hawks circling; dead-quiet.

The car was not hurt, and very slowly they drove on.

Roadblocks were tense. Once or twice they were forced to climb out. It was when Wulf left them on Kironde Heights, with Hesita and Odinga watching, that she felt the walls and roof and floor—of their real house—were fragile as rice paper. She had to walk steadily, and speak evenly, and she had to close her eyes to everything. But it wasn't till night, after John swept her up in his own hungry love, after she rolled away from him, that it was safe to cry. It was safe because the dark was impenetrable. If she breathed through her mouth she could let her eyes and nose run freely, so he'd not hear her cry. And she knew he wouldn't reach to touch her face, because already, in the rhythm of his breathing, she could hear he was asleep.

She waked herself with a nightmare. She forced herself to hold still. She wanted to remember and she must not wake him—but then she saw it wouldn't much matter because it wouldn't take much thinking, not this dream. It was a crowd somewhere. She was supposed to be with Wulf. She was supposed to be in a line with him but every time she thought she was standing beside him it would turn out she was standing by somebody she had never seen, and their plane was about to leave and she had to keep her place in line but she had to go find Wulf or they would never make their plane. And then a stream of children marched through everything and cut off the line and the guards were closing the doors to the runway and something . . .

She stared up in the blackness. Finally tried to creep out of the bed but John woke up. She said the shelling woke her, which it had.

She sat too long in the bathroom. She had to go back in the bed to him or they would fight. It was easier to acquiesce than fight.

When it didn't matter whether they fought or whether they didn't. Their struggles had never budged them. Not a centimeter. A new explosion would not move them any farther. They weren't honest enough for that. The farthest-buried layer of each of them knew exactly how things were and it made them explode and it quickly made them cover it, pile the boards up across the abyss so they would not have to know out loud. Because then they would have to act.

There was only the keeping of the outside calm whatever price she paid.

She crawled back into bed. She let his arm lie over her, and she pretended sleep.

Megan brought them a loaf of bread. She said bread was disappearing and Piet had got some bread from Prudence. John rushed back from the college. He greeted Megan peremptorily. He said, "I just saw Wulf at the office. He had a telegram—his daughter may be dying. He has managed, through the Institute, to get a flight out of Nairobi day after tomorrow. He said he could come by before curfew tonight, so I am asking people then. I hope this is all right with you."

She said, "Of course." She said it calmly. She was aware the ironing noise had stopped. She was aware Odinga was listening from the kitchen. Someone talked and someone yelled from the driveway. The room was full of children shouting about something. She may have looked as if she listened. She even picked up some of the clues, perhaps, of when she was expected to speak.

THIRTY-THREE

On Festive Gatherings

T HE SIZE OF FEASTS AND the height of coffee trees—that's how you gauge the weight and honor, the *ekitibwa*, of a person. It's best when the feast's in the coffee's shade. It can be, because there are venerable groves, groves so old the trunks are thick as eucalyptuses and tall as cassia trees.

You drive a rutted trail through coffee trees. You park by elephant grass. You walk toward singing, or toward reds and blues you see through leaves and through the white-sprigged shoots and branches. You greet. You spread your mat beside the richer mats. You sit *kiganda* fashion, knees bent politely toward one side, and you listen till you catch the flow. It's antiphonal, and it's Luganda. You add your voice. The wind comes through, brings smoke and waves of spice, and the leaf-roof skitters with light.

John was backed against the bougainvillea. He was bent double, which awkward position was because he didn't want to move his junk off the card table so he could bring the card table out. He mixed drinks on a basket stool.

She was sprinting up and down the bank, darting across the porch and in and out of the kitchen and in and out of the closets, knowing this party was perverse beyond perversity or it was John's Tutsi way of keeping a hold of everything himself, once more, or of making her keep her hands on crackers and napkins while Wulf was disappearing off the face of the globe. The party had nothing at all to do with Wulf's desire. It was the last thing Wulf could want when his mind was numb with fear, for his Thea, when he was closed off to them all and most of all to her.

She lugged chairs and Odinga lugged chairs and Prudence was acting like she knew what she was doing, taking her orders from Odinga but joining the guests and acting like part of the family. Prudence helped her spread the mats and pillows. They filled trays with napkins and glasses and baskets of what crackers they had left. People were ambling up the drive and down across the commons and she was gaping in amazement, thinking Who were all these people and where in heaven's name had all these people come from. Yes, news traveled word of mouth before you knew you'd thought a thing. But still. How could people know that Wulf was leaving when she'd just heard herself, and what about the curfew in two hours. She'd never seen these Indian women, and how had Wulf had time to get so widely known.

Was John generous or kinky? With his whitewash projects.

John was running on will. You had to play a role when your good friend abandoned the country, and John would do what John was meant to do. None of the queasy things in your stomach were real at all, John was announcing. This activity was real.

Wulf would be gone in the morning and what in the world would have changed. John would be triumphantly vindicated. Hold on a minute and every snoopy person would forget. Everyone. Forever. Live by will and that is all you need. You will be pronounced quite sane and utterly dependable.

And she was playing along with John. What choice did she have. As long as no one spoke to her. Already when Megan spoke she started to cry and thank the Lord it was Megan. Easier to run up and down the banks than risk a person speaking to her.

She handed cups to packs of children. She filled each cup with a mere one inch of grape juice—Lord knows where she'd get any more—but then abruptly she set the tray down on the ground and ran up the bank—Wulf would get here any minute and she would intercept him, catch him on the far side of the house before any other person got to him.

He was coming through the hedge, carrying something, but he wasn't by himself. Amos Wesikye. And Odinga watching her. She spun back down the bank, bumped into the Indians who were talking about Wulf speaking Hindi with them. The women held out a package to her, something wrapped in peculiar paper covered with odd script with grease coming through so she could smell the spice from the Indian restaurant Chez Joseph. She unwrapped *samosas,* heard snatches around her. Hugh said the journalist who'd been killed had been lured out to the camp. Cranshaw said they most definitely had not been lured, the man had been a fool. The man had been warned and he went anyway. Piet said it was making the British see reason, this murder, and hearing it all made her grasp why people had poured to their shabby excuse for a party. Every person they saw was ravenous for rumor. They would turn out at the drop of a whisper a mile off in the dark.

And John was appropriating Wulf as his own find, as the linguist they had all been waiting for, as if they'd all been waiting for a linguist. So be it. John would fit every murder neatly in the social pattern, so why was she so mortified and torn, if her husband didn't care if she were scarlet why should anyone else here care if she were scarlet and why was she keeping clear of Wulf, fighting off tears, running around like a cretin handing out stale crackers, napkins, pillows to sit on, when he was here right now with her and in one hour he would disappear for good. If the practical joke of this crowd was the last time she would see him, then she would move up close to him and stay pressed close to him. He was in her garden. He was still—now—in her garden. In person. Right this very minute.

• • •

Most of the guests had vanished. The handful left were now in chairs, but she sat down on a mat by Wulf and leaned back against his chair. He put his hand on her shoulder at once, while he kept on talking with Megan, while her body was suffused with heat and while she was going quite heavy and could not would not move even when he took his hand away. While she was catching terror in John's eyes. And for one unguarded moment she let a dart of pity shoot through her but it was only because she was thinking *Go love without the help of anything on earth* and a wisp of that spilled over onto John. She intoned it in her head—*Go love without the help of anything on earth*—while she watched the tops of eucalyptus trees and heard Wulf saying things to Megan while she herself was saying *Go love without the help of anything on earth.* While she herself was watching curfew climb the eucalyptus trees. Curfew would be here, in their garden, when the shadows reached the tops of the eucalyptus trees. And then if you were not inside you would be machine-gunned dead. There was six feet of time now left on the trees. The sun was yellow on the top six feet of trees and she could see that the line was moving up, eating the yellow on the treetops. She could watch the shadows climbing leaf by leaf by leaf, while down below that shadow line the trees were the color of honey and everything around them now was that same color of honey. There were four and one half feet of sun, and she would not see Wulf again.

Amos would drive him to Nairobi, at dawn, at the legal instant light rolled up the curfew.

She answered Megan's question. She explained to the people in chairs about the sun time on the trees. She pointed out the two and one half feet of sun that was left till curfew time. In one foot they would have to leave, or they would all be shot. She was saying that, that they would all be shot—when Hans appeared (Hans, Megan's solitary poet, did not come to parties), and she well knew to keep on talking exactly like she was talking. She, they, all of them let Hans slip in without remark, as Hans wanted, let Hans sit down on the mat and listen to her saying they would all be shot when the sun had left the trees, and while she was saying it she had goosebumps because Hans had walked up Kironde Heights to sit with them on mats. For the sake of Wulf. For the atmosphere of celebrating loss. It was an atmosphere Hans moved in, and he had found it on the mats in her front garden.

Hans questioned her calculations, and he kept his eyes on the trees, while ants and birds and swarming creatures picked at the edge of things. Hawks were circling, and the hill was filling with woodsmoke, and the sun was a foot and a half from the tops of the trees.

There would not be a moment she would have him to herself. Anne was cuddled on Wulf's legs and Lulu was leaning on his shoulder on the other side from Anne, and Michael offered him groundnuts.

Now they'd all gone quiet, thinking their thoughts. Even John left the hush alone.

Until Wulf stood up, when there was half a foot of sun. He said, "Amos and I have the farthest. I will go back to my packing."

He embraced them, each of them, kissed them on both cheeks. He left her to the last, and kissed her also on the cheeks, but he also hugged her closer. And whispered "I will come back. I am not leaving you." Then he was gone, and everyone was gone, and she and John picked up debris in silence and dragged things up the bank, before the dark was absolute.

They opened the package Wulf had left—to John and Agnes, it said. The note named things—Turi, Entebbe, Kironde Heights— and said he would come back. He quoted a line from someone: "I remember a house where all were good to me, God knows, deserving no such thing."

The gift was an icon—a Byzantine face but a black one. She'd stood in front of it for a very long time, and he had noted that. The face was painted on wood. It had a knothole on one cheek.

THIRTY-FOUR

All the Mornings of the World

I F YOU COME OUT IN the early morning, before the haze has quite burned off and the light throws hill-long shadows and while the grass is dripping; if you are alone, and if you step very gingerly and breathe very quietly, the rabbit will keep munching. The wagtail will hold tense an instant—a foot off from your toes, which are damp with grass—and go on with his worm. The barbel will shift notes, but barely so. The turaco will ignore you, like the butterfly. But the sleek blue ibis will certainly pause, gauge the tension, before she consummates the step she's broken up. And after that she will stiffen her neck—a protracted neck—and draw up her knee, and place her foot down gingerly. Her neck will curl to where it once had been, and you will be admitted to the garden, wet-born and shining.

She backed the car out of the garage, down the drive, turned it around, and was halfway down Kironde Heights. She was heading out on errands. It was midmorning. She took no more notice of where she was than she took notice of what she did. She'd been this way for three weeks.

The *thump thump thump* of the mortar and pestle, she never heard that now. People calling out, a woman ambling with water on her head up to a gardener squatting in lilies—she never heard their voices. She scarcely heard the gunshots, though they kept on. School was open. Children trundled back and forth again, dragging bags up hills. It was approximately safe to move around the city if you moved in the middle of the day, if you avoided soldiers. She drove dutifully to shops when she'd heard about bread, or milk, or tomato paste. She graded papers and searched for books to teach her class. And nearly gave up on *The Potter and the Shadow of Death*. It was too bleak for the school and she needed to recognize that.

By the time she noticed, Megan was bending into the road and waving something white. She pulled the car over.

Megan leaned in the window and held out an envelope folded in half. Megan said, "It came in one addressed to me."

She took it, looked down at the thick white square, and noticed it shaking in her hand. She unfolded it, saw the one word *Agnes*. It was printed in black ink.

It took a minute before she looked back up. Megan was watching through the window of the car.

She said thank you to Megan, but her smile was trembly.

Megan said, "Don't torture yourself. Go open it."

She had to escape from Megan. She said, "I have to pick up books for John—the book man will leave at eleven."

Megan said, "Go," and stepped back from the car.

It was true. She had to get to the bookshop quick. It meant she could read it in the Nile Café. She could wait till then. She would sit with a scone and then she'd read his letter. Read it right.

The place was quiet, but the coffee smell was just as it should be. Scarcely anyone was here, no one she knew but Erasmus. That was good, but the spot for cakes was bare, and that was bad. She wanted hot coffee and sweet cream and brown demarara sugar and raisin scones when she opened this letter. If she couldn't have the scones she still could wait for some coffee. She was afraid of the letter. She could at least hold on to coffee.

The envelope sat on the tablecloth. She smoothed it out, studied it. *A-g-n-e-s.* She fingered it. The paper had a silky feel. Shiny. It looked translucent almost. It was not like envelopes out here. It was an oddish size, taller than Patel Press paper that the Red Chinese sent out. This was paper from a different kind of place.

He made beautiful letters. They weren't square and they weren't straight up and down. He wrote them at a slant. The e was open but it had a rounded back. The tail of the g was flung a long way backward, farther back than the starting of her name.

Erasmus passed her, said, "I take some minutes, Madam." Perhaps she looked conspiratorial, because Erasmus stopped, came back to her, said "Yes, Madam?"

She said, "Nothing, nothing."

He said, "You are writing a letter."

She said, "No, I am reading a letter. When I get my coffee."

"Do not wait, Madam. I bring your coffee soon."

"I want to sip my coffee when I am reading my letter."

"It is from your family, Madam?"

"No. It's a letter from the man who knows Luganda."

His face tightened. He said, "No, Madam. Tell me that is not a true thing, Madam, that he has abandoned our country. We need good men to stay here in our country."

She said, "It is true."

Erasmus's face collapsed. He said, "It cannot be, Madam. I believe that that man liked you, Madam. And I believe you liked that man."

He was making her happy, saying these things. She couldn't mention Wulf to anyone. And here was Erasmus intending to talk about Wulf.

He said, "I believe, Madam, that he was good to you."

"He was good to me. But he has left me."

"No, Madam. It cannot be so."

It was wonderfully strange, his being so perturbed. She said, "Many Bazungu are leaving."

He said, "Not the man with the yellow hair. He talked with me, Madam. He knew the names of my children, Madam. He spoke Luganda in the way we Baganda speak Luganda. I do not know white men who can speak a language as he does. He would not leave us."

Hands were going up from tables. A woman was waving a spoon. He said, "I will come back to you, Madam."

She stared at the letter, waited on her coffee. She gave up, picked up the knife, tore it open, and pulled out a single sheet. She saw "My darling" and let her eyes run quickly down, scanning for what she needed. She turned it over and took in the end—"Two more weeks until the Nile Hotel . . ."

Erasmus was back with her coffee. Erasmus was saying, "Madam, it is many years I work in the Nile Café. And no man speaks Luganda like our friend with the yellow hair."

Her grin at Erasmus slipped into bits of laughing. She put the letter down. She poured the yellow cream. She scraped brown crystals from the bowl and very slowly stirred them in.

Erasmus said, "Sometimes a word, he has it wrong. But if I close my eyes with your gentleman, Madam, I believe he is Muganda. I believe he is at home with us Baganda. He cannot leave his home."

She kept laughing. It was genuine laughing, but it did not fit what Erasmus was saying to her.

He stopped talking. He was waiting on her to explain.

She said, "You have known it, Ssebo. The man won't stay away. He will come back and he will sit here and he will speak Luganda with you. Only two weeks we must wait."

Erasmus spoke with a big new happiness: "Very good, Madam. I have seen the man is good to you, Madam."

Erasmus now bent over someone else. Wherever he was moving, she felt him watch her read. It made her glance up from time to time and when she did, he grinned and he nodded emphatically, and she grinned emphatically and nodded, and turned back again to where Wulf wrote, "I sit by Thea's bed and am a guilty blasphemer. You are standing over me. Your arms are in your pockets and your hair is straggling loose and you are studying me and smiling somewhat wickedly and, well, you then appear in a more natural manner, away from me at first—I believe a gauzy net has come between us and then no longer is that net between us . . ."

She caught her breath, slapped the letter in her basket, and abandoned the café.

THIRTY-FIVE

On the Duplicity of Novels

Novels are deceptive. No wonder they were forbidden reading for so long, in so many places. They're all about attachments. But the attachments in these devious books are far more ecstatic, or far more tragic, than our own lives could ever be. In the trashy novels, they're exhaustingly intense. But all of the novels are lying. They're like eighty years of living squashed into a simple pill. Those transporting link-ups the novelists harp on, they just don't come along. Not if we count up years and days and hours. It's the humdrum rituals that keep us turning over. And maybe, for the few who keep their spirits living, it's the textures and the tastes of things, the smells we spin around to find, the trees and birds and kinds of light we search for out the window, possibly the Schubert trio, probably the novel where we lose ourselves—the novel that relates the tragic tumultuous passionate attachments that go on somewhere else.

She hurried through the front door, dropped her books on the sofa, and headed toward the kitchen. Emma was under the ironing

board—no one else in the kitchen. The baby saw her and whim-
pered. She bent and scooped up the baby and headed toward the
clamor. The ruckus was going on out back.

A headless chicken was squawking and flapping at the bank.
Hesita had her hand held out—keeping blood from her skirt. Her
hand clutched a spouting chicken head. Fuweesiky was arching
and spitting from the top of the bank. Paulo's mangy dog was
jumping and yapping at the flapping chicken body. Odinga was
beating back a field rat with a broomstick.

She stood at the back step, in the wreck of bowls and peelings
and stools. She held the baby, gawked at the scene, and over the fra-
cas she saw Megan. Megan was staring, curious, around the edge
of the garage. She skirted the stools and jars and the mortar and
pestle and kept the baby in her arms and came up, grinning, to
Megan. She led her around to the front.

They sat on the camp chairs on the porch. Megan fished in a
basket, pulled out a letter, said, "The only mail that gets through is
mail from Poland."

She smiled calmly. She felt beatific with a baby on her lap.

All of them knew already that Wulf would be returning. All of
them—Megan and Piet and herself and John. Wulf had carefully
written to each of them, and a public letter to herself and John.
His Thea would recover.

Megan said, "I'm waiting every day to hear if my poem was
accepted, and the only thing I find is another letter from Poland.
You might think Amin was calling on Russia already."

Megan jumped up. She said, "I'm going. I know you want to
read it by yourself. I don't like to watch your battle with politeness."

Agnes said, "How can I read with a baby?"

Megan bent down close to Agnes and played with the baby's
hand.

Agnes said, "I've meant to tell you about Wulf . . . why am I so
tongue-tied . . ."

Megan stood up, said, "Because *I* am, I suspect."

She felt Megan's hand on the top of her head. She felt the hand trail down to catch her plait, felt Megan walking off holding her braid, letting it drop without turning. She reached to catch Megan's hand but she was already too late, and Megan did not stop. Megan called back without looking around, "One day."

She sat watching a minute, and then she carried the baby to Hesita.

She closed the door to the bedroom, dropped in the basket chair, and tore the letter open.

The first lines stopped her breath.

They had called his passport in. He would not get another passport for two years.

The hand with the letter fell in her lap. Her eyes closed. Her head dropped back.

When she opened her eyes, she picked up the hem of her skirt and tried to wipe her tears and read the letter but she glanced up at the shadow—John speeding by, his body rigid like a mannequin. She tossed the paper under the bed and dried her eyes more thoroughly. Dully she pulled a book off the table and pulled it onto her lap.

John did not bother knocking. He erupted. He shut the door behind him and stayed where he was, at the door.

She did not look up at once. When she did he was staring at her, breathing like an irate horse. A forced and red-faced breathing. This was meant to agitate her, extort some drama out of her. She despised this blackmail. She would not be pulled and yanked into manufactured theatricals. It was not in her. Maybe months ago it had been in her but it wasn't now, and surely he could see that fact. She didn't care about his anger any longer. Whatever this was it made no difference anymore. She wanted to be left alone. Which was the thing, she knew, that would not happen if she went on pretending to read.

She compelled herself to keep her eyes on him. She made her eyes stay somewhere around his face.

Her eyes began to stray to the window, but she forced them back. Act like he expected and he would leave her alone. Say something normal—like hi. When he was forcing some new melodrama?

She said, "What is it?"

He kept staring. His eyes were stretching wide in horror at her and now he put his hands up to his mouth. Some of the air seemed to leak out of him at that. His shoulders dropped. He reached the bed, lay down on his stomach, and looked bug-eyed, out the window. He had not yet spoken.

She stayed where she was. But she repeated, "What is it, John?"

He said without looking at her, "I can't go on with this marriage."

She did not answer.

She'd had her blow today. She was holding her blow inside herself, with dignity. It did not prepare her for this thrust. One believes the words that one has known are coming—somewhere underneath a person has to have known a thing is coming in order to believe it. She had known Wulf's blow was coming. She believed it. But she did not believe this one. This one was not coming. She did not recognize this person collapsed across their bed.

And something was crashing in her in spite of her refusing to take this in.

John knew of her and Wulf—she'd grown used to that assumption by now. John could press that down because nothing would come of it and John was a man who lived by will. They would be civilized, for as long as no one spoke this thing out loud. But now somebody had said this thing out loud.

A long time the room was silent. And then she said, "All right."

Still she did not move. But she felt wetness down her neck, which surprised her. Like the pain inside her was surprising her. But she would never protest. Her *All right* was exactly what she meant. She would pay what she had to pay. She hadn't known it would come to this, but now she did, and there was something absolute about it that was right. Sealed and pure and chaste. At last. A clarity that made some emotional sense. She didn't have Wulf, and she wouldn't have a family, and there was nothing she could save. No branch she could hold on to. She had leapt and she would not plead innocence. She would go the whole way down through mud and ooze and slime and dark and cold. It was one thing that made sense.

And she knew she was lying. The terror was too cutting. The terror was more cutting than her letter. Her children did not care about Wulf's letter, but they would care about this. They would never become who they were meant to be, not after this. They would huddle and shrivel and be afraid of living. It would happen. Because she would refuse to plead with John.

He stirred. He pulled himself partway up, leaned on the wall, his legs stretched out. This way he could watch her. He said, "Would you kindly refrain from that obscene lip rubbing?"

She dropped her arm in shock that she was rubbing her lip.

He said, "Save that for your other men."

She did not reply.

He said, "No, Agnes. Do not think I am saying this because I've made a new discovery—that you are an adulteress. I've seen your lusting for adultery from the first year we were married. You cannot believe I have no eyes. It's true—perhaps I thought you were a coward. I thought you were basically harmless. Or I was lulled to thinking you cared about your children. Or—I suppose I have been ignorant enough to think you lacked the spirit. Or you had a residual conscience. But I never thought Wulf, who was my friend—he was first of all *my* friend, I did not think . . ."

His voice began to shake. He could not get the words out. He began to slobber. It was not pretty to watch him but she watched him and she began to cry as hard as he was crying.

She crossed to the bed. She sat and she leaned down over him where he was lying on his face. She put one hand on his back. She said, "John. Wulf loved you. He did love you. He loved you first of all. And he loves his wife and child. What he did was not what he meant to do. He resisted it for months. But he thought, like I did, that you would somehow know already. And you would somehow understand one day, maybe not now but one day, that we did not want to hurt you. He loves his wife, John. You are his friend, John. You are still his friend. And he kept on saying you are his friend, even when I did not want to hear—he kept on saying it."

She kept rubbing his back.

She heard children home for lunch.

The door was not locked. Half of her was listening for children. John was not heaving now. But his eyes were open, and they looked wild to her. He said "Go to them. I'm not coming."

She got up tentatively. She combed her hair, powdered the red around her eyes, and went out toward the noise.

THIRTY-SIX

On Liquid Things

Y OU GRAB YOUR SHIRTTAIL, RUB off gook when the dog comes slobbering, or when mosquitoes leave blood-streaks or birds splat on your hair. You reach for a cloth to wipe off sweat or snot or tears, or your various secretions of red and yellow and brown, or the white of your milk or seeds. You rub briskly to keep yourself dry, distinct, to coax your skin to an impermeable wall around your clean-cut form, not to be sunk in mouthy love and gooey birth all streaming labyrinthine openings. You buttress yourself behind dry stone and glass and metal. You slave to hold the razor-edge of the moment, of the cool and compact body when you're twenty-one perhaps. And then one day it happens—the waters dry up. You shrink to rattling. Until the fluids all around you rush back in and suck you back to muck.

John slept on the sofa one half of one night, returned to bed, and kept to his side. They did not touch. He made an elaborate jump when, one time, his leg glanced off hers.

Curfew persisted. Then it trickled away, at least on Lubega Hill.

No arrests till after ten o'clock. John now stayed away till ten o'clock. Each night. She did not ask where he went. He said it was kindness to be rid of the sight of each other. They spoke when they needed the keys and had to know which road would be the safest or had to decide who would stand in line for which form when. She was glad he was gone in the evenings, or halfway glad. She listened to the Last Quartets on the nights the power was on. One night he banged the door open and fell across a chair and slurred some curses. One night he did not bother coming home.

In a few weeks she sensed change. He was watching her too often. His angular vindictiveness was slower.

They spent a good bit of time these days driving back and forth to Entebbe. White colleagues were fleeing Amin. Hugh and Claudia left on SAS to Athens. So did Beryl and the two American families at the bottom of Kironde Heights. She envied them. And she half looked down on them for running out. The Yugoslavs and Russians and the Czechs, on the other hand, weren't going anywhere. They'd take their chances—they got paid hard currency out here and things looked good compared with things back home.

As for their own escape, John wrote letters and hoped. She left it at that. John looked out for his career. They would be leaving with or without a job in not too long, but it wasn't urgent yet. It was Americans who were running out now, and that trait of Americans she did not like to claim. Leaving for the children's sake, always for the children's sake. And what was the children's sake? The children were happy where they were. Megan and Piet weren't leaving as far as they knew.

Safety—and the pending end of a family—they were hourly on her mind. Yet there was a drugged and fatalistic feel to things. She knew they would have to act, oh, for the children's sake. But she could not think very well. The air was out of her. At the moment, living in the muck at the bottom of the ditch seemed right for the debacle that was their lives.

One afternoon Abraham Lasu sat in the living room. They

talked about a student who'd vanished, about what steps to take, and then she heard John say, "No, I am not deserting."

She was somewhat perturbed. *I*. John said *I*—*I* am not deserting he said. Who was this who could speak for her? John to an acquaintance—"*I* am not," not "*we* are not deserting." When did he get to own her voice?

She held her tongue while he talked to Abraham. When Abraham left them, she said, "So *you* are not deserting."

He looked at her hard, sat down, said, "No, I'm not."

Her eyes went cold.

She determined she would not say anything she did not mean to carry out. "Well, then . . . ." she started.

"Just wait," he said. "It's been a while since we have talked. There are things we've not discussed."

"A few," she said. But she felt her fear resurging.

He was looking at her curiously. Then he leaned down. He took her hand.

She stayed rigid.

His head was still bent over, but he tilted enough to eye her. His voice shook. He said very slowly, "I don't know what you want. But I do not want a divorce."

She felt her blood begin to flow. It was a reprieve. For the moment.

She said, "I don't either," and she held on to his hand.

But she did not drop the subject.

She said, "But you say *you* are not going. Where does that leave *us*?"

He sat up, gave a momentary look of surprise, dropped her hand, and said coldly, "Oh, forgive me. I didn't realize what you were quibbling about. I forget your sensitivity. I should have said *we* are not leaving."

"And what gives you that right? How can you sit there and say *we* aren't leaving when we've hardly brought up the subject?"

"I rather suspected neither of us was in the mood to talk. And I remember a few passionate speeches of yours about not running out. So—now—I take it you have reassessed your stand. I take it you assume that we are leaving."

"When I heard *I* am not leaving, Yes. Yes, that changed things quick."

"So you are quite willing to drop your years of idealistic talk—your divide between the sheep and goats—now you scuttle—and merely because I misuse a pronoun."

"You are doing what you always do. As if the way you say a thing has no connection with what your meaning is. As if your speech doesn't touch your self."

"Good Lord, this is nuts—I of all people have never made a move without consulting you. I don't understand why you are doing this."

She waited a minute. Then, in a low voice, she apologized. She said it was the pronoun. He took minutes, sighing, adjusting. Then he reached out for her, and he pulled her close.

This wasn't over. It could not be over. But after the last few weeks it was a sweet release to her to be held warm against him.

She could feel him shaking.

THIRTY-SEVEN

On Walking in the Light

A N ANTHROPOLOGIST WOULD CALL IT gift exchange, these patterned linkages that bind a people. Cowrie shells, ivory, beads and coins; cows and goats and fruit and chickens; women— back and forth to weave the threads of culture. But the weight of the gifts—the constriction in your chest at the unrepayable—you don't read that in a text. You visit a friend in the countryside. You sit in a folding chair, in the front courtyard of the hut. And child after child comes kneeling, bringing you presents that cover the courtyard dirt—stems of bananas, leaves full of eggs, heaps of passionfruit, and avocados and pineapples and papaw. Or your brother-in-law dies at home in the States—your students hear and bring ten shillings each to go toward funeral expenses. Or Amnon presents you with a goat as a farewell gift. Only he knows you can't take a goat on the plane. He hands you the money for which he sold the goat, as a gift for his beloved friend and tutor.

Hans (always he'd be Megan's Hans) had just walked away from her porch. She was sitting thinking of him in the spot where they had sat. Hans knew. Hans's blackness was pervasive, and it absorbed her own blackness. It was good like nothing else was good. Hans hadn't come to visit her because of an attachment to her. Hans had come to let his blackness ooze out over hers.

He had a book in his hand. His finger kept the place in the book. He said he was rereading Thomas Hardy's journals and had found the passage he liked. He said he liked it so much he wanted to read it out loud. Would she mind if he read it out loud to her?

Of course not.

He read: "For my part, if there is any way of getting a melancholy satisfaction out of life it lies in dying, so to speak, before one is out of the flesh; by which I mean putting on the manner of ghosts, wandering in their haunts, and taking their views of surrounding things. To think of life as passing away is a sadness; to think of it as past is at least tolerable. Hence even when I enter into a room to pay a simple morning call I have unconsciously the habit of regarding the scene as if I were a spectre not solid enough to influence my environment; only fit to behold and say, as another spectre said: 'Peace be unto you!'"

In a minute he said, "I like that." And then he played with phrases he picked out, "'Taking their views of surrounding things . . . as if I were a spectre not solid enough to influence my environment.' I am fond of Hardy."

Oh, Hans.

And the orange dress coming toward her was Prudence.

She grew heavier, if that were possible. She had not seen Prudence in weeks, but she'd had bad dreams about Prudence. She and John did not bring up a word concerning Prudence.

Prudence held a package. Prudence's packages were not a good sign. Prudence's loud smile was also not a good sign. Yes the girl was beautiful and yes she watched this face, but she watched it because she envied ice. Prudence's face was a flawless mask. Prudence could go her way behind that mask, and no one suspected what direction she'd be going.

No banana-leaf wrap this time. The bomb was wrapped in *Uganda Argus* pages—Terry Waite's picture she saw, Terry holding a car thief up by the collar. She'd seen that yesterday.

She put the present on her lap. She unfolded to a yellow-green piece of Jjinja cloth. She shook it out and held it up. It was embroidered—WHAT SHALL I DO TO BE SAVED? Embroidery, the Christian woman's occupation. Round the edges of the cloth, little beads were crocheted into scallops. It would take months to make. And this now was Prudence's art?

She said, "When could you have time to make a beautiful thing like this?"

"I did not make this, Madam. I designed it. My aunts have sewed this cloth for you. They requested I present it to you. They know I love you, Madam."

"Prudence, your aunts are far too kind to me. *Paradise Lost* is not worth this." She curled her hands in her lap and smiled at Prudence.

Prudence said, "Madam, you have presented me with the tools with which to make myself. It has showed that you love me, Madam. But what I want to say to you, it is—my life has changed. Because of you, Madam."

"Me? Then may I guess how it has changed?"

"If you like, Madam."

"If it is because of me, if you are being serious . . ."

"I am being very serious, Madam."

"Then, Prudence, I am happy. I think you'll study painting. I think you've given up your idea of becoming archdeacon."

"No, Madam, you have not guessed my change. I am happy painting. I do not want to give it up. But it is useless, Madam. I will give it up for God."

"That makes no sense. Anything can be for God. You know the parable of the talents—I know you do, and you are blessed with a talent. Not many people are so blessed with one as you. So you must use it—that's the responsibility that comes along with talent. It's God-given, like the art. Look at what you've loved." She

pointed to the Rouault print that she had on the wall, the one
with the sun of bleeding blacks and reds and tiny figures walking
in distances.

"One must make a choice, Madam."

"But not this choice, Prudence. Religion and art come from the
same place in us. They are not far apart. Your gift is rare. It will be
tragic for you to turn your back on painting. Put God and art
together. That is the way to go—all African art is a religious art.
Look at Ssajabi's art—he is wonderful, and his subjects are
Christian subjects."

"Madam, I have found my way along the road. I see with wide
new eyes. I will not be ensnared by Vanity Fair any longer. I am
leaving my sins of the flesh. I will study at Lubega College and one
day I will become archdeacon."

Agnes sat still. She had said all she could say.

It was Prudence who said it straight. She said, "Madam, I have
been saved. And you have led me to it."

Agnes was confounded. She said, "You don't mean you're
mulokole?"

"I am, Madam."

"Then I do not understand you, Prudence. I had no part in this."

"But you led me to John Bunyan. I heard the question, 'What
shall I do to be saved?' I understood that very afternoon, Madam.
I understood the way John Bunyan understood, that it was me the
Evangelist was pointing at. You led me, Madam, to the straight-
and-narrow path. Now at last I am walking in the light. Praise the
Lord."

Agnes frowned. She could not lie so blatantly as she would have
to lie now, in return.

Prudence said, "Madam, I hope you will be happy for me. I
know you are not saved. But I make one request of you. You will
come to the Luwero meeting—tomorrow. God has told me you
must come. It is important, Madam. Very important."

She said, "Lulu has not been well. I have to stay at home with
Lulu. I'm sorry."

Prudence said, "Madam, you have been my mother. My spiritual adviser will attend. Then I will be with my family, Madam. The occasion will be a very joyful one."

John. Did this new Saint Prudence mean that her husband John was going to the meeting with Prudence? Was that it?

It couldn't be.

The silence was sick. She considered her words. But when she broke the quiet she said, "Yes, we will come."

Prudence said, "I am praying for you, Madam. I am praying one day you, too, will find your way as I have found my way."

She studied Prudence's face. She hoped for the trace of a smile. But she did not find it. She said, and her voice was spiritless, "Thank you, Prudence," and nothing else. Prudence would leave if she said nothing else.

And when Prudence did go away, she walked to her room, and looked out the window, and thought that life was unpredictable as well as it was sad. And if you thought one time that you had made connections, you were wrong.

She drove with John to the meeting, the meeting of the saved, the *balokole*. Herself and John and that was all. Prudence made her own way. John was morose.

She broke a long stretch of staring out the window. She said, "So your spiritual advising has paid off. Prudence is saved."

John nodded, but barely.

"How did it happen?"

He shook his head.

She frowned at him and persisted.

John said coldly, "I don't know. We are coming here. We are doing what the girl wants. Let's leave it at that."

You could hear the singing from across the valley, through the rustling of mango leaves. Her spirits stirred, sluggishly, but stirred. Absurd, knowing the *balokole*. But the singing was beautiful. Antiphonal. Choral. Repetitive. Sometimes humming. Sometimes wailing, carrying in pulses on the wind, which brought the roast-lemon smell of eucalyptus trees.

The hillside scene was biblical. Groups of men and women were dotted on the slopes. The reds and blues and whites and flowered yellow-pinks were sprinkled down a kind of hollow along all sides. People were streaming down the hills, strolling in from all directions. They sat on mats under scattered thorn and mango trees and eucalyptus trees. A whitewashed church stood on the hill, but it was tiny. It would not hold this mammoth gathering of saved ones who gathered once a month.

She'd been here twice before. *Balokole* grabbed the new-arrived to save them, so of course they'd come. They weren't in the country to anger people, and no one could be blind to the *balokole*, not in this country. The group gave power, and communal backbone. It was the *balokole* in Kenya who stood up to mau mau. It was the *balokole* who stood up to Amin. And no European instigated it. It was African in spirit and in roots and most of all in style. You told it all in public. You walked in the light. Spell it out in public and you are righteous. Keep it to yourself and you are suspect. No matter the casualties, the public judgment is the saving judgment and comes with a forgiveness that is choral and infectious. The spirit of silence is the spirit of the devil.

She was subdued by the conflict. These people were happy, and they might not own a pair of shoes. While she despised this brassy conscience of theirs that they believed in yelling out. While she believed—crush silence and you crush everything that matters. And yet she was to sit here with her husband, greeting in sweet graciousness. That is, she would greet. John was sullen today.

She spotted a sprinkling of whites. She recognized a few persons. An Englishwoman in a splashy-flowered dress. People she had nothing to say to.

She spread their mat far up the hill, in back, where they could slip away. The meeting would last hours.

But they knew too many people. Their hidden spot was not allowed. They were ushered near the front, across the bottom of the amphitheater bowl from Prudence. Prudence had her new saved friends and had her aunts with her. Agnes nodded to the aunts across the singing. She was singing, too. She couldn't help it. John was not.

Her eyes stopped—up the hill not far from them. Odinga. He was watching her. He nodded, not quite smiling, no. She nodded back and turned around.

Of course he would be here. Why had she not thought of this? But then why should he be? Odinga was Luo and this was in Luganda. He was with a Luo man and woman—the woman was not wearing a *basuti*. She had seen the man with him before.

The singing hushed. A man began to pray out loud. The people answered *Alleluia*, or they said *Amen*. Sometimes both, and longer things. The man sat down and the singing started up. Another man in a *kanzu* talked about his fornicating before he walked in the light. He invited others to confess their fornications. It was all in Luganda, most of which was carried off by breeze, but the gist was pretty clear. She watched the crowd, listened to the movement, waited for Prudence to speak. But a woman on the hillside stood up now and outlined her transgressions, and then more men stood up. Already John was looking at his watch.

It was hotter than she thought. She looked for shade nearby, but it was occupied, and there wasn't time to move farther off because here was Prudence standing up. The girl wore a bright blue simple-cut dress, to her knees. She had no other color and no ornament. You had to marvel at this girl's purity of line. The crowd did gawk—the humming stopped. Prudence began to speak.

Prudence was speaking too softly for her to hear more than snatches. But she could guess. The grace that changed her life—she heard her own name mentioned with the story of John Bunyan and a rather lengthy rundown of *Pilgrim's Progress*. The crowd broke into a Luganda version of "Amazing Grace." She joined. It was more moving than the English version, if that were possible. Now came the pattern of confession, which had long been ritualized, and when that confession came out, the sex and the song and the grace could pour down topsy-turvy. The point for the listeners was the sin that brought the change. The sin part brought dead silence. She strained to catch it. It would be more interesting if she could hear. But Luganda was hard on occasions like this, and Prudence's voice had gone lower. She noted several people turn to look at her—at herself, Agnes—or to look at the two of them, herself and her husband. And then the whispering rose around her like an insect whir. What seemed the solid hillside looked in their direction. And she heard one phrase. Clear and repeated—"spiritual adviser," in Luganda. She tried to look at John without appearing to look at John. He was stiff and his face was red. But he was keeping his eyes on Prudence. And then he turned around to her, his wife, and the crowd began to sing.

She didn't need explanation. She froze her expression. She kept her head up, and she kept her eyes down. She knew if she survived this purgatory, she could be stone from now on out. Like Prudence. If she endured this fire, she could not be touched again.

She expected to feel John's arm. She expected John to take her arm and bolt. But John did nothing of the sort. He stayed adamant. He did not sing and she did not sing. The sun and the singing around them burned them to an effigy. She saw nothing. Except she sensed that polite Baganda were turning their eyes away.

She spoke to John in English, without turning her neck, without looking at him. She spoke coldly and nonstop. No one else could hear the lowness of her English underneath the singing. She said, "It is your turn now, John. The crowd is waiting on you, John. Are you planning to oblige the people? You must, you know. This is a first, I believe, for a European here. It must be celebrated. I believe this is a new-invented form of crucifixion. This took a Prudence to come up with."

John said, "I believe they are waiting on you, Agnes. I believe you missed the implications, which had to do somewhat with you and your good Polish friend. But then we lack Prudence's courage. Prudence has walked in the light. Now they are waiting for us to walk in the light. You, too. It's a pity you missed that, Agnes."

She said, "I sense this is a Christian kind of courage. It passes over me. My role here is wife of adulterer. They are waiting on you, John. They will be tired of singing in a minute."

She heard, "Please don't, Agnes." And his voice had changed. It was so strained as to be frightening. She turned around to look at him. He had closed his eyes and his head was bowed. She understood. He was bracing to stand up. Now she dropped her own head and closed her eyes.

John spoke in Luganda. It was halting, but she could hear his clear Luganda faultlessly: that Prudence was a fine courageous girl. That the fall had been his fault. Entirely his. That he was a weak man. He had not known that fact about himself until now. But he prayed for grace. He needed all their prayers for grace. May God and the *balokole* be merciful.

It was brief. He did not mention her, his wife. She was his extenuating circumstance. John had that right to mention her, his mitigating circumstance. But he did not mention her.

Once she looked up. Odinga was studying her.

She let her eyes go back to her own blue skirt. She followed the weave and she pummeled her brain, over and over and over—*Go love without the help of anything on earth.* The meaning was useless but the pummeling was not. The rhythmic beating held her senseless in the bull's-eye-center of the turmoil, until John pulled her through the surge of bodies and the throbbing, singing joy.

They coughed their way through heat and dust. She closed off her reactions. She would not think. She would not consider what would become of her and John. They had scratched and kicked in order to cancel each other and they couldn't keep on too much longer with that. Now there was one thing only—the slapping on blinders toward each other and bailing their children out alive— out of Amin country. Out of *balokole* country.

THIRTY-EIGHT

On the Sun and Sex

I T USED TO BE A rude cliché that people in the south, south anywhere, were happy, simple people. Only now we know it's true—I mean the happiness. And if not forever happy, then at the very least sexier, which is easy to confuse with happier. We've pinned it down at last. Sun people have a corner on a sex hormone, and now it all makes sense: the sun-starved Scots and Danes and Poles who cling to their African dreams; millennia of sun-god worshipers before the Protestant god came measuring things. But then at any latitude, we take our peculiar allotment of hormones, and run it through our busy brains till it's ground into imaginings, unalloyed imaginings. Adaptable to any object whatsoever, as long as it foxes a god who calculates.

It was the Saturday afternoon light. Silent and clear. It soaked you through like fields of loneliness, or peace, and it floated you a long way off.

She lay on the bed, propped on pillows. *The Magic Mountain* had fallen out of her hand, onto her chest, because she'd drifted off. A dog was barking, but it sounded far away. A bird was shrieking and there was the *thump thump thump* of a mortar and pestle like the thickened ticking of a clock, but all of that was hazy like the distance. The sounds might have come from her sleep, which was only a halfway sleep, which was a dozing through an airy finger painting, watery and blue and green and white and billowing.

She opened her eyes. She saw that she was on her bed and let them close, tried to separate her picture from the dozing. Something cold and very stark. To do with time. Something to do with black and white and time.

A mountaintop. Pure white cut by stabs of black. The white was snow, rounded, untouched. She was a black mark on the snow. She was standing on skis. By herself. A solitary hawk was circling her. That was the other stark black mark. She was peering up at the hawk. She was trying to make out the face of a clock—but in the circling hawk. She was very late for something. She knew she needed to know the time and she and the hawk were all there was on the mountain. She was certain, obscurely, that the hawk would help her with the time, would help her grasp the reason that her own time had been wrong.

Her eyelids halfway opened. She was still on the bed, on Kironde Heights.

It took her a minute to remember why, why she could not get off the bed. Her foot was infected and it wouldn't heal unless she kept off it, so she was alone in the house. John and Michael and Lulu and Anne were at Entebbe with the Yugoslavs who lived across the road and who appeared to be blithely nonjudgmental. She was aware of judgment, since their public scourging. Hesita and Odinga were paid to keep their judgment indecipherable, and anyway they went about their own devices on a Saturday afternoon.

She was the single living human on the hill, on the whole of Kironde Heights. It seemed like that on Saturdays. No one would shout *hodi*. No one would trouble her for some child's school form she'd forgotten. No one would gawk at her open streaming sores—she had her leg ulcers again. She could drift with sweet voluptuous drifting. It was medicine that floated her, but she would go quite willingly while this thing visited her.

Her eyes stayed open, followed—out the window—the noiseless hawk that was circling over the valley.

And then, bit by bit, it began to come clearer, the hawk and her picture-dream. In her dream she'd looked at time—direct. She'd been privileged. She'd been taken up high on a mountain and shown the rings of time, and time was the circling hawk.

The very hawk out the window now. Banking so long in its circles it might be holding still.

The hawk had hovered on the Magic Mountain and now it hovered on Kironde Heights—it wouldn't have changed for millennia. Always it was quiet, and circling, and it made sense of time. Time was its circles. If time didn't go in loops and rings then why would you plod on. You would make no sense—nothing would make sense—if time, to you, was one straight line to a future that didn't exist. The end betrayed you. The end was decay. There was nothing but this moment.

But if you consented—in a light like this—if you shifted the image that you carried, if you took for your picture the circle, not the line—then moments would come back to you—in some landscape, in some smell, in some stranger's glance. If you accepted the moments were unpredictable. If you accepted that your life was hovering around you, mysterious. If you consented. If you lay here quiet and watched—then you might tap straight through into living. Into this evanescent floating repetitive thing.

A movement out the window. She raised her head.

Megan. With her head bent, coming up the drive.

She propped up on her elbows to watch this woman she had loved.

It was moving, the sight of Megan. Megan, too, was lugging some world that was all her very own, and Megan didn't have a hint that she was being watched. How odd. That Megan—that people—were hauling worlds—which might be gargantuan spheres, and which might open onto Trebizonds and Zanzibars and multitudinous cities you would never think to guess. You touched a person, and you never suspected that person might be living on those unimagined globes.

She pushed her book off her legs and threw off her blanket. She hobbled to the window, yanked the screen, and called. Megan came over the grass. She handed Megan the key, and hopped back onto the bed and covered her disgusting foot.

Megan peeked around the bedroom door. They smiled.

She moved her legs aside for Megan to sit down.

Megan sat on the bed edge. She said, "You've been crying."

Agnes raised her hand to her cheek. It was dry. She said, "No one but you would notice."

Megan fished in her pocket, pulled out a letter, and handed it over.

She took the letter, fingered it, and smiled at it, but did not open it.

Megan said, "Go ahead."

She said, "Later." And in a minute she said, "It wasn't him that was making me cry—it was more or less this light." She nodded at the window.

Megan glanced out the window and said, "You notice because you're leaving it."

It took her only a second to adjust to Megan's tone, and when she did she said, "You mean you're not."

Megan shook her head, and said inaudibly, "We're not."

She waited more seconds this time, and said, "I thought."

They watched each other.

She said, "Are you scared?"

Megan said, "Yes—no. I don't know. It's right for you to go." In a minute she laughed and said, "It's funny what fears come out— like, I'm afraid my poems will be destroyed somehow. An idiotic paranoia in the face of what's going on."

She said, "Give them to me to take out. We're rats to scuttle. But that's that. There's no way our chaos can help alleviate Amin's chaos. We're useless. We're shell-shocked. We're bankrupt."

Megan said, "Stop. Anyway I came because I kept singing your damned song."

Agnes said, "I don't have a song."

Megan sang a bit: "'Talk of love not hate / Things to do—it's getting late.'" She cut it off abruptly, and said hoarsely, "I don't want you to leave."

They were silent.

Agnes reached out her hand. Megan did not take it. Instead Megan dropped her head on Agnes's lap and her body began to shake.

Agnes froze. She flushed warm. She felt Megan's weight on her legs. She felt Megan shuddering. She felt Megan's breasts pressed on her thighs, very softly on her thighs.

In a minute, tentatively, she put Wulf's letter down and put her hands on Megan's head.

Megan held still for half a minute maybe, and then pushed up. She wiped her eyes, mumbled her apology, smiled very briefly, and went quickly out the door.

She was shaken. She lay without opening the letter.

She had loved Megan. That fact was now a layer of her self; but her self changed. She could not any longer speak that layer, and the silence made her sad.

It was a while before she picked up the letter, looked at the envelope from Wulf, and slowly cut it open.

It was a beautiful letter. It was also sad, but not entirely sad. He knew how they could write, and one day they would meet. Later they would know how they would meet.

She lay looking out the window, rubbing her lip, wanting to believe what he was saying to her.

THIRTY-NINE

On Speaking Softly

YOU LIVE IN THE COUNTRYSIDE in Africa. Your students come to call. You suspect perhaps America has long since dulled your hearing, what with jackhammers out your window, sirens shrilling, shrieking alarms at two and three in the morning. You come to this conclusion because you cannot hear your visitors. And it's not simply the language. Your callers are talking in the barest of a whisper, most of all the girls. You lean closer, you ask them please to shout. Finally you resort to merely nodding at whatever it is they might have come to whisper.

It's many months before you have the wits to grasp the mystery. It's the hierarchical Baganda; it's the superhierarchical Batutsi. They gauge the softness of their voices to the person they address. It's meant to honor. All words to superiors are politenesses and praise. No word of contradiction, no matter how it is one has to act. The ordained use of language is the pleasing of the mighty.

And so, in time, if you're a teacher, you begin to take the deference for granted.

Agnes found a letter in their box, in the shadowy mail aisles. She read it walking home, stopping every now and then to nod, or greet. The letter was from Prudence and it said:

Dear Madam,

I desire you to understand fully that I have walked in the light for Jesus' sake, and that it is also for your sake and your husband's and my own and my aunts' and all persons' sake. My heart is light now, and free, and I know that I am blessed, and I pray that you will one day be blessed also.

But I do not want you to misunderstand, because you have been good to me. You must understand me. I was not fornicating with your husband during the times when you were tutoring me. Of course, Madam, even I, during that past time when I was walking in the dark, even I was not so darkly defiled by sin as that. During that period your husband's love of me was very pure. It was very beautiful. In our meetings your husband would merely caress my mother-glands, that part of my body and that alone, Madam, I tell you truthfully. He never penetrated me at that time. He loved me very gently, Madam, in a manner which held only pure true love. Our love was a pure true love as I believe no one has had before. It was not at all a caress that could bring harm, because it was not a caress of lust. I know you will believe that, Madam, of myself and of your husband. It was only after your husband learned of your own fornications, and when he was in a very bad despair, so bad I feared that he might die, it was only then that I began to comfort him in the woman's way of comforting, the comforting that all men need and that your husband needed more than anyone has needed because of the evil being committed against him, which a man is not capable of bearing. At a time like that the woman's way of comforting was the only way of comforting. It was the only way I saw to make him well again. Now I know that my thinking was directed by Satan, but that is what I believed at that time I comforted your husband. And I wanted you to understand so that you would not think ill of me. I do not want you to suspect that I was wronging you, when you have been my mother.

I never will forget you, Madam. You will be my mother, always, and I pray that the Lord will one day give you eyes to see the light.

Your loving daughter,
Prudence

The letter did not impart the desired effect to Agnes. It did not significantly contribute to a binding together in love.

FORTY

On Saying Good-bye, *Kwaheri*

SEX. THE TRICKSTER. IMAGINE A dead white male declaring—I mean years and years ago—that it all comes down to sex. Let a man work with a woman and it'll all slide down to sex. Let a woman give a man an order and he'll wrestle her down by sex. Snare a woman's sympathy and you have her sex unasked.

It's cthonic psychology. Outmoded. It should not see print these days.

But just suppose you do uncover such a thing. In a novel, say. Be fair. Let a writer have a minute to defend herself. Form is tyrant here, she'll say. Forget the formless muddles that you live. Who wants to read the actual. Take the mocked-up denouement for your worst nightmare of mortification—and be glad you never let things slip so far.

There were still packers, if you knew somebody. Sikhs hoarded boards and nails and oddish-shaped containers and went on boxing up the goods of Europeans because the whites were bailing out, but the Sikhs were not. It was a year until the Asian expulsion.

And in any case a lot of things stayed like they'd always been. Fogs were sluggish. Clouds banked up, drenched you, and gave way to sun. Banana tree pods drooped wettish sultry pink. The reds of the canna lilies hurt. At night when you went outside the smell of gardenias foiled your will and from an unknown slit in the dark, somewhere, a shriek shot zero through your bones.

Michael and Bernie bet each other—who could name which weapon was exploding. It had come to fine distinctions: howitzers were shrill and hand grenades were dull. Their *condo* stories got outlandish (*condos* were the roaming bands of robbers who took your car at gunpoint), but it all meant the air was loaded, not depressed, unless of course you were thoughtful and considered where the country might be headed, or unless you had a friend reckless enough or in despair enough to look a soldier in the eye.

Lulu knew she had to leave Uganda, and so did Anne. But they could not put stock in it. What were they to make of what it would be, when they had never closed a door or kept their shoes on all day long. How could the threat mean anything when the house was noisy with Bernie and Maggie and Emma and Deborah and a packer in a purple-red-pink turban, and when you couldn't tell the house's inside from the house's outside because Michael and Bernie bounced in jacaranda trees and swung the branches down until they touched the windows and they could shout out the color of your underpants.

Odinga felt the differences. He was obsessed with waxing floors. He seemed to know the value of his legs and acted like he meant to stamp them upon her brain. Still, if she were sitting in a room and meant to leave the room, and if Odinga started skating around the red while she was in that room, she stayed put where she was. She let the claustrophobic tension go on pressing down where he showed off his calves. The two of them stayed on, deadly concentrated on their tasks.

His born-againness was notoriously impotent. It never told him to defuse the pressure, which he could do easily by merely waxing down the hall. Or put it another way. Odinga knew. He knew everything about her. And this was the way of their more than intimate entanglement. This was the language that they spoke. The tension was ancient, and almighty, and inescapable.

One of those last drizzling mornings he skated near her knees. She didn't move. She was packing books, studying the pictures. It was a Kiganda art book Megan had given to her. She stared at zigzag lines scorched on a drum. But she was focused on leg-blurs when it hit her, in a shudder, that this day was it. This muggy day. This zigzag pattern. Odinga skating by her feet. There wouldn't be the *thump thump thump* outside. There wouldn't be the tailless lizards— and Fuweesiky batting them. There wouldn't be Odinga. The space would be empty. She would have to fill space on her own, from her own deficient spirit.

She kept her eyes on the zigzags. The legs were fuzzy through her hair because she would not look at them. The legs were hazing near her knees. The legs were black and oily. They gave off gleams from rippling calves. And they were where they ought to be. For this one minute more.

But the legs were gliding slower. The legs stopped moving altogether. Six inches off from her body. Facing her. Odinga's groin at the level of her eyes. She, fully aware of its movement. The movement in her own chest quickening, folding them up alone into this thing, closing them off from all surrounding things. Moving the two of them into an unknown place.

It could have been minutes before she raised her eyes. To his. He did not move. He did not say a word. There was nothing to be spoken. Her unintended promise had come due.

Slowly she rose.

Already she'd obliterated all the lines that gave her self a willed, a daytime, definition. Now a shadowy compulsion was taking hold on her—she would touch this land in a way that branded her, in a way that never anywhere anytime would she be able to deny.

She moved robotically. She locked the living-room door. She walked into the kitchen. Hesita was away. She locked the kitchen door. She came back to the dining room. Now Odinga moved. He followed through the hall. He followed to her room. She turned and locked the bedroom door. Methodically she closed the curtains. She climbed to standing on the bed. She scraped the small high curtain closed. It was the sound from months before when she had climbed on the bed and scraped the small high curtain closed, when she was hiding herself from Odinga. She climbed down from the window and lay on her back. She closed her eyes.

She heard no sound. Odinga was not moving. And in that long arrested moment her own gargantuan insanity assaulted her. She opened her eyes in terror.

It was his eyes that were flaming. He was standing, clenching his fists. His tension was electric.

He said, "Get up." He did not address her as *memsahib*.

She pulled herself to sitting. She did not take her eyes off him.

He said, "I will not touch you. I am not your servant. I am the servant of the Lord. The Lord has driven his pole in me. The Lord is holding me upright. I have fought with the Lord and He has conquered me. His claws are gripping me. I do not bend down to you. You have forgotten your Lord. But you will remember—you did not conquer Odinga. The Lord has conquered Odinga. I pray you return to your Lord. And you remember Odinga."

She answered, but her voice was stunned. It came too low to be heard. She said, "I will remember Odinga."

They held each other's eyes in silence. Until he dropped his own, walked to the door, unlocked it, paused, said *"Kwaheri, Memsahib"* without looking at her. She said *"Kwaheri, Odinga."*

He opened the door and left the room and left her house for good.

FORTY-ONE

On a Breakfast Table

ARE THE LUMINOUS SPOTS PURE dream? Even if you'd lived them? And what can you say about them, if they ignore all politics and race and poverty; and genocide and plague.

You say they come from far away, from a barely believed-in site.

Yet they underlie the way you see; even, for instance, the way you imagine a meal.

The breakfast will be laid out on a porch. The vines must only halfway close you in, and you must have some gauzy streaks of early morning sun. That's possible if you're a southerner. It's harder to have banks of bougainvillea, or drifting woodsmoke. Harder still to get the thump of the mortar and pestle, or the hornbills, or to suspect you live outdoors where over breakfast, early morning, visiting girls will wait on the grass and hum. Or a man in a long white robe will stop, with blades of grass glued to his toes.

For a while you'll take their word, after you've fled Uganda— that it's good you have a telephone because a telephone connects you in the way you want connection. But you will be wrong to believe them. And it may take years before you grasp what you are missing—that the virtual body is a cold body, lonely, with wires in the place of blood and veins. While you remember a spot where the air was live—chaotically alive—but warm and sweet and flowing, filling the chasms yawning inside you.

They stayed at Megan's the last night, before they headed for Entebbe. (It was not John's choice, to find himself with Piet. But then the subject of Prudence was not likely to come up.) In those last days there wasn't time to dwell on dreams. Yet the one she had the last night was tenacious. It hung on whatever she was doing. Of Odinga of course. But in this dream Odinga was a deacon or a minister—or at least he had John's robes on. He was standing where Prudence had stood in the meeting of the saved, in the amphitheater, only it was really the amphitheater at her mother's college at Randolph-Macon where she used to go sometimes with her mother when she was little and where they used to do Greek plays but now it was confessions in this amphitheater and she knew she'd be the subject of Odinga's confession—only she didn't really mind, as if everybody knew already and everybody wanted things exactly the way they were. But then she herself wasn't truly herself either. She was trim and small and black—clearly she was Prudence but she was sitting with Megan and they were leaning on each other as if they were meant to be that way and then Odinga's talk was not, after all, about her—or she didn't hear that. Odinga merely held up a stick and he kept on saying "this pole," "this pole," like he was blaming this stick for everything when it was clear he was proud of his weapon, that he was threatening the crowd with it.

She woke up with the feeling of great muddle. It wasn't a bad muddle. It was thick, but almost comforting—she was caught in the muddle along with everybody else, everything and everybody clumped in one shape-shifting mass. Even time. Because the time was now and the time must be her southern childhood and the time must be ancient Greece as well—all by way of that very same amphitheater. Religion was intertwined with sex and black was interchanged with white and male got confused with female—and the amphitheater was the place of the drama and of the entertainment, too, maybe it was the place of events you were meant to remember, events that made up history—weren't the stories in Greek amphitheaters full of blood that spewed out from the bedroom and the family? But—but the amphitheater was the confessional as well—where a person came for judgment, or for communal forgiveness. It was the place to force the messy bedroom into order. Except the sorting wasn't working—the boundaries to everything were shifting and that made judgment premature or quite impossible because the place for humiliation seemed to be turning into the place for pride.

Or she was reaching for such things, meaning to chew on them. Oddly, it wasn't until hours later—when they passed the turnoff to the Port Bell Road—that it came to her that Wulf had been there too—that the pole wasn't merely Odinga's upright stiffness. The pole was her Pole too, in the center of her dream. And when she discovered Wulf was there the dream felt right to her; not quite yet comprehensible—except perhaps from the hawk's-eye view—but somehow as it should be.

Mysteriously, before they started for Entebbe, Hans said to her, as if there were no question: "We will meet again—I intend to see *The Potter and the Shadow of Death*." And then, quite methodically, he came up to each of them—Michael and Lulu and Anne and John and herself—and kissed them on both cheeks.

Now they were cramped with bags and hats and sugarcane and branches of gardenias. They halted at the turn of the Heights. Prudence was there waiting.

John pulled the Peugeot over. Let Prudence saunter up if Prudence wanted—first to John's side of the car.

Then they edged around the curve, onto Bataka Road. She was rummaging for Lulu's shoes. She had to root in four odd bags and when she did look back she saw Odinga. For the first time since he'd left. He was standing by Prudence. Not waving. Watching stoically. She saw Prudence take Odinga's arm. She saw Prudence lift up Odinga's arm, as if she meant to search his skin for something. It was an odd and an intimate movement for two so freshly born again. She turned around. She did not care to be a witness. Lulu was leaning out the window shouting *Kwaheri kwaheri* to Odinga.

The airport roof was sprinkled with friends and students, black and white, who had come to see them off. That was the custom here— these ceremonial gatherings—but in the state of their disgrace, she had not thought it would happen.

They themselves were in a line of fleeing Asians, crossing the runway to the waiting 747 and battling the wind. The sun was high but the wind came off the lake and it was higher. Hair and bags and saris and skirts were snapping out loud in the wind.

The plane took off over whitecaps—the lake was choppy in the wind. They circled over the water and headed out above the light green patches of papyrus swamp.

They were quiet. John took her hand, but both of them were somewhere else. It would take a while to know where it was they were.

The swamps were gone. They were flying above banana trees and hills of coffee flowers, which trailed sprays of white along the green. They flew north across the cotton fields, and the tangle of the Sudd, and the tannish-green savanna, and the black Nile glinting through sand.

She closed her eyes. Which closed off nothing at all.

Once she felt the plane shake. Her eyes popped open—she was looking at a skeleton and she drew her breath in sharp.

The skull was a reflection, in the window glass. But it came from where John sat and it was not his face. It had gaping holes where eyes and cheeks had been. She found her own face in the glass. There were deep black hollows where her cheeks had been. Empty sockets that had been her eyes.

She shut her eyes against the dread, and when she opened them, to check on the skulls, the sun was glancing off the pane and what she saw was an aqua line and not the skeletons. The line was rising off the horizon. She leaned forward. She narrowed her eyes.

It was the Mediterranean Sea. It was a white-shadowed line, where the yellow sand met aqua. It was vivid. It was beautiful. It said in a minute they'd be out of Africa.

She sensed a hubbub from the people in the plane, but she did not look round at them. From some new angle of the wings the plane, out the window, was made of blinding sun, exploding light, blazing off the metal and into the cabin and the passengers were gasping, buzzing, calling, straining to see out the windows. Michael and Lulu were scrambling over each other and Michael was saying "I saw it first, I saw it first" and Anne was twisting round from the seat in front and banging a fist on her mother.

"Yes, yes, I see," said Agnes. But she kept still, in confounding light, with her forehead pressed on the pane.

The line down there had come too quick. The border had come much much too quick.

And what was it they, or she, or he, or anyone at all could ever grasp—beyond immaculate pain—when a line like that came up so quick. What would they do—when they had crossed that thin white line.

The shadow of their 747 would touch that line in two quick heartbeats more.

But it came on them too quick.

They could not know what they would be—beyond this pristine pain—when in one beat they had crossed that line, and crossed that water, and banked, and dropped, and waked up, and discovered they were displaced persons. Strangers. Occupied by harsh and ancient sunlight, vast and echoing. Left to go love. And without the help of anything on earth.

Glossary

✂

asante (Swahili) thank you

ayah word from India for children's nanny, common in the British Empire

Baganda people of the kingdom of Buganda

Balokole (Luganda) the "saved" group of Christians

Bantu peoples of varying tribes that dominate Africa from Uganda to the Cape

basuti (Luganda) traditional long Victorian dress with puffed sleeves still worn by Baganda women

Batutsi the Tutsi people of Ruanda, sometimes called Watutsi because the *b* is pronounced almost as softly as a *W*

Bazungu (Luganda) white people

Buganda the country containing the Baganda people, the most powerful kingdom of Uganda

bwana (Swahili) sir

condos (Luganda) robbers

debbie large rectangular tins that once contained kerosene, now used for carrying water in East Africa

dduka (Swahili) small shop

ekitibwa (Luganda) honor

habari (Swahili) How are you?

hapana (Swahili) no

hodi (Swahili) Are you at home? Called out by a visitor at the door

jambo (Swahili) hello

kabaka (Luganda) king

kale (Luganda) okay

---

*In Bantu languages, the prefix helps determine the meaning and grammatical usage of the word. For instance, take the root *ganda*. The prefix *ba* indicates plural persons, *mu* a single person. *Bu* indicates the country of the *ganda*, *Lu* gives the language, *ki* the adjective, etc. *Uganda* is the Swahili form of the word.

kanzu (Swahili) long white robe worn by men in East Africa (from the Arabs)

karibu (Swahili) Come in. Called out in answer to *Hodi*

kiganda (Luganda) adjective referring to *ganda* people or things

kitenge (Luganda) bright cotton figured print marketed exlusively in Africa in the sixties and associated with Africa. It was, however, a Dutch marketing ploy, one which lifted the designs from their former colony, Indonesia.

kwaheri (Swahili) goodbye

Luganda the Bantu language spoken by Baganda

memsahib (Swahili) madam

michungwa (Luganda) orange juice

Muganda a person of the Baganda people

mulokole (Luganda) one of the "saved" group of Christians

m'zuri (Swahili) well or good

ndiyo (Swahili) yes

nnyabo (Luganda) madam

okukola (Luganda) to work, or "for working"

okuwumula (Luganda) to rest, or "for resting"

omwami (Luganda) Mr.

omukyala (Luganda) Mrs.

sais word from India for keeper of the horses, common in the British Empire

sana (Swahili) very

samosa spicy Indian pastry popular in East Africa

shamba (Swahili) homestead

Simba (Swahili) lion, but also referring to the rebel movement in eastern Zaire in the 1960s

ssebo (Luganda) sir

ssekibobo (Luganda) most important chief in Buganda, under the kabaka

toto (Swahili) little one, often a servant's helper

waragi (Luganda) local liquor

webale (Luganda) thank you

Author's Note

This novel is a work of imaginative fiction; it is not autobiographical fiction. While the setting is drawn from memory, all characters, their acts and words as well as the psychological underpinnings of the central marriage, are the products of my attempt to craft a story.

I would like to thank various persons and groups who have helped to make this novel possible. First, for funding some of my time through summer grants and a sabbatical, my appreciation goes to Converse College, to the Virginia Center for the Creative Arts, to Yaddo, the MacDowell Colony, and the South Carolina Arts Commission. Individually, for their long hours of reading and reacting to the manuscript, my thanks go to Georg Gaston and Jean Dunbar; and for making publication possible—to Michael Congdon who dared to represent this first novel and to make sensitive suggestions; and to Laura Hruska at Soho, for her warm appreciation and receptiveness. Also I thank Mary Shand Rule, Bonnie Auslander, Cecile Goding, Rita Weeks, Susie Jackson, Danielle Raquidel, Frances Thompson McKay, Kathy Underwood, Eun-Sun Lee, Lillian Wamalwa and Libby Paul for their helpful comments. I am grateful for other forms of help given by the Converse English Department—Charles Morgan, Karen Carmean, David Taylor, Rick Mulkey, Susan Tekulve, and Laura Brown; and finally to the late Sally Cary Edwards, first reader, first critic, and first with encouragements.